GOING DARK

GOING DARK

MELISSA DE LA CRUZ

UNION
SQUARE
& CO.

NEW YORK

UNION SQUARE & CO.
SQUARE
& CO.
NEW YORK

ISBN 978-1-4549-4764-6 (hardcover)
ISBN 978-1-4549-4766-0 (e-book)

Library of Congress Cataloging-in-Publication Data

Names: De la Cruz, Melissa, 1971- author.
Title: Going dark / by Melissa de la Cruz.
Description: New York : Union Square and Co., 2023. | Audience: Ages 14 and up. | Summary: When nineteen-year-old Josh returns from Rome without his budding influencer girlfriend Amelia, he immediately becomes a suspect in her disappearance, but as college sophomore and hacker Harper attempts to clear his name, she unearths secrets from both Josh and Amelia's past.
Identifiers: LCCN 2022037200 (print) | LCCN 2022037201 (ebook) | ISBN 9781454947646 (hardcover) | ISBN 9781454947653 (trade paperback) | ISBN 9781454947660 (epub)
Subjects: CYAC: Missing persons--Fiction. | Social media--Fiction. | Secrets--Fiction. | BISAC: YOUNG ADULT FICTION / Girls & Women | YOUNG ADULT FICTION / Social Themes / Prejudice & Racism | LCGFT: Novels.
Classification: LCC PZ7.D36967 Gn 2023 (print) | LCC PZ7.D36967 (ebook) | DDC [Fic]--dc23
LC record available at https://lccn.loc.gov/2022037200
LC ebook record available at https://lccn.loc.gov/2022037201

For information about custom editions, special sales, and premium purchases, please contact specialsales@unionsquareandco.com.

Printed in the United States of America

2 4 6 8 10 9 7 5 3 1

unionsquareandco.com

Cover design by Whitney Manger and Marcie Lawrence
Interior design by Marcie Lawrence
Cover art by Fatima Baig

For my dear friend and agent,
consigliere, therapist, producer, and more.
Man of many hats and talents,
Richard Abate

PART 1

THIS BIRD HAS FLOWN

CHAPTER ONE

JOSH

The plane bucked with unexpected turbulence on its final descent, sending Josh's stomach into his chest and causing him to grip the armrests so tightly his knuckles turned white. He'd finally dozed off while watching the in-flight movie when he'd been jolted awake by the sudden drop. Instinctively, he reached out to the seat next to him, only to find it empty. Of course, he'd forgotten. Amelia hadn't boarded with him.

Gray clouds whizzed past Josh's window, so thick he couldn't even see the wing tip's blinking light. The ground below was still shrouded in darkness, and he couldn't see the city lights either. It was sometime past ten, and the sun had set, but his circadian rhythm was off. He'd been in Europe with his girlfriend Amelia for the past two weeks, and his body tried to tell him that it was sometime in the early morning so he couldn't sleep. Besides, he'd never been an easy flier. The turbulence didn't help. The midflight meal of an open-faced sandwich and tiramisu was starting to rebel in his stomach. He squeezed the armrests as the plane dipped again, making the cut on his palm sting. The pain helped distract from the nausea roiling in his gut every time the plane shimmied and shook.

The cut on his hand was fresh and surprisingly deep. He'd had to change the gauze during the flight but it had already soaked through. He regretted not going to the hospital to get stitches, but it was too late now. Whenever the cut stung, it reminded him of Amelia.

Every time he rested his phone in his palm to check for a text or picked up his bag to scroll through photos on his DSLR to look at her face, he recalled that the trip was over and she wasn't there.

Movement across the aisle caught his eye. The pretty woman in 13F crossed herself with one hand while clutching her armrest with the other. She noticed him looking and smiled, the kind of smile that was nervous and a little embarrassed. Josh smiled back at the woman because it was the polite thing to do. She couldn't have been much older than he was at nineteen, and guys who looked like him were used to pretty women smiling his way. Still, he wasn't interested in taking advantage of the fact that his girlfriend had abandoned him in Rome.

He couldn't believe Amelia had actually not shown, especially when she'd been the one who bought the tickets, booked their hotels, arranged their itinerary. Tickets to Europe weren't cheap, especially since they were both college students.

Thoughts swirled in Josh's gut, as sickening as turbulence. *Were they really done? Was that it? Months of dating, over like that?* He didn't even know what he'd done wrong. It had been the perfect vacation, a literal dream come true with his dream girl. And now, all he had was an empty seat next to him.

It had been a miserable ten hours without Amelia.

At the Leonardo da Vinci International Airport in Rome, he'd gotten in line to check in, head on a swivel, expecting to see her rushing up behind him. While he stood in line, he held his phone tightly, waiting for something, anything—even a breakup voice mail. But nothing came.

When it was his turn at the check-in counter, the attendant took his boarding pass. He glanced around the concourse, hoping to see Amelia's blond ponytail swinging behind her. She was obviously still mad at him, but she had time to board. He hadn't worried, even then.

The attendant loaded his luggage onto the conveyor belt and it disappeared through the leather flaps into the bowels of the airport. To think, Amelia had packed his suitcase for him while he checked them out of the hotel. She'd tucked all of his souvenirs and clothes away, expertly folding everything with the skill of a veteran traveler so it all fit like Tetris pieces.

Josh sat in a row of chairs near the Four Winds counter, keeping an eye on the queue for Amelia. He waited. And waited. And waited. He passed the time by buying a small, personal-sized bottle of red wine from a vending machine, a novelty for an American visiting Rome for the first time. He downed the whole bottle before he realized it was gone. The wine was supposed to calm his nerves, but it only made his stomach full of acid and turned his tongue purple. The clock inched closer to departure time. Josh couldn't wait for Amelia any longer.

He went through security with no problem and bought an overpriced cappuccino at an espresso cart. He wanted to get one last taste of an authentic Italian coffee before returning to the real world. Amelia had been the one to introduce him to espresso.

"*Ess*-presso, Josh. If you say *ex*-presso, I think an Italian person is legally allowed to kill you," Amelia had said on their flight over, her eyes alight with teasing.

He drank his cappuccino as he mindlessly scrolled through his phone, cycling through Twitter, Instagram, TikTok, over and over again, hoping to find any distraction, before inevitably opening his text conversation with Amelia only to close it again. An apology from her would have been nice, especially after all the things she'd screamed at him.

While he was in line to board, he got a text, but it was from his roommate Derek in California.

Boarding? Derek was never one to type out a paragraph in a text if one word could work, but he was loath to use emojis, a firm stance that Josh could appreciate.

Yeah. Almost to my seat.

Get me anything?

Josh grinned and texted back, **Absolutely nothing.** Derek would know he was lying.

Josh had bought him two pairs of socks: one pair featuring the Vitruvian man and another with the pope's face on them.

Asshole, texted Derek. **Fly safe.**

They'd been best friends since they'd met freshman year at San Diego State. Like Josh, he was an artist, specifically a painter, though his major was in finance. Derek and his girlfriend Tori were made for each other, and probably headed for the whole kids and white picket fence life.

Before, Josh could have imagined a similar future with Amelia. She was special, someone worth holding on to, keeping close. Now, all he had left were photographs on a camera and an empty seat beside him.

All his past relationships had been intense. He loved with his whole heart, but what he had with Amelia was different. She was everything.

A flight attendant made Josh switch off his phone for departure. Still no text from Amelia. Where was she? The engines had roared to life, and the plane vibrated beneath his shoes. Rome fell away as the plane took off and the seat next to him stayed empty. The acid from the cappuccino and the bottle of wine sat high in his stomach, but it was nothing compared to the anxiety swirling in his gut.

It hadn't really set in, not until he was well over the Atlantic and they turned off the lights in the cabin for everyone to sleep. Were they over?

Unable to help himself, Josh purchased in-flight Wi-Fi. Amelia hadn't posted on her social media, which was unusual for someone like Amelia Ashley, rising Instagram model and travel writer. No sad Insta stories about breaking up with her boyfriend while gazing at the Trevi Fountain, or some Roman ruin. She was an enigma in so many ways, even if her whole life was online. The Wi-Fi charges were starting to rack up, so Josh switched off his phone. There would be plenty of time to talk to Amelia later.

The selection of movies on the transatlantic flight was lackluster, but Josh picked one so he could at least get comfortable enough to try to get some sleep. He'd even popped a Xanax to help him get settled. Waiting for the pill to kick in, he scrolled his camera, only half-watching the movie, staring at the photos he'd taken of their trip.

Amelia was so beautiful. He could stare at her face all day.

It had started off like a perfect Roman Holiday, just like the movie with Audrey Hepburn and Gregory Peck. One picture of her posing in front of the large windows overlooking the tarmac at the airport when they first arrived, another of her looking over her shoulder in front of the

Colosseum, another of her grinning over her wineglass at a small restaurant where he'd had the best ravioli of his life, her high cheekbones illuminated softly in the candlelight.

The plane landed, tires thumping heavily on the tarmac at the San Diego International Airport. As it taxied up to the gate, Josh texted Derek that he'd landed and that he'd be home soon, but he didn't expect a response. It was Friday night and he knew Derek was probably busy with Tori, letting off some steam before fall semester of their sophomore year started. Tori had become Josh and Derek's pseudo-roommate because she stayed over all the time, but she didn't pay rent. Josh didn't mind though; it kept Derek happy and occupied and Josh enjoyed the apartment to himself when they were out most weekends.

Tori had been the one who'd introduced him and Amelia. He could still remember that feeling when he first saw her several months ago, as if she'd drawn him toward her by an invisible string around his neck. Tori had invited her to his birthday party, and the moment he saw Amelia, he knew she was the one. His last relationship had ended terribly, but Amelia made him realize he could love again.

Tori loved playing matchmaker. Of course, she'd been right. Amelia was perfect—everyone said so. Everyone loved her, but the best part was that Amelia loved *him*. His heart ached to hear her say it again.

The line of passengers moved down the aisle and Josh slipped on his Dodgers' cap and triple-checked that he had his camera, his phone, his passport, and wallet all in his carry-on. He stayed for an extra minute to help a couple of elderly women get their bags down from the overhead bin. Their smiles were big, and their laughter girlish as he handed them their bags.

"Oh, thank you, young man!" one of the women said. Her glasses made her eyes look gigantic. "Chivalry still exists in this day and age. See, Flo? What a gentleman."

"It's no trouble at all, ma'am," he said, with a wink.

The women giggled. He left, feeling better about finally being home.

×××

At baggage claim, Josh stood at the carousel, waiting, as the final suitcase was picked up and carried off. He heaved a huge sigh.

His bag had not made the flight.

He went to the customer service area, where he joined a long line of annoyed travelers. Still no text from Amelia. He filled out the lost baggage form, circling what his bag looked like from a huge catalog of pictures. It used to be his father's. It was an old-fashioned leather suitcase, covered in stickers, with a gold handle and clasps that always made him feel like an adventurer from the movies whenever he opened it. This was the first time he'd ever lost his bag on a flight, but, then again, he was aware that this kind of thing happened all the time. But the acid from his stomach had returned. He'd packed almost his entire wardrobe in that suitcase. What was he supposed to wear for the first week of class?

The night was warm and welcoming as Josh stepped out to the line of taxis ready to whisk travelers wherever they needed to go. It was hot but dry. California heat was different from the Roman kind. Rome's felt older somehow, even though he knew it wasn't really. It was thicker.

Amelia had joked that she could eat the air like cotton candy when they first stepped outside after arriving.

Josh hailed a cab and got in, feeling adrift without his suitcase. He checked his phone again. Still not a word from Amelia. The last thing in their text conversation was one she'd sent before their trip:

Hotel Artemide

Via Nazionale, 22, 00184

It was the address of their hotel in Rome, in case one of them got lost. They could just hold up their phone to anyone who could help. She was always prepared that way, always thinking ahead. He liked that a lot about her.

He missed her. He wished things had gone differently, that he'd had her at his side on the trip home, falling asleep on his shoulder. That would have been a nice punctuation mark on the story of their trip. The vacation had been so much fun until it wasn't . . .

Josh sighed. His pride told him not to, but he knew he should.

He started to type to tell her that he'd landed in California, but after a moment's pause, he deleted his message, shoved his phone in his jacket pocket, and rested his head on the window. The glass felt cool on his forehead. When she was ready, Amelia would reach out to him. He knew there was no talking to her when she was angry, and by the looks of it, she was beyond reasoning with.

Hell hath no fury like a woman scorned, as they said. And Josh was smart enough to know that him talking to her before she was ready was a recipe for disaster.

When the cab dropped him off at his apartment, a two-story complex of which he and Derek rented the bottom floor, he was semi-relieved he didn't have to haul his huge suitcase inside. He was too tired to do much besides open the door and flick on the light. Derek's cat, Munch, waddled over to greet him.

Immediately, Josh's mood brightened. "Hey there, buddy-boy. Miss me?" He kneeled down and scratched Munch behind his black-and-white ears. Josh and Derek had rescued him from a shelter when they got their apartment. He was old and the shelter was ready to put him down, and their lease technically didn't allow pets, but Derek convinced the landlord to let them keep him. "I bet I missed you more," Josh said. Even though he was Derek's cat, Josh was attached to him.

Besides Munch, the apartment was empty. Derek and Tori were probably at her place a block north, so Josh went to bed. He dumped his carry-on near his bedroom door and flopped backward onto his mattress, barely doing more than taking off his pants and shirt, shedding the gross international travel feeling. With Munch already asleep at his feet, Josh lay in the dark, staring at his phone, chewing on all the things he wanted to say to Amelia, before finally typing:

Miss you.

He paused his thumb over the SEND button, then finally hit SEND before he could talk himself out of it. **Sent: 11:07 PM.**

He didn't expect an immediate response, but he wanted to see those dots appear to show she was typing, to show that she was thinking about him. He fell asleep never getting any answer back.

His text went unread.

CHAPTER TWO

JOSH

"What do you mean she didn't come home with you?"

Tori's spoon hovered over her Cheerios as she stared at Josh like he'd grown a second head.

Josh had woken up that morning to find Derek and Tori had come home sometime during the night while he was asleep. He hadn't even heard them come in. Jet lag had knocked him out. Based on the smeared makeup Tori had around her eyes as they ate cold cereal at the breakfast bar, spanning the length of the kitchen, she and Derek had gone out to a club last night. Derek, still hungover, had his head buried in his arms, slumped over the counter. He lifted his head though when Josh said Amelia missed the flight.

"She didn't show up at the airport?" he asked.

"No," Josh said. He stirred his cereal, drowning the marshmallow charms and letting them bob back to the surface. "I waited for her but—"

"What happened exactly?" Tori asked. She and Amelia had been friends since before Amelia had started dating Josh in February. She was practically the polar opposite of Amelia in looks—dark-haired, dark-eyed, dark-skinned—but like Amelia she was gorgeous. No wonder Derek was head over heels for her. She and Derek already acted like they were a married couple. Josh had been their third wheel until Amelia. Tori had liked Amelia immediately—everyone did when they met her. She was a magnet.

Josh cleared his throat. "Right before our flight, we got into an argument. We were at a cafe, eating before we needed to be at the airport, and . . . she blew up at me."

"Did you say something? Did you do something? People don't just blow up . . ." Tori crossed her arms and looked skeptical.

"I don't know. I mentioned something about our next vacation. Maybe Iceland to see some volcanos. And she freaked out. I swear, I have no idea what happened. It took me totally by surprise. She flew off the handle and stormed off. Took her bags and left. We'd already packed for the flight and everything. And she just . . ." He gestured with his spoon.

"For real?" Derek asked. "Where did she go?"

Josh scooped a spoonful of cereal in his mouth and shrugged. "I have no idea. I texted her last night but she didn't answer. Do you think she dumped me?"

"Josh, what is wrong with you?" Tori's voice had taken on an edge of accusation. "You left your girlfriend in a foreign country?"

Derek had lifted himself up from the counter. "Bro, that's kind of messed up."

Josh balked. They made it sound like he'd dropped her off on the side of the road and sped off into the sunset, leaving her in the dust. He was starting to feel like he was on his heels, defending himself from . . . he didn't even know what. It wasn't like he'd *meant* to leave without her.

"She knew when our flight was leaving, she was the one who booked the tickets in the first place! I waited for her at the airport forever. I had to go or I would have missed my flight! Look, I thought that's what she needed. To blow off some steam. Alone. She did it all the time."

"What do you mean all the time?"

Josh hadn't used the right words. "She went off on her own a lot. She had friends in the city too. You know how she likes walking alone. It wasn't so weird to me."

Dating Amelia had been an adventure on its own. When they weren't going out to dinner, or to the movies, or studying at home, she would take him on real-life "expeditions," called geocaching. With some coordinates and a good pair of hiking boots, all she needed was her phone and her GPS, traipsing through the wilderness like an adventuring tomb raider in search of hidden treasure in empty fields or at the beach, caches left behind by fellow enthusiasts. She loved puzzles of every kind. It made for great content on her blog.

Josh wasn't the outdoor type and didn't find it as much fun as Amelia did. She often went by herself.

Tori dropped her spoon into her bowl and scrutinized Josh, mumbling something like "Can't believe you."

Derek dragged his hand down his face and propped his head up with his hand. "You didn't try to stop her?" he asked.

"No," said Josh. "Like I said, she was furious. I figured she needed some space. Me talking to her wouldn't help."

"What did you do to her?" The suspicion in Tori's eyes wasn't lost on Josh.

"What? Nothing! I swear! I didn't do anything."

"Yeah, sure."

Josh sighed. This was not how he had expected his return home would go. "Okay," he said, bracketing the air with his hands. "We ate together. We talked. Everything was normal. We had a few glasses of wine, then she flipped out. It all happened so fast, I barely even knew what was going on. But she was the one who started it. Why am I the bad guy here?"

"Did you say anything else?"

Josh's face felt warm. It was all a blur. "I don't really remember. Like I said, we had a few drinks." He wondered if she could tell he was holding back.

Tori dipped her head toward him. "What happened to your hand?"

All eyes moved to the bandage on Josh's right hand. He flexed it. "I cut it. I was picking up a broken wineglass."

"Josh," Derek groaned. "I know you, man. I know you were trying to be nice and give her space, but come on. At least check up on her."

"She didn't answer my text."

"Call her."

The time on Josh's phone when he tapped the screen said it was just past eight in the morning, so it would be five in the afternoon in Rome. Derek was right. He needed to call her.

Derek and Tori exchanged glances with each other while Josh waited for the first ring. It never came. It went straight to voice mail.

Amelia's chipper recorded voice sounded tinny against his ear. He could almost picture her when she recorded the message, imagining her scrunching up her nose and sticking out her tongue whenever she was being silly. "Hi! This is Amelia's phone. Amelia's busy right now. Leave a message or text like a normal person."

Josh waited for the beep. His heart had lodged itself in his throat and he sounded like he was talking through a bubble. "Hey, it's Josh. I'm . . . I'm sorry about everything. Please call me. Please. Okay. Bye." He always sounded stupid on phone calls and he cringed when he hung up.

"No answer?" Derek asked.

Tori pushed away from the counter. "She's probably still pissed at you. I'll call her." Tori grabbed her phone from where it was charging on the dock and flipped her braids over her shoulder as she dialed Amelia's number. She too got a voice mail. Josh could hear Amelia's recorded voice from where he sat, but she didn't leave a message. "I'm texting her. We'll see what's up."

"I'm sure she's okay. She could be on a flight right now, and her phone is off," Derek said. It was obvious that Tori had started to panic, but Derek was always the calm one, finding a reason for everything.

Josh resumed eating his cereal. It had gone soggy. The lump in his throat hadn't gone away. Nothing bad had happened to Amelia. To think otherwise was absurd. There had to be a better explanation. Bad things didn't happen to people like Amelia Ashley.

The moment Amelia walked into any room, everyone looked at her, couldn't take their eyes off her. She radiated confidence, and poise, and a brightness that was hard to ignore. Josh felt like the luckiest guy in the world when he entered her orbit. By then, she was already popular on Instagram. She had several hundred thousand followers and was making a name for herself online. Josh hadn't been the first, or the last, person to notice how special she was. Girls like Amelia Ashley were one in a million.

Tori was overreacting. She was worried about Amelia, but she hadn't been there. She hadn't seen Amelia walk away. He wasn't going to grab her by the wrist and make her stay if she didn't want to. He wasn't that type of guy.

Munch jumped up on the counter and butted his head against Josh's arm. He was begging for food. Derek scooped Munch up by the stomach and carried him to his empty food bowl by the door, where he poured in some cat chow.

"I'm sure it'll all be fine," Derek said. "We'll try calling her again in a while." He squeezed Tori around her bicep and brought her to him, folding her up in a hug. Tori was stiff at first but she melted into his arms. His own arms ached for Amelia. He always liked holding her, smelling her neck. Would he ever get to hold her like that again?

Josh scooped another spoonful of cereal in his mouth, but his appetite had vanished. He was already having a bad day, and now he was getting the third degree from Tori about something he didn't have any control over. He sighed loudly, making the two of them look at him. "I'm just . . ." he started. "The trip was really great, we were having a great time, but then everything went wrong so quickly. First Amelia walks out on me and then I lose my bag . . ."

"Lost your bag?" Tori asked.

"The airline lost it. It had all my stuff in there. It's not helping my mood." Josh regretted packing almost everything in his closet. Amelia had teased him when she saw him pack twenty-five pairs of boxers. She'd counted. "Why do you need so many? What, are you expecting to shit your pants every day of our trip?" She was kind of vulgar, but in a fun way.

He ate another spoonful of cereal. Tori was right. He had been thoughtless. He should have stayed in Rome, tried to find Amelia, tried to get her to calm down, tried to get her to come with him to the airport and return home, but it was too late now. All he could do was wait for her to call back. Munch returned to Josh's side and knocked his head into Josh's hand, demanding to be petted, and Josh scratched him under the chin. "All right, buddy-boy," he said. "Heard you loud and clear."

✕ ✕ ✕

Despite Tori's call, Amelia remained radio-silent.

She never called Tori back, even as the hours wore on from the day and into night. It was unlike Amelia, who was so attached to her phone it might as well have been another appendage. Derek assured Tori that everything would work out, that she was probably somewhere without signal. Josh had to believe it too. It was all he could do.

There was still nothing on her social media either.

Josh tried to get back into some semblance of his routine, but there was nothing to unpack. His luggage was still in transit somewhere. He fell asleep almost instantly on the couch with Munch dozing on his chest after he'd tried to find something to watch on Netflix. Tori and Derek had gone out to enjoy the rest of their Saturday, even though Tori kept saying she was worried about Amelia. Josh had only meant to close his eyes for a few minutes, listening to a boring documentary drone on like a lullaby, but he couldn't stay asleep for long. He woke up several times, starting with a jolt, imagining that his phone had gone off in his hand, but it had only been a phantom ring. So every time he jolted awake, he'd scroll through Netflix only to fall asleep again.

Netflix was pushing true crime documentaries and terrible reality TV shows at him, since Amelia used this account and loved both of those genres, sometimes swinging rapidly between them. To go from a woman crying in front of a camera, talking about how beautiful her daughter was before she was murdered, to a house full of beautiful twenty-somethings screaming at one another about who slept with whom was emotional whiplash that Josh could hardly understand. Maybe it was because Amelia liked people, enjoyed learning about how they thought or how they expressed themselves. She liked watching people tell their stories, open up some raw part of their soul in front of a camera and spill something they might not have intended to. The deconstruction of a person on-screen. Josh wasn't a fan of either genre, but he hardly spoke up about it, even if Amelia would look over at him in the middle of a particularly gruesome episode about a child killer and ask, "Is this too much of a bummer?"

He'd always say no. He'd always lie. For her.

As he dozed, he couldn't help but remember seeing her that last time as she stormed off, her blond hair catching the light as he called out to her.

"Amelia! Amelia, come back!"

He hated to admit it, but it felt like she was punishing him, even in his memory of her. She ignored him now, just as she did then. Even in his dreams, she taunted him by pretending he didn't exist. He was a ghost.

The third time he'd jolted awake, it was dark outside already. Josh checked his phone reflexively, like it had become glued to his hand, but still his text to Amelia from last night was unread. He felt terrible. His head hurt, his skin felt hot and cold at the same time, even his eyes pounded like a DJ was blowing up the club. When Derek came home alone later that night Josh knew something was wrong. His stomach churned with a queasy discomfort, and it wasn't because Derek had picked up some dinner for them at the worst Chinese takeout place in North Park. (They couldn't be picky, it was the cheapest.) It was because Derek asked, "Still no word?"

That meant Amelia hadn't contacted Tori yet. Somehow that was worse than not contacting Josh. Amelia and Tori were friends. If Amelia wasn't even talking to her, that meant something was wrong.

That something had happened to her.

"No," Josh said. He sat up from his prone position on the couch, making Munch open one eye from his perch on the mountain of Derek's clothes. Josh massaged his eye sockets with the heel of his hands. He could feel Derek watching him as he unpacked the takeout dinner. Already the apartment was starting to smell like grease and egg. Normally Josh wouldn't have minded, but it was making him sick.

"What do you want to do?" Derek asked, nudging his glasses up his nose. "Shouldn't we call her parents? Or tell the police?"

"I don't know how to get in touch with her parents," Josh said. "It's not like I have their contact on my phone." He'd checked. He didn't. But why would he? He'd never met them.

"Well, someone's got to tell them that she didn't come back with you," said Derek.

Josh checked his phone one last time, just in case, finding nothing before he threw it across the couch defeatedly. "The police? What would they even do? Go to Italy?"

"I dunno, maybe they've got some kind of cop network thing where they ring up a buddy in Rome who can do them a favor? I don't know how cops work. Or maybe they call the FBI? At least, that's how it is on TV."

"The *FBI*? She hasn't even been gone that long."

"You don't need to wait twenty-four hours or whatever to report a missing person. At least, I think I saw that somewhere. Like, if you can be reasonably worried that a person is in danger, you can say something. And I think this qualifies."

"You really think she's in danger?" Josh asked.

Derek shrugged. "No one's heard from her. She's probably not in trouble, because what are the odds? But you want peace of mind, don't you?"

Josh sighed heavily. He really didn't want to bother the police with this.

"Worst-case scenario," Derek went on, "it's all just a big misunderstanding. You won't get in trouble for that, if that's what you're worried about."

Josh wasn't worried. He hadn't done anything to her in the first place. "Amelia isn't in danger. She's the most capable person we know."

"Yeah, but we know that sometimes capable people don't get a say in who wants to hurt them."

"Don't."

"Sorry. I'm just with Tori on this one. It's weird that she's not responding to anything. What if someone did hurt her?"

Josh couldn't help the heat that came to his face. He didn't want to believe that. "No. There's got to be another explanation. We shut off our phones on the trip to avoid roaming charges. I bet she's doing exactly that. She's just hanging this over me, making me squirm."

Derek handed him a bowl of fried rice but Josh wasn't hungry. He rested it in his lap while Derek sat next to him on the couch, his legs twisted up underneath him while he blew on his food to cool it down a bit. "You must have really pissed her off, huh?"

Josh stared at the peas and fried egg in his rice and sighed again. He was getting really good at that. "I swear. I didn't do anything."

"Come on, man. We know women don't just fly off the handle over nothing. What did you do?"

"Derek. Look at me. In the eyes. I am telling you, I. Didn't. Do. Any. Thing."

Derek didn't say anything but raised his eyebrows and chomped down on his forkful of rice. If he didn't believe him, he didn't say it. But Josh wasn't lying. He wasn't perfect, by any means, but everything at the restaurant went down exactly as he'd said. He knew it didn't make sense, and that was why it was so hard to believe, even for him.

Derek took a moment to chew, swallowed his food, then said, "Okay, fine. Alternative ideas. Do you remember her friends' names? The ones she stayed with in Rome?"

Josh racked his brain. "The last name was Sparkle or something. Spark, maybe? Speck?"

"Maybe you can reach out to them, see if she's crashing at their place?"

It wasn't a bad idea, but Josh didn't have their contact info. They'd been Amelia's friends. He'd only tagged along when she said they'd been invited over to stay a few nights for free in their apartment together before heading to the Hotel Artemide for some alone time on the final leg of their journey. Amelia had seemed so excited about having a friend in town. Staying there was definitely a possibility. It was one of the few places she could go.

"Maybe they're friends with her on Facebook or Instagram," Derek said.

"Instagram probably." Josh reached for his phone and Derek handed it to him.

Josh opened Instagram and immediately saw Amelia's face looking back at him. It was the last picture she'd posted on their trip and Josh's heart squeezed painfully in his chest. He opened her profile.

The last time he'd checked, she had over a million followers. Now it was closer to a million and a half. But she only followed three hundred people, mostly people she knew in real life. He opened the list and scrolled through the list of names, scanning faces, searching for something familiar.

Derek had commandeered the TV remote and picked something on Netflix to watch, but it became background noise as Josh scrolled and scrolled, scanning through the profile pictures and names. His rice had gone cold by the time he found the profile.

Sarah Speck. That was her. Same glossy curls, same winged eyeliner. She was an Instagram influencer, like Amelia, so she had a few million followers too, but the profile he found was her personal one, set to private, probably so she could keep her business and her personal life separate. He couldn't see any of her posts from his account, except for her profile picture and biography, which also meant he couldn't send her a direct message. He sent a follow request and all he could do after that was wait.

Josh forced himself to eat the rice that had gone cold and absently watched TV with Derek. Munch had claimed a spot in Derek's lap, sniffing the fried rice curiously. While his eyes were on the screen, Josh's mind was six and a half thousand miles away, in Rome, watching Amelia walk away from him over and over again, like she was stuck in a time loop.

What if she really had dumped him and was with one of her friends in Rome? What if she had left him for another guy? Jealousy made his cheeks hot, not quite a boil, but a simmer nevertheless.

Now Josh was checking his phone for other reasons. He kept refreshing Instagram, waiting for a response from Sarah Speck. It was the middle of the night in Rome where Sarah lived, but he checked anyway. He finished his dinner without even realizing it and cleaned his bowl in the sink. Derek wasn't even watching the TV either. He was texting Tori, no doubt, and scratching Munch on the head.

By the time Josh sat back on the couch, he was checking his phone again, out of habit. This time, it paid off. Sarah Speck had accepted his follow request.

"Got her," he said.

Derek bolted upright. "Amelia?"

"No, her friend. The one I mentioned. Instagram."

Josh typed a direct message to her. It was early in the morning, but she had been on her phone. She must have been a bad sleeper. He wanted to keep it brief.

Hey, he typed, I'm not sure if you remember me. I'm Josh, Amelia's boyfriend. Is Amelia with you?

Thankfully, the little dots appeared in the direct message as she typed a reply.

Hey Josh! Of course I remember you! What do you mean though? She's not with you?

Josh's heart sank into his stomach, battling with greasy fried rice for dominance.

Have you seen her? he typed.

Not since you guys stayed over. What's going on?

Josh knew this didn't mean anything. It only meant that she hadn't gone to her friend's house like he'd thought she would. She had to be out there somewhere. But where had she gone?

CHAPTER THREE

JOSH

Monday rolled around and the time for speculation had come and gone. Amelia wasn't answering texts, or calls on her phone, or posting on social media.

Derek wanted to be the optimist, reminding them of Amelia's free-spiritedness, but Tori—being the only girl in this situation, as she constantly reminded both of them—was on the verge of panic. And no one knew how to contact Amelia's family. Josh still wasn't sure what they could do about it, but something had to be done, and his options were becoming limited.

Even so, Josh didn't want to sit around the apartment all day worrying. If he didn't go to school, then Amelia's disappearance would feel real, a twisted rationale that got him out of bed. It was the first week of his sophomore year and he didn't want to make a bad impression with his professors, not when he was finally starting to take some of the classes focused on his photography major. Going to school meant things were normal.

His first class of the semester was Abnormal Psychology at ten on Monday morning. It was a general course, chosen from the list available, to round out his year. But it seemed interesting enough to Josh at the time when he enrolled. Knowing how the depraved operated was inherently interesting. Normally he paid attention in class (they cost too much per credit *not* to, he figured), but today he sat in the back row of the lecture hall with his laptop open, his brain anywhere but on psychology. Amelia had invaded his every waking moment.

The professor stood at the podium at the bottom of the lecture hall and spoke into a microphone to address the two-hundred-some students sleepily staring back.

"Good morning," the mousy professor said. He had large, coke-bottle glasses and gray hair that reminded Josh of a Brillo pad. "My name is Dr. Brumble. Welcome to Abnormal Psychology. Seeing as it's the first class of the year, I wanted to address you all and welcome you to the semester ahead. As most of you are aware, this is a general course, touching on the basic concepts in my field. My teaching assistant here—where are you, yes—my teaching assistant Reece Sanchez will be your first point of contact about the material you go over on my syllabus."

Josh looked up politely from his computer screen at the TA. He thought the name had sounded familiar, and seeing him only confirmed it. Josh would recognize that mop of caramel-colored curls a mile away. Reece was a senior now, but when Josh met him he'd been a junior. The last time they spoke, Sanchez had been flirting with Amelia at a party thrown by one of his frat brothers. He was the type of guy Josh hated: handsome, smart, and rich, based on the Rolex that caught the light from the lecture hall. Sanchez flashed an easy smile at the giggling girls sitting in the front row. Josh rolled his eyes. He knew he wasn't going to coast by in this class, thanks to Sanchez. He still didn't forgive him for cornering Amelia at that party. He remembered it like it was yesterday.

He'd gone to the bathroom, having had one too many beers, only to come back to find Amelia missing from the spot on the couch they'd claimed for themselves in the thrum of the party. He'd searched everywhere for her, finally spotting her blond hair partially obscured by Sanchez's red polo shirt, his arm propping himself up on a wall and simultaneously blocking Amelia's exit.

Josh felt strong when he yanked Sanchez back, making him stumble but giving Amelia some space. Her wide eyes darted between them as Sanchez had smiled sleepily at him. "Hey, man," Sanchez slurred. "Easy there." His breath stank of tequila.

Immediately, Josh's face was on fire. He was drunk too and knew it, but he'd had enough presence of mind to back off. He put up his hands, placatingly, in a show of courtesy. He shouldn't have touched him, but Sanchez didn't seem to care.

"This your girl?" Sanchez had asked, wobbling his head.

Josh and Amelia had only just started dating. He wasn't sure how she'd wanted him to answer, so he said what his drunk heart told him to. "Yeah. She is."

Amelia took him by the hand and smiled at Josh. "Let's go. Nice meeting you, Reece Sanchez." She said his full name, a habit Josh later learned was a quirk of hers. It was like she was putting a face to the name, a name to the face. She often called him Josh Reuter, *Joshreuter*, like it was one full name on its own, like Cher or Beyoncé. He loved the way she said it.

While Sanchez introduced himself to the lecture hall, going over the syllabus for the semester, Josh returned to his computer screen. His thoughts continued to circle around Amelia. He expected to see an update from her accounts online, some sign that she was active, but all her accounts remained unchanged since he'd last seen them. The last time her blog had been updated was a week ago.

Her blog, Amelia Eats, was her claim to fame. She had started it a year before, covering food and lifestyle. Naturally, comparisons were drawn to her style and technique. She wrote like Anthony Bourdain, skillfully crafting articles about little-known eateries and restaurants in towns up and down the West Coast, and finding culturally significant hideouts that saw a boom in customers once she wrote about them. It helped that she was beautiful, and brilliant, and funny. Other guys might have been intimidated by her.

She went viral. You could see why. She had great taste, often breaking down the complexities of a dish into simple, approachable ways that made people fall in love with food again, even if it was just about the little cafe down the street that made a good sandwich. She could write about a blueberry and a reader would think it was made of gold.

Not just online foodies noticed. Major publications did too. *Vogue* featured her in an article about up-and-coming influencers, which skyrocketed her following. People paid attention to what she wore, where she ate, who she was with. She was making a real name for herself.

Josh scrolled through her blog, almost hearing her voice as he skimmed the last article she'd written. It was about a gelato shop they'd visited together, Centro Storico in Rome. She was more adventurous, encouraging him to try a pistachio flavor that he had been reluctant to taste. He liked it more than he thought he would. Who would have expected a layer of saltiness to be so welcome in a dessert? She'd given him a knowing smile and said, "See? You just have to trust me."

He'd do anything for that smile.

Amelia had worked hard to make a name for herself as an influencer, even though she hated the term. He remembered her laughing about the job title listed on a convention VIP badge when she was asked to speak at a YouTube convention, the place where she'd first met other creators like Sarah Speck.

"Content creator," Amelia had said. "That sounds so pretentious. What does that even mean? Content, please. I write. The concept of content creation makes me feel like a machine."

But it made her money. Lots of money. Advertisers loved her, brands were eager to work with her. She was entirely real and that was hard to come by online. Where the whole world looked fake, she wasn't.

Money didn't lie. She paid for their Rome trip with it. Josh knew a few people who would kill for her kind of audience. But it also meant that she was always on her phone. Whether it was because she was responding to comments, or uploading a story to Instagram, or recording a video for her YouTube channel, she was always online, even if she was at the gym or in the bathroom.

So then why wasn't she texting anyone back?

The lecture had started and Josh barely noticed.

× × ×

What's going on with Amelia?

The DM from a stranger later that afternoon took Josh by surprise. Hardly anyone ever DM'd him. He wasn't an influencer like Amelia, preferring to stay behind the camera instead of in front of it. Rarely did he make an appearance in her grid, and even then, people had to go digging to find his account. The fact that someone did set him on edge.

He didn't have as many followers as she did, but he'd seen a bump since they'd started publicly dating. Overnight, his photography Insta had gone from three hundred followers to over twenty-five thousand, all because she featured him in one of her Q&A videos. He was a private person, and he wanted to stay that way.

Josh's fingers hovered over the screen of his phone. Even from the safety of home, he couldn't escape the nagging question about Amelia.

Munch stared at him expectantly, as if he too was wondering what Josh was going to write. Josh wasn't sure what to say. He didn't want to sound ignorant, and he didn't want to sound careless. He truly didn't know where she was or if she'd needed a break from a seemingly endless job, always grinding, always doing more.

He decided to leave the message on "read" and closed the app.

He made Munch dinner. Derek still wasn't home from his afternoon class, and Josh wanted to get a head start on the required reading for Abnormal Psychology. But once his phone started buzzing, it didn't stop. It started as a trickle, then turned into a waterfall. His lock screen started filling up with notifications from Instagram and Facebook.

@jreuter_photography **Is she on break?**

Someone has to look into this! *@jreuter_photography*

It's weird that she hasn't posted her weekly recap. Any updates? *@jreuter_photography*

The messages and tagged posts kept coming, and they didn't stop. His phone was literally blowing up. It kept buzzing until he had to turn off its haptics.

He nearly jumped out of his skin when his phone rang, buzzing for real against the notifications. His phone almost never rang, and it was from a number he didn't recognize. He let it go to voice mail. If it was important, they would leave one.

Twitter was no better.

What is going on? *@ameliaashley @jreuter_photography*

Secret wedding? Much love! *@jreuter_photography*

I'm dying to know what's going on. *@ameliaashley @jreuter _photography*

The only way people would be asking these questions was if someone had said something.

Sarah Speck.

Heart racing, Josh went to her public profile, the one full of photos of her makeup looks, and found she had uploaded an Instagram story. Set against a red-and-white background was a paragraph of text:

Hey Glam Fam! I'm worried about *@ameliaashley*. *@jreuter _photography* asked where she was yesterday, since she was supposed to fly home with him but didn't. No one's heard from her. She might be missing. Anyone have any leads?

Josh felt like he'd been bricked over the head. She'd just told millions of followers that Amelia was missing. *Missing.* There was no proof that she was missing, she was just . . . gone. That was different! Amelia Ashley—had gone dark.

This was all his fault. He regretted reaching out to Sarah. She'd tagged him, putting his name out there, opening the floodgates, and a sinking feeling took hold of him as he set up his laptop at the table. He couldn't help but think the internet had sunk its fangs into him. And it was only the beginning. Hours felt like decades as the conversation started to pick up, gaining momentum with each unanswered question.

All the posts he was tagged in, all the DMs, all the hashtags he ignored. He couldn't respond to all of them. Plus, what would he even say? He didn't want to make people freak out, but it was too late now. Sarah Speck had led the charge.

Josh was going to lose this battle, whether he liked it or not. Once an audience latched on, it was hard to shake them off. He hated the attention. That was Amelia's domain.

Is everything okay?

What's going on?

This is crazy.

Did you two break up?

Where is she?

What did you do to her Josh?

Over and over, the words from anonymous users online swarmed in his head like wasps. His phone rang again. He barely noticed.

The world started to feel a lot smaller when eyes had turned toward him.

"Come on, Amelia. Where are you?" he mumbled, staring at her blog, Twitter, Instagram, and YouTube. Still no update. He waited for her to swoop in and clear everything up, but it never happened.

Someone on Instagram had tagged Josh in a post. It was a screenshot of the last photo she'd uploaded to her Instagram, a photo he'd taken, of her eating the pistachio gelato that she liked so much. She had her head tipped back, her face toward the sun, eyes closed. She looked so carefree and happy. It belonged in a magazine. Overlaid over the photo, direct and to the point, was:

WHERE IS AMELIA ASHLEY?

Blood rushed to Josh's ears. Automatically, he blocked the account that tagged him, but knew it wouldn't be enough. This was getting too real, overwhelming him like a crashing wave. Operating on instinct, he unfollowed everything that had to do with Amelia. He unfollowed her Twitter and Instagram, and unsubscribed from her YouTube channel. He needed space. He needed distance. He couldn't breathe.

It backfired. Almost instantly one person noticed. It started an entire avalanche of screenshots of his activity. He'd messed up. Badly.

Why is Josh unfollowing her accounts?

Where is Josh?

Hello? Josh! What's going on?

#WhereisAmeliaAshley

#WhathappenedtoAmeliaAshley

He navigated to his settings and deactivated all his accounts. His phone immediately went quiet.

Peace. Finally.

He held his head in his hands, able to breathe again after what felt like someone had been holding a pillow over his face, and he nearly jumped out of his skin when his phone rang again. Third time. Two voice mails.

Automatically, he answered.

"Mr. Josh Reuter?" the voice on the other end asked.

"Uh, who's calling?"

"This is the San Diego Police Department. When would be a good time for you to come in for some questions?"

CHAPTER FOUR

HARPER

WHERE IS AMELIA ASHLEY?

The first time Harper Delgado saw the post, she scrolled past it. It didn't even register in her brain that it was something worth paying attention to. Among the rest of her feed, it looked like an ad, and the question faded into the background as she continued to scroll while she took the bus to her house in Valencia Park. The man sitting next to her shifted and spread his legs, forcing Harper to wedge herself up closer against the cold metal wall. Her exposed knee touched something sticky, and she regretted wearing shorts today.

It had been a long day at school. She was starting her sophomore year at San Diego State and already she felt the weight of coursework bearing down on her. Scrolling mindlessly through Instagram was the one place where she could shut her brain off and veg for a few moments before, inevitably, she had to get back to reality.

The second time she scrolled past the post, it was shared again but this time from a different person on her feed. The repetition made her pause. This wasn't an ad. This was different.

This post had been shared by one of her old high school friends. Now Harper's interest was piqued.

The caption below it said: **Spread the word.** *#WhereisAmeliaAshley*

She googled the name Amelia Ashley. Instantly, a bunch of hits came up for the pretty blonde she saw in the post, but there weren't any recent news articles about her. All Harper understood was that Amelia was some kind of travel and food influencer, but she'd never heard of her. Harper mostly followed pet Instagram accounts and climate activist profiles, often vacillating between climate change anxiety and cute puppy videos like a pendulum. She didn't have time to do any other research. The bus was reaching her stop, so she pocketed her phone and pressed the button to be let off.

✕ ✕ ✕

Even at home, there was no escaping it.

"What's with this Amelia Ashley girl?" Lucy, her younger sister, asked.

Harper looked up from her coding homework. It took a second for her brain to process thought into English speech again; she'd been working on Python for so long, she'd almost started thinking in sources and indentations.

"Oh yeah," she said. "I saw that too. I think she's some travel influencer. Something to do with food?"

Lucy seemed unhappy with the answer and she leaned on the doorframe of Harper's bedroom, a clear sign that she wasn't going anywhere.

Lucy was still in high school, so she was always glued to her phone. By the looks of it, she'd just gotten home from after-school practice. She was still in her cross-country gear, her dark hair damp with sweat and pulled back in a high ponytail. Harper hadn't exercised in years, but Lucy made up for the both of them. She was always running everywhere and didn't seem to care that Harper was in the middle of working on something. "I'm seeing this girl all over," she said. "I figured you'd know something."

"I thought it was an ad for a movie or . . ." Harper didn't finish her thought. She traced her thumbnail over her lips as she reread her lines of code.

"Me too, but a ton of my friends were talking about it. I figured since you're the resident techie, always online and stuff, you'd know what it was about."

Harper made a noise of agreement, not committing to anything in particular, as her eyes went over her code, looking for any errors she might have made. She didn't find any. She was good at what she did.

She hadn't thought about Amelia Ashley since the bus. The name had come and gone from her head, as fast as the Santa Ana winds. "Mom home?" she asked.

"Not yet," said Lucy. "I guess she went missing after going on vacation to Rome with her boyfriend."

"Who, Mom?"

"No, Amelia. I'm reading about it on Twitter."

"That's really sad," Harper said. Any time a girl went missing was sad, but Harper felt it was particularly typical of everyone to care when the victim was a pretty blond girl who was probably loaded. People with teeth that straight didn't *not* come from money. Harper was well aware of how pretty white women enchanted society. Girls with brown skin like hers disappeared every day and people on the internet barely batted an eye. Harper went back to her coding. Classes had just started and already she felt like she was swimming in due dates.

"She was dating this dude who unfollowed all her accounts right after she went missing. Acting super suspicious. Crazy sad. I hope they find her okay."

"Crazy," Harper said, only half-listening. "Luce, can't you see I'm working?"

"Yeah, jeez. *Sorry* for bothering you!" Lucy threw up her hands and disappeared down the hall.

Harper sighed and tried to focus on the lines of code in front of her, but the universe was hell-bent on causing more distractions. Her own phone buzzed with a text message. This time it was from her client.

Is it ready yet?

Harper sighed. She unlocked her screen and typed back: **No, but for an extra 500 I can get it to you by this evening.**

The text bubble appeared, then disappeared, then reappeared again as her client figured out what to say. Harper waited.

Fine.

Harper smiled.

She had figured out a way to put her talents to good use. She was good with computers and made a few extra dollars on the side by doing some not-so-legal coding for clients who were willing to pay. This client in particular was asking for her to do his homework for him at San Diego State. She wasn't above charging him more for her services. If he was willing to cheat, he could pay for it. Harper knew what she was doing was wrong, but it paid the bills and took care of her family.

Harper was about to set her phone down when it started to vibrate. A different number was calling, one she didn't know. If she wasn't in the business of doing strangers' homework for a living, she would have let it go to voice mail, but she answered.

A breathy, high-pitched voice was on the other end. "Hi, is this Harper Delgado?"

Harper spun around in her swivel chair, heart thumping. Had one of her clients snitched? "Who's calling?" Harper asked, suspicious.

"My name is Tori, Tori Chapman. I got your number from a friend of mine you helped a while back."

Harper had first started out writing code after one of her friends last year began to suspect that her boyfriend was actually married at the time. Harper made an app that sent copies of his text messages to the friend's phone, a little tech vigilantism. The friend offered to pay her four hundred dollars for her time. Turns out, her friend's suspicions were true, she dumped him on the spot and paid Harper in cash. For once Harper wasn't late on her credit card bill. It snowballed from there.

She developed code and programs to be installed on phones, tracking everything that happened on the screen without the user finding out. Her clients mostly consisted of jilted lovers trying to prove that their significant others were cheating on them. It was a depressing line of work. There were always more desperate people who wanted to know for certain that they were in a toxic relationship, and with a few taps on the screen they would find out the truth. Harper was making more money writing a few lines of code for one client than her mom did working all month at the library. In today's world, Harper had to get creative. The rent on the family's two-bedroom apartment in Valencia Park had gone up and the extra income was a much-needed relief, even if

Harper wasn't exactly honest about how she'd been able to chip in. Mom and Lucy would be fine if they kept thinking she was making a lot of money tutoring.

"My friend said you were really good at what you do and I need your help now," Tori said. She sounded winded, like she was walking briskly while talking. Harper could hear cars rumbling in the background.

"Oh," Harper said. "Yeah, I'm Harper. What's this about?" She really did have a soft spot for helping people, even if that help was less than legal. Morally dubious, one might say. But in Harper's opinion, sometimes it took a little dirty work to shine light on truth.

"One of my best friends is missing, you might have heard by now. Her name is Amelia Ashley."

Hearing the name again made Harper's ears burn with interest. Harper tapped her fingers thoughtfully on the desk as she remembered what Lucy had said. Vacation. Rome. Boyfriend. This girl just kept popping up, like the universe was sending Harper a message.

"Ah, yeah," Harper said, then added, "I'm sorry about what's going on. It must be really stressful. But what do you think I can do for you?"

Tori paused, as if taking a moment to gather her thoughts. It got quieter, as if she'd stepped indoors. Her breathing was ragged and shallow, and Harper imagined her heart was racing.

"I need your help finding Amelia. I don't want to believe something terrible happened, but it doesn't feel right. Her boyfriend, Josh, he's one of my closest friends too, so I feel guilty even asking for this, but . . . I feel it in my gut. I don't have proof but something is *wrong*."

Harper tugged on her lower lip and winced. This was way beyond her expertise. "I'm not the police," she said. "I don't solve crimes." She didn't think of herself as a detective. Far from it. She'd be the last person in the world to wield a badge.

"I know you're good with computers, I know you can track phones and you can get information a lot of people can't otherwise. You're a hacker."

Harper's eyes darted to the door, in case Lucy had come back, but it remained empty. She didn't want her sister overhearing. "I'm not a magician," she said, lowering her voice. "You should call the police."

"I did, but they're slow. Please," Tori said. "I don't have a lot of money, but I can try to get you whatever you need. I know, it's a lot to ask, but . . . Amelia could be in trouble or . . ." A small sob escaped her and Harper's breath hitched. "It's been days, I'm afraid I'm too late."

Even if Tori was flush with cash, Harper still wasn't sure she was up for the job. She could help jilted lovers get proof that they were being cheated on, but finding a missing person half a world away was a lot to ask. Hearing Tori's panic made her insides go cold.

"I'm sorry," Harper said. Doing something like investigating a missing person would be exposing herself to law enforcement, potentially attracting attention when it was the absolute last thing she needed to keep providing for her family. "I can't do anything."

She could almost hear Tori's heart breaking on the other end. "Okay," Tori said after a long moment. "Thanks anyway."

When she hung up, Harper sat at her computer for a long while, staring at her homework as guilt gnawed at her insides.

Curiosity got the better of her and Harper saved her work and then saved it again, just to be sure. With a few quick keystrokes, she pulled up Amelia's Instagram profile and opened a picture of her with her boyfriend, Josh, or rather half of his face. He'd ducked out of the frame, as if shy, but he was smiling. The face looked familiar. All she did was stare at a computer all day, but she had a knack for remembering faces. Josh went to school with her at San Diego State.

Something about this Amelia Ashley girl was mysterious and strange. And the fact that Josh Reuter went to school with her felt close enough that she should at least be aware of the case. This wasn't some stranger; this was in her orbit.

Harper did the bare minimum first. She googled Amelia Ashley's name again, this time finding more results, the hashtag campaign #WhereisAmeliaAshley from Instagram had carried over to Twitter. The news was spreading like a virus. Lucy was right—everyone was talking about it. Harper got the feeling this was only the start of seeing this Amelia Ashley's name everywhere. Only one online newspaper had written a story so far.

Amelia Ashley, Beloved YouTube and Instagram Influencer, Missing?

Harper skimmed the article. Food blogger, wannabe Anthony Bourdain, devoted following, blah blah blah. She got the picture. She knew it was none of her business, but she couldn't help that her curiosity had been put into a stranglehold.

Harper saved her work a third time and put her computer to sleep, then padded into the kitchen. She found Lucy making some cinnamon-butter toast, her signature "lazy person churros" as she called them, while the TV was on in the living room.

"Is the dude she dated being questioned? That Josh guy?" Harper asked.

Lucy shrugged, scraping the butter over the toast. "Probably, right? I don't know."

Harper went to the fridge and took out a small bottle of orange juice.

"Interested now?" Lucy asked, a spark in her eye.

"Maybe. Not like I can do anything about it though. It's just weird, is all."

"Why do you think it's weird?"

Harper took a swig of orange juice and swished it around in her mouth for a moment before answering. "I go to school with the guy."

Lucy's eyebrows shot up. "No way."

"Yeah, he's in my Abnormal Psychology class. He sits in the back row, behind me."

"Six degrees of separation. You're practically famous," Lucy said, sarcastically.

Harper swatted the air by Lucy's arm and Lucy cried, "Hey! Watch my trash churros."

"It's not about me," Harper said. "I'm just saying, it's weird. I remember seeing him in class today." She shrugged. "He seemed normal. Like, not even worried."

"Ooh, creepy. Like, total sociopath vibes?"

"No, more like oblivious vibes. You'd think if someone made their girlfriend disappear, they wouldn't be acting so normal."

Lucy took a bite out of the corner of her toast. "That's the perfect cover though, right? Play the dumb boyfriend who has no idea where his poor, innocent girlfriend went?"

"Yeah, maybe," Harper said, then took another swig of orange juice. Her conversation with Tori still rang in her head. "Something about it is just weird, that's all."

"You keep saying that. Why?"

Harper wasn't sure how to tell the truth, especially about the call with Tori. "A lot of people are worried about her."

Lucy screwed up her face, her cheeks full of toast, and she hissed out a laugh. "Is that a crime now?"

"No, but . . ." She trailed off, staring at the magnets on the fridge, lost in thought. Something tugged at her heartstrings. There was a lot of injustice out in the world. Not knowing what happened to a loved one was probably one of the worst feelings in the universe. She stared at Lucy for a long moment as she leaned on the counter, idly watching the TV and nibbling on a corner of her toast.

Without another word, Harper left Lucy in the kitchen and went back to her room. She called Tori, who picked up almost immediately.

"I don't want your money," Harper said, talking quickly before she could change her mind. "And I can't promise anything, but I can promise I'll do some digging. It won't hurt to look around. Send me everything you have about Amelia."

CHAPTER FIVE

JOSH

Josh waited, alone in the interview room. Interrogation room, really. He understood the game here. They'd made no attempt to disguise the camera blinking away, pointed in his direction from an upper corner of the room. He'd agreed to come in for some questions, and this was the only place to do it.

The officer who greeted him at the reception desk when he first walked into the police station ten minutes before his scheduled appointment with the detective asked him if he wanted anything to drink. He'd asked for water. Condensation had started to sweat on the outside of the paper cup, and by the time the door to the interview room opened and the detective walked in an hour later, the condensation had turned into a puddle, making the paper soft.

"Hey, Josh," the detective said, closing the door behind her. "Thank you so much for waiting. The copy machine is my nemesis."

Josh didn't want to seem rude. He hadn't expected a female detective. She could have been his mother's age, with tawny brown hair pushed back from her forehead with a headband. The headband was an odd choice in his opinion. He hadn't expected a detective to wear one. It was the kind you might find in a pharmacy—cheap and practical—but it made her look girlish, despite her power suit and sensible heels. She smiled at him, the creases around her eyes deepening when she did, and he, of course, smiled back.

He half-stood out of his chair and shook her hand. "Yes, hi," he said. "Detective . . . ?"

"Hindmarsh. But please, call me Catherine." Her eyes flicked down at his hand for a moment before she smiled wider. She was attractive for an older woman, not that Josh was interested. He just noticed these kinds of things. "Please, get comfortable. This won't take long, I promise. Just a couple of routine questions—dotting some t's, crossing some i's, as they say."

Josh smiled at her joke even though he didn't find it particularly funny. He wanted to appear good-natured, despite how his insides were roiling with nerves. He knew how this looked. He knew what might happen next and he tried to put his best foot forward. "I get it completely. No trouble at all. Do you have any update on Amelia?"

Detective Hindmarsh set a large legal pad down on the metal table between them and leaned back in her chair. She readjusted the headband and sighed. "Unfortunately not. We're actually having some more trouble than we thought on that front." Josh moved to ask why, but she continued, "International cases and the like can be a little slow going, you understand. We just have a few questions to ask."

"Of course, anything I can do to help."

"Thank you so much." She had nice brown eyes, and Josh felt more at ease. "So, from what I understand, you were dating Amelia."

"Yeah, for a while now."

"You two were exclusive . . ."

"Entirely. We're not really into anyone else."

"Awesome. So you two decided to take a trip together. Tell me about that."

Josh cleared his throat. "Ah, yeah. She loves to travel, and well, we found the trip of a lifetime. We booked tickets to Europe, planning to stay for two weeks, seeing the sights. Paris, Rome, the works."

"Like *Roman Holiday*," Detective Hindmarsh said, midway through taking notes.

"Yes! Exactly. Vespas and everything." Hindmarsh smiled at that.

"And Rome was the last place you saw her, correct? What was the name of the hotel you stayed at? Or maybe an Airbnb?"

"Hotel Artemide. I've got the address on my phone if you need it."

"That's great. Yes, please."

Josh pulled out his phone and opened up the text conversation with Amelia, displaying the address of the hotel for her to copy down. "And do you have a phone number with that?" she asked.

"I don't, sorry. Amelia did all the planning. She bought the tickets, she organized the trip."

"No worries. We can google it." She wrote quickly, her handwriting a scribble across the page. Between pauses in the conversation, the only sound in the room was the pen scratching on the paper.

"Tell me more about your itinerary. You had no idea that she would decide not to come home with you?"

Josh shook his head. "No. She bought us both round-trip tickets. To think she'd leave me, it was a surprise, but I trusted her that she knew what she was doing."

"And you decided to come home without her?"

Josh knew that question was coming. "Yes, I didn't want to miss the flight. I wasn't sure what else to do. So I left."

Detective Hindmarsh hummed thoughtfully as she wrote, nodding all the while. "So, when was the last time you saw Amelia? Do you have an exact time? Place?"

"Yeah, actually. We had a lunch reservation at this restaurant called Il Gusto right before our flight. She wanted to get one last bite of food in Rome before we were going to fly back together. But we went our separate ways after dinner, and she didn't show up at the airport. I couldn't miss the flight, I'm in school. So I left without her. I know it looks bad, but . . ." Josh decided to leave it at that. Detective Hindmarsh was still writing.

"I see," she said, only looking up from the page when she was done taking notes.

"I really wasn't worried about her. She had friends in the city."

Detective Hindmarsh nodded. "Okay. And did anything happen out of the ordinary before that? Did you two fight at all or . . . ?"

Josh grew quiet. He remembered what happened, her almost flipping the table on him, out of the blue. He blinked and took a moment. "No," he said. "Nothing."

"If you're trying to protect her—"

"I'm not. Everything was normal. We were happy." He wanted everyone to know that Amelia was perfect. Derek teased him sometimes that Amelia had been too perfect for someone like Josh, a gentle ribbing that only slightly rubbed raw. He didn't want one little detail to get in the way of being able to find her.

Detective Hindmarsh analyzed him for a moment. "You don't have to lie, Josh. No one's in trouble. If we can find her, or if you know where she is, there's no problem."

"I swear. I last saw her at Il Gusto and then that was it. She hasn't messaged me since."

"Nor have you messaged her. Except to say MISS YOU." She'd seen his chat history with Amelia when he showed her the address of the hotel on his phone.

"I wasn't sure what else to do. I thought we broke up." It hurt saying it out loud.

"How about your luggage? Do you think we could take a look at it?"

"The airline lost it. It still hasn't arrived yet."

She sucked her teeth. "Hate it when that happens." But he heard something else in her voice.

"I'm not lying. You can call the airline, I swear. You can check it, but it's only got my clothes and some souvenirs. If I had it, you could go through it. I don't care."

"Okay, we'll make a note of that." Detective Hindmarsh wrote something down, then asked, without looking up, "And how did you get that cut on your hand?"

The air in the room felt ten degrees cooler. Either the central air had just kicked on, or Josh was starting to feel like the conversation had taken a turn. He didn't know how many ways he could tell the truth without everyone thinking he was lying.

"I cut it on some broken glass. It's nothing." He pressed his thumb into the palm of his hand.

Detective Hindmarsh clicked her tongue. "We've all been there, haven't we?" Her voice was flat and unreadable. Josh had the sudden realization that he was dealing with a seasoned professional. He'd been thrown off by the headband. She was better at this than he'd thought. How could he prove to someone like her that he hadn't done anything wrong?

Josh's chest felt tight. "I want to find Amelia as much as anyone. If anything bad happened to her because I left . . . I don't think I could live with myself. I don't know how to make it right."

"Well, you've been extraordinarily helpful so far. We'll check in with the hotel, see if they've got any information we can use. Your timeline really puts things into perspective."

Josh chewed on his words before he asked them. "Do you think I had something to do with her disappearance?" The question hung in the air for a beat, like a cloud of smoke that neither of them could bat away. Josh's heart thudded painfully in his chest.

Finally, Detective Hindmarsh smiled again, bringing back that charm. "Thanks for coming in today, Mr. Reuter. We'll be in touch."

✕ ✕ ✕

Josh knew he was in deep shit.

Outside the precinct, he took a moment to breathe and gather his thoughts. The afternoon sun was warm and peaceful, the exact opposite of Josh's inner turmoil. He felt jumpy and frightened, mostly at the idea that the police were watching him from the windows of the precinct. He needed to be calm, normal.

But how could he possibly convince people of the truth when all they saw was the boyfriend of the missing girl, the only person to see her last? He felt like he was going crazy. How could this be happening?

As he walked down the sidewalk, keeping his head low and his eyes down, he texted Amelia.

They think I had something to do with you being gone. Amelia, this isn't funny. Please, please call me.

He hit SEND and, like his previous text, it went unread. His insides churned. If she really had run off with someone to make him jealous, or she had wanted him to come crawling back to her on his hands and knees, this had gone too far.

But what if someone had taken her? He should have run after her, he should have protected her. Instead, he thought he'd been doing the right thing, letting her have her space. He'd learned the hard way that girls needed breathing room. His stomach churned.

He needed to be smart about this. He needed to stay cool and collected—his whole life was on the line now.

The moment Josh got home, he closed the door behind him and slid to the floor. There was no oxygen in the room. Everything felt too close. His skin was too tight on his body. He needed to think, but all his mind could do was race, and he couldn't keep up. It felt like he was being dragged behind a moving truck, choking on dust and dirt and forced along for the ride.

He didn't get off the floor in the entryway for some time. Only when Munch waddled over demanding food did he move. Even then, as he scooped food into Munch's bowl, Amelia's laugh chimed in his memory.

How was he going to get out of this?

✕✕✕

As soon as he could, Josh called Hotel Artemide and asked to speak to someone who could help. The receptionist spoke broken English, and Josh didn't know any Italian, so the conversation was short. The only word he knew in Italian was *grazie. Thank you.* But no one had seen or heard from Amelia since that day.

Online, word spread that the Italian police had started their own investigation. He had a Google Alert set up to email him whenever her name was mentioned in the news. Josh started sending text messages to Amelia every hour.

Please be okay.

I'm begging you, please come home.

Please. I'm scared for you.

I miss you.

All unread. Still, he sent them.

He never hurt her. He wasn't the guy that everyone wanted to make him out to be. He needed to prove his innocence, and to prove his innocence, he needed to find her.

✕✕✕

The next day, a knock at the front door felt like a slap in the face. Josh yanked it open, irrationally hoping that Amelia had come home, only to find that it was instead Detective Hindmarsh and another police officer Josh didn't recognize. A police car sat parallel-parked in the street.

"Hey, Josh," Detective Hindmarsh said. She smiled at him, that same warm smile she always had. "Can we come in?"

Josh's heart jackhammered. "Did you find Amelia?"

Detective Hindmarsh shook her head. "We haven't, no. Do you have a moment?"

"Sure, come on in." The apartment was empty, except for Munch, who greeted the police with his tail high. He rubbed up against Detective Hindmarsh's legs, leaving a streak of fur on her pants in his wake. "Sorry about him, he likes you."

"No problem at all. Cute cat! This won't take long. We just wanted to ask you some questions, and maybe if you were willing, we could take a look at your room."

"Do you have a warrant?"

"Do we need one?"

Josh's heart was in his throat, choking him. "No. I just . . . Anything I can do to help." *Anything I can do not to look guilty*, he thought. He gestured deeper into the apartment. "Please."

Hindmarsh held out an arm in front of Josh, blocking him as the officer moved inside first. Then she asked, "Amelia spent a lot of time here, didn't she? Maybe she left something behind?"

"She slept over a lot, yeah. But she didn't live here. She's got an apartment a few blocks away. I'm not sure what will be helpful here."

"Anything at this point, really, is better than nothing. We're starting off on our heels here a bit." Detective Hindmarsh smiled again, brightly, like she was chatting with a friend.

Josh knew this was a bad idea. But turning them away would look like he had something to hide. And he wanted to appear helpful, to *be* helpful. He loved Amelia so much, it was making him crazy, crazy enough to let police search his place.

He told the officer where his bedroom was. Josh and Detective Hindmarsh stayed just outside the doorway, watching from the hall. Josh had no idea what he'd be looking for.

"Have the Italian police helped out at all?" Josh asked.

Detective Hindmarsh seemed surprised he knew about that. "They haven't yet, but we're remaining optimistic."

The police officer didn't touch Josh's things, but he looked around with the keen eye of someone looking for anything out of the ordinary. Josh wished he'd made his bed today. He looked like a slob. He wasn't sure what they were hoping to find, but if it could help rule him out as a suspect, it would be a start. Proving his innocence meant that they could focus on the real mystery.

"You're a good student, Josh?" Detective Hindmarsh asked.

"I try. I think that accounts for most of it."

"What are you studying?"

"Photography."

"You didn't want to go to an art college for that?"

The cop got down on his knees and he looked under Josh's bed. All he would find was a sock that had escaped the laundry basket.

"San Diego State just worked for me. I like it a lot, made a lot of friends."

Detective Hindmarsh said, "You seem like a popular guy, if you don't mind my saying. Do you go to parties?"

Josh hardly saw how that was relevant. The beat cop had opened his closet and turned on the light. "Sometimes. I'm not a total shut-in.

Are you looking for anything in particular?" He switched his focus to the officer by his closet. It was empty.

"Taking a quick look, nothing to worry about. Just doing our job," Hindmarsh said.

The beat cop didn't seem to find what he was looking for. He shut off the closet light, closed the door, and shook his head.

Detective Hindmarsh clapped her hands. "All right then. If you find anything that you might think could help us find Amelia, let me know." Detective Hindmarsh gave Josh her card, her name printed in neat block letters with her phone number and email.

He hadn't expected that they would be leaving so quickly. Josh showed them the door, Munch begging for more food all the while, and just as Josh opened the door for them to go out, an unmarked van pulled up and blocked the police car in.

Josh's gaze made the detective and the officer notice. A man in a T-shirt and board shorts got out of the driver's seat, clutching a clipboard, and moved to the back of the van. He brought something out that made Josh's heart sink.

"Josh Reuter?" the guy asked. He pronounced his name like *rudder*.

"Yeah. That's mine."

It was his lost luggage from the trip, delivered at literally the worst time.

Detective Hindmarsh looked at the luggage, obviously noting the airline's bag tag wrapped around the handle.

"Say, Josh, how about we continue this back at the station? And bring that along."

CHAPTER SIX

JOSH

They'd taken Josh's suitcase the moment he got to the station. He couldn't say no. Rather, he could, but doing so was asking for even more trouble. Besides, there was nothing in there that would be of any importance, and giving it to them was the best chance at proving his innocence.

"Am I under arrest?" Josh asked. Did he need a lawyer? Should he call his parents?

Detective Hindmarsh watched him carefully from her seat across from him, both of them in the interview room once more. She eyed him, and Josh felt like he was under a microscope, anxiety bubbling up in his throat like bile. Nobody, especially not the police, believed him. Even Josh was starting to doubt what really happened. He revisited the events of that day, over and over, constantly churning his memories like maybe he'd find something there that he'd missed.

"I swear, I didn't hurt Amelia. I don't know how many times I have to say it."

"Understand something, Josh. We're just ruling out all of the major players here. We looked into the hotel, we ran into a brick wall. If we're going to find Amelia, you're going to have to start cooperating with us."

"I am!" What did she mean a brick wall? Detective Hindmarsh watched him. Heat bloomed on Josh's cheeks. "How do I prove to you I didn't do anything?"

"You can start with telling us what really happened that day."

Josh closed his eyes and took a steadying breath. He opened his eyes once more and held his forehead in his hands. "We sat down. We had a table on the street where we could watch people walking. Amelia liked watching people."

"What did you have to eat?"

"I ordered a pizza. She ordered a pasta. I also ordered a bottle of wine. Red."

"Was that the glass you cut your hand on?"

"Yes," Josh said, closing his eyes again. "It broke."

"How did the bottle break?"

"It fell over when Amelia kicked the table."

"Why would she do such a thing?"

"I don't know."

"Josh—"

"I don't know!"

"It's okay. Take a breath. All right. Start from the beginning." Detective Hindmarsh's pen hovered over the page.

Josh couldn't help but feel like he was losing control, and the thought of losing control made him angrier than he wanted to appear. Losing his temper now was equivalent to admitting guilt. He took a steadying breath and forced himself back to that day. "Everything was fine. I was keeping an eye on the time. We had to make our flight. She packed while I checked us out. I came back up to the room and she said she wanted to grab a bite to eat before we needed to be at the airport. I said sure—I was getting hungry—and we went to this restaurant she'd been talking about going to the entire trip. Il Gusto. It had a little outdoor seating area, and we got a table. We ate, everything was normal. And when we were done, I checked the time and said we needed to go so we could get through security and that's when everything changed. I'm getting chills remembering it now. She looked at me, like I was someone else. Someone . . . She looked at me like she wanted to kill me."

Detective Hindmarsh had gone stone-still. "Why would she do that?"

Josh palmed his forehead again. The skin of his hand felt cold, but the skin on his forehead felt hot. "I truly have no idea. I never hit her, never hurt her. God, I could see myself marrying her. I said we should plan another trip together, maybe someplace cool like Iceland, but she looked at me and said . . ." Josh debated whether or not he should continue, but if he had any hope of finding Amelia, he had to be honest. "She said, with this look in her eye, 'I hate you so much' and then she attacked me."

"Attacked you?"

Josh winced. "She jumped up from the table, kicked it, and started clawing at me, going for my throat. I only pushed her to get her off."

"And you never touched her like that before?"

"Never. Not in a million years."

Detective Hindmarsh's eyes seemed to bore right through him. "And you have no idea why she would do such a thing?"

"Not at all." Josh breathed the words, at a loss. Amelia was one of the most levelheaded girlfriends he'd ever had. She wasn't prone to flying off the handle over the simplest of things. Once, he'd caught her snooping on his phone, searching for evidence of cheating with other women, but he didn't think she would do anything like that again. "I don't know how else I can prove that she totally flipped? I don't want to make her sound crazy, but it was like I was talking to a different person. Do you think . . . Do you think she had some sort of medical emergency? Like maybe, she was having some sort of episode and I didn't know any better? I should have known it was too weird for her to just walk away like that . . . Why did I let her go?"

Detective Hindmarsh's eyebrows shot up as she wrote his story. "Do you know if her family had ever had some sort of medical history like that?"

Josh shook his head. "I don't know. She never talked about anything like it before. But I've never met her family. I'm not sure they were close."

"You'd been dating a while and you never met her parents?"

"Is that weird?"

Detective Hindmarsh frowned. "Not particularly. But if she truly did have some sort of medical emergency, this changes things. Getting hold of her family would help."

"Have you spoken to them? Told them what's going on?"

Hindmarsh kept writing. "We'll call some hospitals in Rome, see if they have anyone matching Amelia's description who's in psychiatric care. Thank you for your candor." She didn't answer his question.

"She's not crazy."

"I understand. But we want to make sure she's safe. Were there any witnesses? Anyone we can contact who can corroborate your story?"

Josh thought about it for a moment. "The waitress maybe? There was another couple sitting out there with us. They pulled her off me. But I didn't get their names, or really remember anything about them.

I was so shaken up." Josh took a breath. "Detective, I'm sorry. I haven't told anyone about this. I didn't want her friends to think she had lost her mind, but . . . I know, I shouldn't have kept it from you."

"Telling us sooner could have helped, but we know now. We'll do some due diligence, make sure we can get our timeline in order."

There came a small knock on the mirror. Detective Hindmarsh let out a small sigh and she got up. "Excuse me. It'll be only a second."

Of course, Josh knew that there were other people on the other side of the mirror, watching, but the knock rattled him. His heart beat in his throat. He knew cops didn't interrupt interviews for nothing. Had they found Amelia? Was she hurt? The wait was agonizing but Detective Hindmarsh came back a couple minutes later, now holding a manila envelope.

She said nothing as she set down the folder and took her seat.

"Is it Amelia?" Josh asked, his throat tight. "Did they find her?"

"Not yet." Her jaw was set, and Josh knew something was wrong. He clenched his fist, so hard it hurt the cut on his palm. He kept tearing it open. Blood already started pooling inside the bandage.

Detective Hindmarsh leaned back in her chair. It squeaked on its hinges. The wait was worse than anything before. He couldn't take his eyes off the folder. Josh felt like he was being dangled above a shark tank. Finally, she said, "We ran some tests on your bag, like I said, checking off some boxes. But we found something that was awfully odd. We found blood in your suitcase."

Cold sweat dripped down Josh's armpits. "What?" Nothing made sense anymore.

"Blood, Josh. Know how something like that got there?"

Josh had to think about it, but his thoughts rushed so quickly it was like trying to grab onto a speeding train. "Maybe when I cut my hand? It bled a lot at the time. I had to pull some glass out of my skin. Maybe it got on something? I was in a rush to get to the airport."

"Hmm. Maybe. What's your blood type?"

"O-negative. I donate blood a lot." If they needed proof, the nurses at the clinic would vouch for him. He was popular there.

"I see. Well, the type we found in your suitcase was O-positive. Amelia's type is O-positive."

The periphery of Josh's vision had started to darken. He blinked a few times, not quite sure he was hearing things correctly. Blood rushed in his ears, and he felt like maybe this wasn't happening. This couldn't be happening, but Detective Hindmarsh stared at him with a level, unwavering gaze. He almost didn't hear when she asked, "Why would her blood be on your clothes in your luggage?"

"I have no idea." He knew he said the words, but he wasn't sure his mouth moved.

"Why don't we talk about what happened that day? The truth, this time."

PART 2

TERMINALLY ONLINE

HARPER

Tori emailed me a ton of data on Amelia, so I'll be sorting through my findings and organizing all my thoughts here. I'm trying to get a clear picture of who she is, but I want to make sure I'm not going crazy either. What I've found is hard even for me to wrap my head around. What Tori sent me is . . . disturbing. I've made notes, checked some facts, for my own records. I don't plan on sharing this with anyone else, not until I know what exactly happened here. I want to try to get a timeline of events down because maybe then it'll paint a clearer picture of everything happening up until now. There's something about this case that doesn't seem right, but I want to be sure. I want to know exactly what happened.

I've got transcripts of Amelia's YouTube videos, blog posts, even some Instagram captions that I hope will shed some light on who exactly Amelia Ashley is. She shared so much of her life online, I wanted to pick the stuff that seemed important.

I hope I can make sense of everything.

—HD

CHAPTER SEVEN

AmeliaAimlessly YouTube Channel
Day in the Life - Vlog #498
Uploaded on March 2

Amelia: I've never donated blood before. This is so scary. I hate needles! Do I sound like a wimp? I'll bet a lot of you watching are like, psh, please, Amelia. Get over it. I don't know why! It just freaks me out. Does that make me sound like a baby?

[HD: Amelia is lying down on a medical bed in a blood dona-tion truck. She's—for lack of a better word—glowing. This girl is exactly what being telegenic is about. She's got her blond hair pulled back in a ponytail, and it flips over her shoulder when the nurse comes over and inserts the needle in her arm. She's got the face of a cheerleader, perky and bright, with stunning blue eyes. Even when she cringes, she's still pretty. No wonder people are drawn to her. This video has 214,000 views. About donating blood. Ad revenue of a video with those kinds of numbers is nothing to scoff at. I'm in the wrong line of work.]

I talk when I'm nervous. I'm so sorry. I sound like I'm rambling. You can't see her, but the nurse is laughing at me. Yes, you are! [Amelia laughs.] It's okay! I'd laugh at me too. I probably look like a loon. This is so scary, but I'm okay. I can do this. I can do it. I hope I don't pass out. Imagine if I passed out right before my date with Josh tonight. It'll be our first date, officially boyfriend-girlfriend. I'm so excited, the kind of nerves that are wiggling around in my stomach. Not really butterflies, but something that makes me feel like I'm alive.

Tonight is going to be amazing. We're going to a restaurant called Jin's House. I'm sure a lot of you who live here in San Diego know it. For those of you who don't and are planning your trip, it's the best Korean place in town and it specializes in Korean street food, like *dakgangjeong* and *tteokbokki*. They make their own noodles for you right there in the restaurant. I'll be posting a full write-up on my blog, so you can read all about it. I've been looking forward to eating there for forever, and thanks to you guys I finally got a reservation! Chef Jin's nephew heard about my channel, and I just about passed out for real when they asked me to come for dinner. They really liked my previous videos for the Copper Door, the cutest falafel joint (which is the best in town, if you haven't read my review, by the way, I'm linking below), and they were really excited for me to try their food too. Chef Jin also agreed to let me film some B-roll, so I can get some really great footage to put up on Instagram. I always ask the chefs if it's okay to do stuff like that, with them being so swamped and all. I'd hate to bother anyone, you know how I am. They're usually pretty happy to share their talents though! I'm so excited that I get to see Chef Jin in action, and you guys get to come with me too!

[HD: Her editing style is very snappy. She knows how to navigate the camera, make sure a shot never lingers too long or too short. She can frame what she's filming in a way that's pleasing to the eye. It helps that she's attractive. From what I can see, most of her audience is female. I have to double-check, but it's somewhere in the 90 percent range, aging younger, 18–26-year-olds. People are inherently interested in a pretty girl doing the things they wish they could do. She talks to the camera like I'm her friend, and I almost believe it. She's a girl putting herself out there, and it resonates with viewers.]

All done? Oh my gosh. That went so fast! I did it! Yay! Wanna know a secret? I'm only here to get a snack and apple juice. I'm totally joking. Oh gosh, I get my own card?

[HD: Amelia holds up her Red Cross card, while she happily eats a packet of graham crackers. She's blood type O-positive.]

✗ ✗ ✗

Amelia Eats: A Blog
JIN'S HOUSE: SIMPLY DIVINE
By Amelia Ashley
Posted on March 3

My mom always said that the best things in life often come wrapped in paper bags: school lunches packed with love, handmade Christmas presents under the tree, treasured old school books ... There, one can find the divine in simple packaging.

Jin's House is University Heights' best-kept secret here in San Diego. Nestled between a pharmacy and a laundromat on Park Boulevard, you might be forgiven for missing it. You can look for the sign out front with the steaming bowl in the South Korean flag's colors, though you shouldn't worry about getting too lost if you follow your nose. If I had been blindfolded, I imagine I would have been able to find my way by following the intoxicating smell of kimchi alone.

Josh stood waiting for me in front of the large windows and I could see just how small the restaurant was. It might barely fit ten people inside, including Chef Jin Seo-yeon, a small Korean grandmother who hunches over the heat like hundreds of *halmoni* elders who came before her, passing on their precious knowledge. To get a reservation here is akin to eating in the chef's own kitchen.

Like me, Josh never had the chance to visit Jin's House before, and he's buzzing to get inside, based on the smile he flashes when he sees me coming. Jin's House doesn't have a dress code, but this was our first official date, so he'd worn a nice blazer over a striped T-shirt. I went for comfort, feeling a little underdressed in my floral sundress. But when you're about to eat Korean street food, you can expect to get a little messy, and that's the best part.

"Welcome to the Splash Zone," I told him, which made him laugh. Come to Jin's House and don't be afraid to get messy.

Jin's House's claim to fame is the *tteokbokki*. If you like spice, this is the dish for you. Stir-fried rice cakes float in a radioactive red soup, made from fiery chili paste (*gochujang*), the inevitable stain maker. For the uninitiated, Korean meals are served with several side dishes called *banchan*, sometimes so numerous there's hardly any room for you to rest your elbows. Perhaps it's a method of ensuring that patrons remember their manners in the presence of Chef Jin.

Spicy cucumber salad, garlic-seasoned spinach, stir-fried eggplant, fish cakes, braised beef . . . I ran out of room in my notebook trying to list them all. I had totally forgotten to buy a new one, but now I have an excuse to return to make sure I can give you a complete list here. If there's one thing to take away from experiencing authentic Korean cuisine, it's that you need to arrive hungry. You will not leave on an empty stomach.

I didn't know if it was the *tteokbokki* that put me in a good mood or something else, but as about the twentieth side dish was squeezed onto our table, all I could think was that coming to Jin's House with Josh was one of the best ideas I'd ever had.

(Don't let my swooning detract from the review of this restaurant. I might truly, madly, deeply like this boy.)

[HD: Amelia inserted a photo with the article. This is the first photo we have of Josh Reuter. She posted it to her Instagram the same day she went to donate her blood. He's a relatively attractive guy. Not my type, but easy on the eyes. He's got brown hair and brown eyes, with a jawline like a movie star. He's looking at the camera, obviously one Amelia had taken, chopsticks pinching kimchi hovering over his mouth. He's got a sparkle in his eye, and anyone can tell he's into Amelia.]

The air sizzles with sound and smell, and the atmosphere is dimly lit but romantic. You might just forget that anything else exists outside of this place. I'm not eager to return to the real world yet, even as I relive my time there as I write this. I've been bewitched, enchanted. The smoke of the barbecued ribs clouds my senses, like a dream, and I'm drifting off to Neverland.

Chef Jin didn't have time for me to interview her. She was busy with the other tables that had booked reservations, and I didn't want to bother her. But her work is extraordinary. Her hands are strong and sure as she moves around her kitchen with unbroken focus and finesse. She doesn't even break a sweat. I've linked to posts on my Instagram, where she allowed me to take some videos to show her in action. As I watch Chef Jin's hands transform basic ingredients into a meal that I will never forget, I think of a history that sustains, of memories that linger.

Before we left, full to bursting at the seams, Chef Jin wrapped six house-made *dalgona* candy (honeycomb toffee) in paper for us to enjoy on our walk home. Josh and I couldn't resist them, even though we'd already eaten like kings. We shared each and every one.

Simply divine.

CHAPTER EIGHT

AmeliaAimlessly YouTube Channel
Ask Amelia - Q&A - Boyfriend Edition
Uploaded on April 20

[HD: This is one of several Q&As that Amelia posted to her channel, but one of only a few that Josh has been featured in. At this point, they've been dating for a few months, note the date the video was posted. Amelia gets a lot of comments and questions on her videos, and she does whole videos interacting with her community that way. In this video, she and Josh are sitting in her bedroom. It's pretty typical as far as aesthetically pleasing bedrooms go. Not exactly my taste, but who am I to judge?

She's got a four-poster bed with fairy lights strung around the headboard, lots of pictures on the back wall (she had a video once where she redecorated her room and showed that they were pictures of Josh, of her friends, of places she's been. Thailand, France, Colombia, and Australia. So perfect they almost look like they're taken from a magazine. Her walls are wallpapered with gold foil. It might seem tacky, but with Amelia it seems very natural. Lots of commenters adore her bedroom.

The rest of her room is pretty sparse. She's got a desk where she does all her work and a lamp. I'm surprised. I didn't really take her for a minimalist, but it's cozy. She seems to film most of her more personal, chatty videos in here. The rest, she's out on the town.

Since it's a Q&A, Amelia and Josh are sitting side by side on her bed. Even though she's got a full face of makeup, she looks really casual, like my little sister. She kind of reminds me of her in a way. She's wearing an oversized sweatshirt that drops over one shoulder to reveal a sports bra, and her hair is up like she's just got back from the gym. Josh too is looking super casual, with a soft-looking T-shirt, his dark wavy hair pushed back from his face.]

Amelia: Hey guys! Welcome back to my channel. As you know, or if you've never been here before, I'm Amelia Ashley, back with another video for you. Yay! Today I figured we'd be a little more laid-back, a little more cazh—

Josh: Cazh?

Amelia: Yeah, casual. You know, *cazh.*

Josh: Did you make that up?

Amelia: What? No! You've never heard that word before? You're kidding, right? [HD: Josh smiles and Amelia nudges him with her elbow and turns back to the camera, her eyes sparkling.] **He's teasing**

me! Gone and ruined my intro. Meanie! Well, so much for introductions! Thanks, Josh. Everyone in the comments, say, Thanks Josh!

[HD: Josh rolls his eyes, but he seems to be having a nice time. He doesn't look awkward on camera at all. If I were him, I'd be so nervous. Amelia's got 700,000 followers at this point. If I knew that this video could be seen by 700,000 people, I might die of stage fright. By the way, she has over 5,000 comments of people thanking Josh. (I'm guesstimating. I'm not going to count that many. But it's a lot.)]

Josh: Okay, so what are we doing? How does this work?

Amelia: Well, I asked a bunch of my Instagram followers to send me questions, and I got almost two thousand questions, which—thank you! So much! All of you! I feel bad I could only use so many. We should do more of these in the future, yeah? Together?

Josh: If that's what the people want! I don't think I'm all that interesting.

Amelia: Shut up, people want to get to know you like I have! I guess the secret is out—we're Official. God, I hate using that word but, what else are we?

Josh: You prefer *going steady*?

Amelia: That sounds so corny.

Josh: We're sidetracked again! What are we doing here?

Amelia: Right, I picked fifty questions, sent in by my followers, aimed at both of us. I've got the ones for you on my phone, and, Josh, I'll send you the ones to ask me. Here. You got it? Okay, great. So now we go back and forth and ask each other questions, and maybe we'll get to know some stuff about each other, and the community will learn about you too!

Josh: Okay, I'm game. Who goes first? You or me? You go first, it's your channel. I mean, I'll ask you a question first.

Amelia: Ready!

Josh: Amelia, what is your favorite book?

Amelia: *Peter Pan*!

Josh: [laughs] No hesitation!

Amelia: Oh my gosh, it's the best story. I grew up with it. Absolute classic. Have you read it?

Josh: No. I don't read a lot. Not as much as I used to at least.

Amelia: Because Josh isn't a nerd like me.

[HD: Amelia is endearingly self-deprecating.]

Josh: That's not true. You're smart and beautiful—the total package.

Amelia: You're just being nice. I always have to have a book with me, especially when I'm traveling. It's the best way to pass the time. And *Peter Pan* is the perfect companion too, all about traveling and new adventures. I wanted to be Wendy Darling when I was little. She was my favorite.

Josh: I used to love reading those mystery books. What were they called, Boxcar Children? Hardy Boys, stuff like that.

Amelia: Ah, so reading mystery books is the key to your mystery, I see. Okay, next question. Josh, what's your favorite article of clothing?

Josh: That's such a hard question. Maybe my shoes?

Amelia: Oh my gosh, you have, like, one pair.

Josh: Why would I need more than one pair? They're shoes!

Amelia: So practical.

Josh: Next question. Amelia, what are three things on your bucket list?

Amelia: Easy. Go skydiving in Hawaii, see a Galápagos turtle in person, and finish a marathon. I'm gonna throw it back at you. What are three things on your list?

Josh: Oh, I don't know. I haven't really thought about stuff like that.

Amelia: Not even a little? Like, if you were told you had a week to live, what's something you would do?

Josh: Um. Maybe go to the Grand Canyon, take photos—

Amelia: Oh yeah! Josh's photos are incredible. I'll link his stuff down below. It's insane. He's so good. His Instagram is so pretty.

Josh: Aw, thanks. I don't know if they know this, but yeah, I go to school for photography. I want to do it for a living. Maybe take pictures for *National Geographic*. I guess that'd be on my real bucket list—get a picture in there.

Amelia: Okay, here's another one.

Josh: Go for it.

Amelia: Sammy B. wants to know, What's your favorite animal?

Josh: Cat.

Amelia: Didn't even have to think about it! So fast.

Josh: Cats are the best! They just chill, and it's awesome.

Amelia: You guys, Josh's cat, Munch! He's so cute. He's a rescue!

Josh: He really is the best. I'm not sure what I'd do without him. He's better than most people I know. I'm not even joking. If anyone says they hate cats, they're just a bad person. You can tell a lot about someone if a cat likes them.

Amelia: Very opinionated, I see.

Josh: Okay, next up. Amelia, gun-to-your-head—Where's the one place you want to travel next?

Amelia: Umm. If I could drop everything and go? I'd really love to visit Rome.

Josh: You've never been? I'm shocked. You've never told me that.

Amelia: Oh, it's just so cliché, you know? Like, the foodie loves Italian food, surprise-surprise. This next user asks you, Josh: Do you believe in ghosts?

Josh: Of course not.

Amelia: Not even a little? Nothing spooky or scary ever happen in your life?

Josh: Never! Ghosts aren't real. Wait, you don't believe in them, do you?

Amelia: Listen. [This makes Josh laugh.] I was in this cemetery and saw this figure—

Josh: No way! Did it float and go "Boooo"?

Amelia: I'm serious. It was all pale, and I could see through it, and—you don't believe me.

Josh: Of course I don't. I think you *believe* you saw something.

Amelia: I know what I saw!

Josh: [smiling] Sure, Ams.

Amelia: Okay, fine. You, who's watching this, let me know in the comments if you've ever seen a ghost or believe in the paranormal. Tell me your ghost stories, or if you know of any good ones. Real ones! Maybe I'll compile some of the best ones and do a video about it later, read real-life ghost stories for everyone.

Josh: Oh no! Don't encourage her.

Amelia: My community will hit you back with your science and reason!

Josh: [laughs] You're cute when you get flustered.

Amelia: That's why you set me off?

Josh: I don't mean to. You're adorable when you're worked up.

[HD: He buries his face into the slope of her neck and they topple out of frame, laughing. They seem like they're made for each other. Complementary duo, evens and odds, ketchup and mustard, peanut butter and jam. I want to know more about them.]

CHAPTER NINE

AmeliaAimlessly YouTube Channel

Day in the Life - It's happening! - Vlog #509

Uploaded on May 29

Amelia: Oh my gosh! You guys won't believe it!

I'm going to Rome!

I can't believe it myself.

[HD: Amelia is pink-cheeked with excitement. She's holding the camera, swinging us around as she walks through her apartment. It's like we're with her, spinning around the hills like Julie Andrews in *The Sound of Music*. She looks truly happy. I can't help but feel sick. Did she have any idea what was going to happen in Rome?]

Later this July and into August, we're taking the trip of a lifetime. I just bought the tickets. It's going to be amazing. Josh and I had been talking ever since that Q&A we did about our bucket lists and since we're both on break from school, I figured why not go for it? It's summer, we only have one life and might as well spend it with each other! Long story short, I found these super-cheap tickets online, and we're going to do a week in Paris, and then we're going to be in Rome to spend our last week of freedom before school starts. I'll link in the description some of my travel tips and guides for how you too can get cheap flights. But not only are we getting super-cheap flights, but my friend and—you might recognize her—YouTube makeup guru, Sarah Speck, a.k.a. Glam-o-llama, is letting us stay at her place for a few nights.

[HD: Amelia inserts Glam-o-llama's profile picture in her video. She's a makeup artist I've heard of, but I've never watched her videos. She's got silky dark hair and icy violet eyes. I'm convinced she's wearing contacts, but I guess that's part of the look. She stands out from the crowd, even if she's not wearing mermaid-scale eyeshadow or turning herself into Angelina Jolie through the pure magic of contouring. From her Wikipedia page, she does lots of beauty looks as well as Halloween- and holiday-themed makeup videos. She's very talented. I am jealous. I can barely put on mascara.

I'm not sure how these two know each other, if they've always been friends or what. The mystery deepens. I realize I'm going to have to scan through Glam-o-llama's channel too, to figure out the timeline. I'm giving myself a lot more work.]

Go check out her videos. She's a doll, not exaggerating. I'll link to her creepy doll makeup look. [Amelia puts her hand over her mouth, her eyes bright and dazzling.] I'm still so excited. I can't believe it's happening. I've been waiting so long to visit Rome. I've mentioned it before, but I've always wanted to visit the Vatican. I've always loved the art. Something about it is divine. [laughs] The Sistine Chapel is definitely going to be my first stop when we get there. Although, are we allowed to film in there? I'll have to ask. Who do you even ask about something like that? I would hate for the pope to be mad at me. [laughs] As if I'm not already a lapsed Catholic in need of confession.

Did you know the Vatican is technically not part of Rome? It's called a city-state. It's so funny to think that a thing like that can exist in our day and age, sectioned off from the rest of the world within a city. It has its own laws and rules, like a totally independent island, even though it's right in the middle of an ancient city. It feels like it's from a time long ago, or something out of a fairy tale. I can't believe I get to see it with Josh.

✕✕✕

AmeliaAimlessly YouTube Channel
Ask Amelia - Q&A - Questions and Advice
Uploaded on June 12

[HD: We're back in Amelia's room for another one of her Q&As. This time, she asked for people to send her personal questions and she would respond to them. On top of reviewing food and talking about travel hacks, she also seems to care about her community a lot. A lot of people have rallied support for her, especially financially. She doesn't have merch, like a lot of other YouTubers, but she makes money from ads and followers on her Instagram and she's got a pretty significant following on Patreon, where she uploads a lot of her more private and personal videos. At this point, she's just reached a million followers and she wanted to give back to her community. It seems like she really cares.

I've edited the transcript, revealing the information I see as relevant.]

Amelia: Okay, the next one is from Anonymous, who writes, "Dear Amelia, I've been dating this person for two years now, and I'm not sure if I'm happy. I feel like I'm constantly having to apologize for things I didn't do, and I don't want to make it sound like my partner is crazy, because I could be a better partner too. But I always feel like I'm walking on eggshells whenever I'm around them. What do I do? How can I say what I feel in case it hurts their feelings in the process? Thanks. Love you. Anon."

Okay, wow. There's a lot to unpack here, but I think you already know the answer to your question. You said you're not sure if you're happy, and I think that's the key phrase here. If you're not sure, then maybe you're really not. If you were happy, you would know, wouldn't you?

You wouldn't have to question whether or not you're feeling these emotions bubbling up inside you. I think, if it's safe for you to do— because I know sometimes it's not—but if it's safe, you need to talk to your partner about what's going on. They might not have any idea. Sometimes the things we're feeling are invisible to those around us, and people aren't mind readers. They're not going to be able to understand right off the bat that, because you've gone quiet, you're dealing with something.

[HD: Amelia looks down at her hands, and then squints back up at the camera, like she's trying to find the right words. She's unusually soft, but still sincere.]

You know, Josh and I don't have this perfect relationship either. It might shock some people, ha, especially my viewers, but we're normal. We fight sometimes and that's okay! Well, I wouldn't say fight. We argue. *Argue.* Mostly about petty stuff that gets under our skin. Neither of us are to blame. We sometimes take it too far, say things that we want to take back, do things . . . It's what happens after that really matters, how we treat each other and what we do about it going forward. My mom always said I was mature for my age, and I think some girls my age are still getting used to being honest about their feelings because our whole life we were told that we need to be polite, not to make a fuss, not to make noise. It's rude to deny a hug, it's rude not to smile, it's rude to say what's on our mind. But that applies to guys too. They're told to man up, don't talk about what's bothering them, until it explodes. I've seen it firsthand, I know what that's like, boy do I know.

It's okay to talk about your feelings, share them, even if it's uncomfortable or awkward. I encourage you. Be honest with people around you, be kind, but be honest. If something doesn't feel right, say something. If someone is hurting you, speak up. You don't have to smile, you don't have to make nice. You can be kind, and still know that you're a person who deserves kindness back. But only if it's safe. That's the most important thing. Get somewhere safe first, if you have to. I hope there are people out there who can help if it's not. I know how lonely it can be. But you deserve to be happy. We all do.

Uh, yeah. Sorry, that got a little deeper than I intended it to be. Of course, be honest with the person about your feelings and if they're not willing to change, then you need to take your happiness back for yourself. But give them a chance, let the other party make an effort to be better, to do better.

I really admire people who can do that, who can face their feelings. I know for me sometimes it feels like my own feelings aren't my own, like they're apart from me, and I need to grab them by the shoulders and face them head-on to make any sort of sense of what I'm feeling.

That's why I love this community so much, you all are so supportive and helpful, even to each other in the comments and offline. It's honestly the best feeling in the world to know that good people exist in the world.

CHAPTER TEN

AmeliaAimlessly YouTube Channel
Paris mais oui! - Day in the Life - Vlog #510
Uploaded on July 25

[HD: Amelia abroad. She doesn't look like the average American tourist. She's still got her hair up in her signature ponytail, but she's wearing large sunglasses, a leather jacket, and silver bracelets and earrings. She blends right in with the Parisians she interacts with. She has a whole series of her two days in Paris, visiting the Louvre but also stopping by a small bakery that had "the best croissants, seriously" in the city, as well as visiting Notre Dame. Josh makes a rare appearance.]

Amelia: Oh my God, okay, so the craziest thing just happened. I'm still not even sure it was real, but it's so cool. So we were walking around Notre Dame, and Josh was taking some photos of me, and this guy came up and asked us if we were tourists. So we said yes, and then he asked us if we wanted to see Paris like real Parisians and invited us to this club. Club something. Club Nightmare. Josh got, like, super protective of me. You did!

[HD: Amelia pans the camera to focus on Josh walking beside her. He too is wearing sunglasses and an easy smile. He's got a large DSLR camera in hand, looking at photos on the flip-out screen.]

Josh: Amelia, that guy was trying to scam us. Maybe planning to mug us.

Amelia: He was not!

Josh: He super was.

Amelia: Josh got all up in his face and scared him off. I think you were just mad that he was hitting on me.

Josh: Not like that. The guy was a mega creep. What strange person invites you to some underground club you've never heard of? Skeeved me out.

Amelia: Oh come on. We're fine. Nothing happened. Not when I've got you to protect me. What happened to your sense of adventure?

Josh: We're easy targets. Tourists, with expensive cameras, and you're hard to miss. Look at you, you're gorgeous. He was probably trying to lure us somewhere and rob us blind.

Amelia: You should write a book, honestly. You're so paranoid. You think everything is like, this big deal.

[HD: Josh doesn't answer, he just smiles.]

Amelia: Do you really think he was going to try to rob us?

Josh: Would you really have gone to some secret nightclub with a stranger?

Amelia: No way. With you maybe!

Josh: That's my point. He might have been planning something bad.

Amelia: Mais non, monsieur! Zis is too, how you say, oar-EE-bluh!

[HD: Josh laughs.]

Josh: Fine, look up the club! See if it's real!

Amelia: Oh yeah? Should we?

[HD: Amelia brings the camera into a small cafe where they get food and sit at a table. Once she's there, she frames the shot so that she and Josh are in full view, scrolling through her phone. Amelia's face lights up and she holds the phone to the camera. The camera doesn't have time to focus, but if you pause the video, you can see a blurry image of a Google search result for Club Nightmare. Josh sips a cup of coffee, smiling, knowing that he lost a bet they hadn't even made.]

Amelia: Told you! It's real, proof is in the pudding. We should go.

Josh: We definitely should not.

Amelia: We should! We will! When was the last time you went to a swanky nightclub in Paris?

Josh: Never. And you think I want to start now?

Amelia: Sense. Of. Adventure, monsieur.

Amelia Eats: A Blog

CLUB NIGHTMARE—LIVING IT DOWN WITH THE DEAD

By Amelia Ashley

Posted on July 26

The entrance to Club Nightmare was an old, unused subway station. It had been cordoned off with a lazy wrapping of police tape, but Josh and

I slipped through, following the voices of other patrons heading down a dark tunnel that led to the Parisian catacombs. Like any normal person, I was wary of following strangers into a tomb. I almost turned back, but Josh took me by the hand and I thought, Well, if I die tonight, at least it would be one hell of a story!

But fear not, dear reader. As I'm writing this, I'm back in the hotel, cozy and warm in a fuzzy bathrobe, so you can rest easy. For now, let me paint you a picture.

Club Nightmare was a not-so-secret secret, a pop-up event for the so inclined to get a different perspective of Paris. We were invited by a mysterious man who promised us a good time, and since we were only in town for a little while, we figured why not! You only live once!

As we walked, it was so dark I had to use my phone's flashlight to see. I wish I hadn't, because staring at me from the walls of the tunnel were thousands of human skulls.

[HD: Amelia inserts a picture of said skulls. It's creepy.]

Their cavernous black eye sockets and jawless grins followed me down the hall, guiding us like ferrymen of the underworld toward the swelling sound of dance music, the bass thumping through the stamped dirt path.

Paris is well-known for its maze of catacombs beneath the city streets. Rumor has it that it's the home of six million people, their final resting place in a patchwork web of tunnels, ossuaries, and quarries spanning an estimated three kilometers. Aboveground, the land of the living. Belowground, the land of the dead, and we were among them— only visitors passing through. Josh and I had purchased masks before coming, having heard about the dress code online.

Josh had chosen a skull mask, a ghoulish one with grinning teeth, not knowing just what would be awaiting us down in the tunnels below. I chose a Venetian Carnival mask. Its features were for a woman's face: a perfectly pert nose, wing-lined eyes, and a bright red lip. It felt like fate, seeing as we were heading to Italy (Rome, not Venice, but close enough) the following morning. If I were the superstitious type, I would say it was eerily similar to my own face, down to the bright red lipstick I had chosen for the occasion. But I'm not one to shy away from an omen, and I just had to have it. (Beware the markup. The masks in Paris are not cheap.).

Our masks covered our whole faces, mine immediately making my skin sticky and damp with my own breath, but I didn't care. The anonymity, the ability to hide my face from the world, pretend to be someone else even for a little bit, awakened something in me that I didn't know existed. In Paris, a city new to me, I wanted to be unknown.

The thrill of what we were about to witness seemed to fog the air, drawing me closer, pulling me on toward a certainty most mortals don't want to think about. The inevitability of death makes life a little more beautiful, doesn't it?

Club Nightmare was located in a grand hall, reminiscent of a gothic cathedral. Sloping archways made of femur bones, a chandelier made of fingers and spines, candelabras of tibia and fibula (okay, I'm not an anatomy expert so I may be taking some creative license here, but you get the idea). The only modern addition was a masked DJ on a stage, stationed between thousands of laser-lights, catching the haze of the smoke machine. House music is not one of my preferred genres, but the way my blood beat in sync with the rhythm, it seemed as if my body had other ideas. Hundreds of people were already dancing with the dead. I would be one of them.

A bouncer stopped us before we entered, and I almost reached for a coin to hand our ferryman to the underworld, but he was only checking for bags. We didn't bring any with us, so he stamped our hands and we were allowed to pass.

We stepped into a world that felt like it was on the cusp between life and death, teeming with its own heartbeat made of music and lungs made of bodies breathing the same musty air. It felt as if our every move were being followed by the watchful, gaping eyes of our hosts.

Josh whisked me into the crowd and it swallowed me whole. The heat of hundreds of people, both living and dead, pressed on me from all sides. I lost myself in the music as Josh's hands wrapped around my waist. All hesitations he'd had about coming here had evaporated. He'd been nervous beforehand, but something in him had shifted too. There was confidence in his grip around my body, the way he pulled me into him. I couldn't see his eyes through his mask. I couldn't hear him, even if his lips were right against my ear. All that was left of Josh was the grinning skull, smiling at me through the dark, his arms solid and sturdy beneath my fingers. The faceless bodies around me, masked and anonymous, slithered and slid around us like demons.

Club Nightmare truly lived up to the name. It felt like a fever dream, as if I were walking through a nightmare conjured by an evil spell. And I wanted more. I was drunk off the danger.

Everything about this place should have made me feel uncomfortable. From the mere claustrophobia of being trapped underground, packed into a small room with hundreds of strangers, suffocating behind an overpriced Venetian Carnival mask. And yet, Josh's hand on the small of my back, his steady assurance that he was still there calmed me. Death itself could not reach me here, for I was touching it first.

When I die, hopefully sometime far in the future, I wouldn't mind being buried here among the watchers of Club Nightmare. Place my skeletal remains among the masses, let me become the six million and one. Scatter my bones to lead the way for future travelers, roaming the path between life and death, let my hands hold a candelabra, let my spine support the chandelier, let my skull smile at those who smile back.

I can't wait to get to Rome, but my soul is back in those catacombs.

× × ×

AmeliaAimlessly YouTube Channel
Day in the Life - Vlog #515
Uploaded on July 29

[HD: Amelia is on a high-speed train. She's curled up in a row of seats near the window where the French countryside is whizzing past. She's wearing an oversized sweatshirt and her hair is up in a messy bun, but she doesn't look sloppy. She's just casual enough that she looks cute, rather than lazy. I can't help but wonder how long it really took her to get her hair like that or to put on her makeup. Why do we expect everyone who posts stuff online to show only their best self?]

Amelia: Sleepy day on the train! I've never been on an overnight train before. Josh is off getting some snacks for us at the food cart. He doesn't know a lick of French, so I think it'll be a fun surprise what he can manage to order. [laughs] We're making our way from Paris, and we'll be here on this train for the next half-day or so. The motion of the train is oddly comforting, like being rocked to sleep. Let me know if you've ever been on an overnight train before! The rest of the world is spoiled by public transit while those of us in the States have to rely on cars to get us anywhere. I actually love this. I'm so jealous. See, these seats fold down to make one bed, and then, up here is a bunk. There's a ladder here. I get to sleep on the bottom bunk and Josh gets the top. I know what you guys are wondering, are we that serious together? No, not yet. We're taking it slow. I think it's so great how so many of you watching and following along with these videos care so much.

[HD: Amelia intercuts her video with B-roll of the train. The vibration of tea in a paper mug, trees whizzing past the window, Amelia fluffing up the sleeper-car pillow. Amelia writes in a journal and reads from her book, an old and well-used copy of *Peter Pan*, and it looks like the aesthetic of my dreams. To travel like her would be so much fun. But not everyone can do what she does. I think a lot of her appeal is that people want to live vicariously through her. She's doing the thing everyone says they want to do more: travel the world.]

It's so crazy to think that we'll be in Rome soon. My dream is finally coming true, it's really happening. To be honest, I was a little afraid at first, coming here with Josh. I wasn't sure if this was something I wanted to do. I know it sounds backward, but I was scared that if I finally achieved this one thing, what else would there be to look forward to afterward, you know? What else did I have going forward? It's like when people peak in high school, and they look back at their past and can't move on. I don't want to look at this trip and think this is where I peaked but at the same time . . . I can't help but feel like I'm going to wake up any moment and it'll be over.

I'm just a little lonely, that's all. I don't know what my future has in store. I don't want to talk to Josh about it, just because I don't think he'd understand. [Amelia sighs.]

They say all roads lead back to Rome and I wonder if any roads lead away. Maybe there's an untried path for me. I know I'm nervous, but I want to make sure that I can find new dreams after this one. I have so much to do still. So many adventures. I can't help but feel like I'm Wendy Darling, soaring with Peter Pan off to Neverland. "Second star to the right and straight on 'til morning!" This is only the beginning.

PART 3

NUMBER-ONE SUSPECT

CHAPTER ELEVEN

JOSH

Josh peered through the blinds, pushing them apart with his fingers ever so slightly to get a look out the window. The car was still there, parked inconspicuously. The driver, only a shadow, moved behind the wheel, where he'd been all morning.

The police were watching him.

"He still there?" Derek asked.

"Yes."

He turned back to Derek, who stood behind him, his arms folded across his chest, like he was giving himself a hug.

"Listen," Josh said, "I know what this looks like—"

"What this looks like? Josh! Why was Amelia's blood in your suitcase?"

Ever since they'd found it, the cops kept his suitcase as evidence in their investigation. But without a body, they didn't have enough to hold him at the precinct. They let Josh go, both parties understanding that Josh was now Suspect Number One, and they would be watching him. They'd had an undercover cop car and eyes on him ever since, in case he tried to skip town.

"Derek, you have to believe me. I had nothing to do with that, I swear. If you don't believe me, I'm not sure how I'll be able to get through this."

"I believe you, I really do, but you have to be honest with me, bro. Why was Amelia's blood—"

"I don't know!" he snapped. Derek's face immediately morphed from concern to shock. Josh had practically bitten his head off. He took a moment, then another, and put his hand on top of his head, grounding himself. "I'm sorry. I'm . . . sorry. I'm under a lot of pressure right now. Kind of freaking out."

Wide-eyed, Derek said, "I can see that."

Josh took another second to breathe. He felt like the world was slipping out from under him and he had no control, nothing to grab onto to steady himself, and all he could think about was Amelia. "I feel like I'm going crazy. I didn't do anything. I didn't touch her! You know me!"

"I know you're a good guy. You and Amelia are perfect. But I'm not sure how much my opinion about you counts with the police."

"It's absurd. All of this. I don't know what blood they're talking about. I have no idea how that got there . . ." He racked his brain, trying to find an explanation.

Derek was doing his best to be helpful. "What if this is all just one big misunderstanding? Do they know if it really is Amelia's blood? Why weren't they able to tell right away, like you see on TV?"

"It's not like that in real life. They had to send it to a lab to get it tested, and even then it could take weeks, there's such a huge backlog."

"So they're going off it because of the blood type test? Is that it? No other evidence?"

"They're looking for their suspect, and they'll use whatever methods they have on hand."

Derek swore under his breath. "So, what, they're not going to arrest you—just watch you? Is that really how they're going to spend their day? Don't they have other stuff to do?"

It was true, Josh felt like a prisoner in his own home, even when he knew he'd done nothing wrong. How Amelia's—or *someone's*—blood got in his suitcase was completely beyond him, beyond understanding, beyond reason. No matter what he said or did next, it would make him look guilty and it was starting to drive him mad.

At least Derek seemed be on his side for now, but trying to convince the internet, basically the whole world, that he was innocent was getting harder and harder each day. What happened to "innocent until proven guilty"?

Josh looked out the window again, peeling back the blinds. The shadow in the undercover cop car was moving around. It was lunchtime, no doubt they were enjoying a sandwich and whatever else a stereotypical cop on a stakeout would eat.

"This sucks," Josh said.

"Have you called your folks? Maybe they can help."

"It'll break their hearts." Josh's own ached. "There's nothing to tell. I didn't even tell them I was dating anyone . . . I wanted to wait 'til they came for parents' weekend in October."

Hearing the weariness in Josh's voice, Derek dropped the topic. "What about school?" he asked, pivoting.

"I'm still figuring that out. I don't exactly know how to tell my profs that I'm involved in a *murder* investigation."

"You should tell them something." Derek took a seat on their couch, his fingers locked together, elbows on his knees. "Otherwise it might be a bigger mess down the line."

"Yeah, you're right, I should go to school."

"Is that really such a good idea? I mean . . ."

"Well, what is it then? I don't know what to do! What would you do if you were in my shoes?" Josh asked.

Derek shrugged. "I'd try to help find Amelia."

"I can't exactly do that, can I? She won't respond to my texts, or any of my emails. I can't *fly* to Europe either—they'll think I'm fleeing the country. If I sit at home all day, scouring the internet for anything that might help, I look guilty. 'Why is he hiding? Doesn't he want to show his face? He's up to something.' If I go out and try to live a normal life, I look guilty. 'Look at him, he's not even trying to help. Doesn't he care about her? He's up to something.' I can't win." Josh pulled himself away from the window and flopped on the couch next to Derek.

Derek cringed once Josh had laid out his entire conundrum. Everyone looked at the boyfriend when a beautiful, talented, smart girl went missing.

"It still doesn't make sense about Amelia's blood . . ."

"It's not Amelia's blood!" Josh's own blood pressure was through the roof. "It can't be! I didn't do anything! Derek, man, come on! Please!"

"Fine, fine. If it's not your blood, and if it's not her blood, whose is it then? Do you think the cops planted it there?"

Josh had heard of worse things before. Several famous cases had made the news about how police planted evidence to convict innocent people of crimes they didn't commit, provided physical proof of their guilt for a jury, sentenced helpless people to rot in prison for years, all because they wanted to get their prime suspect behind bars. It looked good for a department to close cases, even if they'd seemingly gone cold. Sometimes police—anyone with that kind of power really—felt pressure to get the bad guy, even if it meant jumping the gun.

"It's possible but . . . I have no idea what happened." He shook his head, remembering Amelia's face before she'd attacked him.

Derek asked, "You never blacked out? Or got so angry you forgot . . . ?"

Josh gave him a withering look and Derek held up his hands in surrender. "Look, I only ask because I want to help you. It's not enough to say you're innocent. You gotta do something to prove it."

"Literally impossible," Josh said. "How do I prove I *didn't* do something? How?" He knew he sounded desperate, but the walls were closing in every minute he was stuck in the house. Anxiety ate away at his insides and he felt like he was going to implode.

Derek sighed. "My dad's got a friend, a lawyer, you might want to—"

"No lawyers!" Josh jumped to his feet.

"Josh, dude. Stop. A lawyer can help."

Josh had started pacing, rubbing the stubble on his face. "It makes me look guilty."

"If I were you, I'd rather look guilty with a lawyer's help than guilty without one. You said it yourself: You look guilty either way."

Derek was right, but Josh didn't want to give in. As the days passed and Amelia remained missing, it was looking like something really had happened to her, something that was beyond Josh's control. If a lawyer could help him with the blood, Josh could at least start proving his innocence and finally get to the truth.

Josh stopped pacing and took a deep breath. "Fine," he said. "What's their contact info?"

✕ ✕ ✕

On campus, Josh felt all eyes on him, burning into the back of his skull like hot irons.

Talk about Amelia's disappearance cast a shadow on the student body, and the moment Josh walked into the police precinct with blood in his suitcase, he had become persona non grata.

News of her disappearance had hit the mainstream. So little was known about Amelia's background—or even where she was from, which only added to the mystery surrounding her. So far the media had kept his photo out of the articles, but word had spread quickly on campus about him.

In Abnormal Psychology, no one wanted to sit next to him, as if he were contagious or perhaps he would lash out and anyone unlucky enough to sit next to him would go missing next. Two hundred or so classmates and everyone was watching him. Word spread fast at San Diego State, and Josh couldn't hide, even if he sat in the back of the atrium.

Strangers Josh had never spoken to, let alone even stood close enough to exchange air molecules, kept glancing at him between taking notes on their laptops. Josh tried to focus on his own notes, tried to get back to a sense of normalcy, but he couldn't focus on anything. Everything was always about Amelia, Amelia, Amelia.

Time was ticking, and the longer she stayed missing, the more pressure would be put on Josh, crushing him to death.

He'd set up email alerts whenever Amelia's name was published online. His inbox had been inundated for days. He ignored the lecture and looked through all the articles.

A recent one in particular caught Josh's eye, making all his muscles stiff. A woman had been interviewed by a gossip magazine, *Talk Now*. The article was titled: **Suspect in Amelia Ashley disappearance exhibited inappropriate behavior on plane after disappearance, witness claims**. Appalled by the lie, Josh opened the article and read it. It included a photograph of the woman, the one he recognized from 13F on the flight home.

Josh could barely hold it together long enough to read her quoted statement:

"I got a sense that Josh Reuter—I didn't know his name at the time—had been acting strangely. It put me off immediately and I only learned about what happened to Amelia later. That poor girl! I saw his photograph on Sarah Speck's Insta and I just knew he had done something. He kept smiling at me on the flight, creepy, like he was watching me. It gives me chills just thinking about it!"

Josh had to close his laptop before he exploded. The internet was full of speculation and rumor and straight-up lies. Amelia walked off on her own and Josh was left dealing with the blowback.

He'd only smiled at that woman on the plane. He didn't even talk to her. That stupid smile of his was going to get him killed.

He stormed out of the lecture hall, ignoring his classmates' stares. Coming to school had been a bad idea.

✕ ✕ ✕

At home, he couldn't rest. The unmarked police car was still out there and Josh felt like he was trapped in a cage. He threw himself down on the living room couch and got to work. The woman from 13F had said she'd seen something on Sarah Speck's Insta, so he went to her account to see for himself.

When he opened the app on his phone, his heart stopped.

Sarah had posted his face in her stories, a picture taken from Amelia's blog post when they went out on their first date. She'd inserted his name and an arrow pointing at his stupid smile. He stared at his own face, completely dumbstruck, until Sarah's story switched over to Sarah talking to the camera.

"Everything is happening so fast," she said, the hashtag **#Whereis-AmeliaAshley** overlaid on the bottom of the screen. "I spoke with the police about Amelia's disappearance because I couldn't keep it a secret anymore. I heard a fight between Josh and Amelia days before she went missing. Several witnesses at my house can verify this. It's horrible. I'm starting to worry that something terrible has happened. I told the police everything I know. Josh Reuter isn't telling the truth. They found blood in his suitcase that might be hers and that can't be a coincidence, can it?"

Josh dropped his phone and it clattered to the floor. Munch walked over and sniffed it, tail high.

Lies, all lies. Everyone would believe her. And no one would believe him. He was powerless and now Josh was everyone's new favorite villain.

His face would be everywhere. He couldn't hide. The dogpile had started.

His fingers were stiff and cold, his chest felt too small for his lungs. It was like a bad dream and he wanted to wake up. All he had was a charming smile that was losing potency every single time someone uttered the question: Where is Amelia Ashley?

Reality seeped into his bones. Panic flitted through his thoughts. She was gone.

Without Amelia, or any sign of her, it wasn't a matter of he-said, she-said, but he-said, and she's-missing. It didn't take a grade-A detective to figure out that something wasn't adding up.

He picked up his phone from the floor and forced himself to do the one thing he didn't want to do: call his parents. His father, who answered, said the same thing Derek had said:

"Get a lawyer."

"But, Dad, it's too—"

"We'll pay for it. This is non-negotiable. I know you didn't hurt her, but we need to protect you no matter what."

Josh paced back and forth in the apartment, gripping the phone like a vise. His heart felt like it was going to smash out of his rib cage. He knew not to put up a fight though. His father, a land buyer, traveled around the country dealing with ownership rights and property battles. This was not his first experience with the legal world.

"We've been through this," his father said, his voice level and calm. "You need a lawyer. End of story."

Josh pressed his fists into his eye sockets, making himself see stars. Even with his eyes closed, he saw Amelia walking away from him. Walking. Never looking back.

He put the phone back to his ear. "Okay," he said, nodding. "I know."

After he hung up, he rooted around in his front pocket, finding what he was looking for. Derek had written his dad's friend's contact information on a scrap of notebook paper.

Setting his jaw, he dialed the number and finally asked for help.

CHAPTER TWELVE

AmeliaAimlessly YouTube Channel
Day in the Life - Vlog #516
Uploaded on July 30

[HD: Amelia made it to Rome with Josh. This video is snappy, hardly letting a clip linger longer than a second, showing everything in quick succession: the walk along the train station framing a sign: BENVENUTI A ROMA, a shot of a pair of police officers laughing with each other, Fiats and Vespas speeding down the street. Some footage is captured by Josh, as Amelia leans on a railing overlooking the ruins of Foro Romano, or points at the winged statues on the bridge to Castel Sant'Angelo, walking through the winding tunnels of the Colosseum, tossing a coin into the Trevi Fountain. Rome is bright and sunny, both earthy and urban, with paved streets but green trees. Paired with music, it's like a tourist promotional video for Rome. I wouldn't be surprised if Amelia got a sponsorship from the tourist office to do it. (I'm mostly joking, she would have mentioned getting sponsored, but I can check later.) Amelia looks genuinely happy to be in Rome, if not a little tired.]

Amelia: We did it! We're finally here. After—what was it, Josh? An eighteen-ish-hour train ride? There was a pit stop in Milan between there, and I'm basically dead on my feet, but we're here! We made it!

Josh: [off camera] We made it!

Amelia: We had to get all the touristy stuff out of the way. See the sights and all. My favorite part actually was seeing the fountain. It was a lot smaller than I expected! I always thought it was this huge pool, like a swimming pool or something. I guess photos I've always seen made it look way bigger, just like the *Mona Lisa*. She's the size of a postcard, I swear. But I threw a coin into the fountain over my shoulder for luck! I couldn't leave Rome without doing some stereotypical tourist thing. What about you, Josh? What was your favorite place so far?

Josh: Definitely the Colosseum. But to be fair, the Colosseum didn't have anything as crazy as what happened at the fountain.

Amelia: You're right, it was crazy. At the fountain, there were some protests, I think. I'm not really sure what it was about. My Italian is mostly centered around food ingredients, but there was shouting and someone put red dye in the water. The fountain is usually this pale blue, really pretty, almost as pretty as Josh's eyes. [HD: Josh makes a noise off camera that makes Amelia grin.] But there was this huge seeping stain of bright red right in the middle. People were screaming, it looked so real.

Josh: It really looked like blood.

Amelia: You don't think anyone was hurt, do you?

Josh: Nah, I wouldn't worry about it. I think there would have been more people panicking.

Amelia: It was so gross either way! You know how I am about blood. Ew. I'm going to throw up just thinking about it. But we didn't stay too long after that because it was getting crowded. So here we are! We got ourselves some gelato, one of my all-time favorite desserts, and we're basking in the afternoon Italian sun.

Josh: I'm glad we're not jet-lagged.

Amelia: So yeah, Josh and I are going to my friend Glam-o-llama's apartment so we can drop off our stuff. She's letting us crash at her place for a few days before we check into our hotel. We can't take advantage of her generosity forever! So we're going to hang out with Sarah for a few hours, relax a little bit, and then we'll head out for a night like real Romans. That sounds weird. Romans, like I should be wearing armor or something. What do you call a person from Rome?

Josh: Uhh. [HD: Amelia pans the camera to him where he's thinking, looking up from his own camera. He looks almost exactly the same as I've seen him in class.] I think it's still Romans? But you're right, it makes it sound like we're time travelers.

Amelia: Okay, don't hate me. But I'm gonna say it.

Josh: [smiling] Don't say it.

Amelia: I'm gonna say it!

Josh: Help, I can't stop her!

Amelia: Can't stop me! "When in Rome!"

Josh: Could you be any more of a tourist?

✕ ✕ ✕

AmeliaAimlessly YouTube Channel
Day in the Life (ft. Glam-o-llama) - Vlog #517
Uploaded on July 31

[HD: Josh has taken over the camera for Amelia. She's wearing a crop top, paired with sunglasses and high-waisted jeans. Her suitcase is a purple hardshell that's sitting next to her as she stands on the doorstep of an elaborate-looking, red-painted door. It's got a brass knocker in the shape of a lion holding a ring in its mouth, and just by the looks of it, this building is expensive. You can hear the rumble of cars in the background, and people talking in Italian in the distance.]

Amelia: Do I look okay?

Josh: You look great, don't worry about it. Haven't you two met before?

Amelia: At Creator Convention last year!

Josh: So what do you have to worry about?

Amelia: Nothing, I guess. I just feel like such a slouch next to her.

Josh: You are gorgeous. Trust me. Just knock on the door already.

Amelia: Okay, yeah. Yeah! Here we go.

[HD: Amelia knocks three times and after the first knock, you can hear a small dog barking wildly on the other side, sounds like it's about ready to chew someone's face off. Amelia cringes at the camera, embarrassed that she caused such a disturbance, but the door clicks open.

Standing in the doorway, a little Yorkie with a pink bow, calm now under her arm, is Glam-o-llama herself. She's got a full face of makeup, and is looking extraordinarily fabulous in tight jeans and a flowing cashmere top. Her hair is perfectly curled and draped over one shoulder. She looks like she just stepped out of a photo shoot. She smiles when she sees them, flashing perfectly white pearly teeth.

Glam-o-llama, real name Sarah Speck, is an American expat who moved to Rome to pursue her career launched from her incredibly successful YouTube channel. Early twenties, slender, and graceful. She's got her own makeup line that you can find in most department and drug stores, and she's starting up her own fashion line as of this writing. She's doing very well for herself, indeed, based on the look of the house.]

Sarah: *Ciao bella!*

Amelia: Hi, Sarah!

[HD: They hug, and Amelia is a little awkward with the double cheek kiss from Sarah. But it's endearing. She's blushing.]

Sarah: And you must be Josh! [She shakes his hand off camera, the camera shakes a little bit when she does.] Welcome! Welcome! You are just in time. Come on in. Are we filming for the vlog?

Amelia: I hope you don't mind—

Sarah: Hello, vlog viewers! It is I, Glam-o-llama, and welcome to my humble abode.

[HD: Humble abode it is not. As Josh follows Amelia inside, we see the full expanse of this "flat" in Rome. Everything is pure white, from the walls to the ceiling to the furniture. White marble, white oak, white rugs. The place is immaculate. On the far wall are huge windows with a balcony overlooking the brownish-yellowish water of the Tiber River, snaking through the city. A fireplace sits dark and empty in the living room, flanked by pure white sofas.]

Sarah: Come on in! Step inside, don't be shy. Everyone's already here, but you're just in time. Over here is the sitting room. You can kick your feet up and lounge. Then over here, we've got the kitchen. Say hi, everyone! [HD: The kitchen and dining room are also pure white, open to the rest of the house. Three other people are seated at the dining room table in various poses, all of them waving to the camera.] I'm sure you all know Amelia. She's staying with me while she's here on a trip. Amelia, I'm not sure you've met the rest. There's Juro—he's that big video game guy, and then that's Alex—he's a journalist, and that's Grace—she also does travel vlogs!

Amelia: Hi! Yes! I've seen all of your work. This is great. A surprise, but great.

Sarah: I didn't tell you everyone was coming over?

Amelia: No! It's okay though, totally fine! I just wasn't expecting people. Alex, I think we met at CreatorCon a while back.

[HD: Alex Ciupa, a.k.a. RealNewsNow, is a legitimate journalist. He does international news as well as some travel videos, focusing on topics for American viewers that might not otherwise be covered on the news. Like Sarah, he too is in his early twenties. He's got brown hair and dimples, and he's wearing a blazer.]

Alex: Of course I remember you, Amelia Ashley! Your videos are incredible, you really capture the spirit of a location. Really good stuff. I love your work.

Amelia: [smiling at the camera] Well! I try!

Sarah: And how could I forget? Everyone, this is Josh, Josh Reuter. Amelia's boyfriend.

[HD: The group greets him in turn. I'll do some more research. I'm sure the police have already interviewed the people here, but it's worth looking into.]

Sarah: Come on, I'll show you two to your room.

[HD: Amelia waves Josh to follow her as the group at the dining room table continues their conversation. Sarah leads them through the living room once more and down a narrow hallway.]

Amelia: This house is incredible, Sarah!

Sarah: Right? It used to be Montalti's. She was one of Rome's most prominent architects of her time, and I just had to have it. Yeah, it's a little small, but she's home. Sweeping views of the river, marble floors, big bathroom with lots of lights, what's not to love?

[HD: A little small? Okay, lady.]

Amelia: It's gorgeous. Really. Right, Josh?

Josh: Incredible.

[HD: He doesn't sound all that enthusiastic. In fact, he sounds a little miffed. I'd be a little put off too. This place looks like a museum, not a house.]

Sarah: Here we are! The guest room. You two have your own bath, your own balcony. Anything here is yours. My personal recommendation is the Jacuzzi.

[HD: The room is gigantic with a plush four-poster bed and open double doors to the balcony. The curtains blow in the breeze. It's almost like a honeymoon suite.]

Amelia: Oh my God, Sarah! This is amazing! Thank you so much! How can we ever repay you?

Sarah: Not at all, hon. Make yourself comfy.

✕ ✕ ✕

Amelia Eats: A Blog

A LESSON IN PATIENCE

By Amelia Ashley

Posted on August 2

When in Rome, don't expect to start your evening meal until at least nine o'clock. It's bad manners to break off the conversation and the passing of bottles of wine to interrupt the flow of the evening.

And when you have a chef like Fulvia Beneventi in the kitchen, you don't want to do *anything* that might jeopardize your dinner.

Josh and I are staying at my friend's apartment in Rome. She graciously invited us when she heard we were in town and we were lucky enough to dine with some of her contemporaries in the city. Sarah employs Fulvia as her personal chef, and while she doesn't speak a lick of English, her risotto speaks the language of the gods.

Risotto, a result of standing vigilantly over a pot of rice while it gently cooks in scoops of broth, was already one of my favorite dishes, and, thanks to Fulvia, I'm quite sure I've ascended to another realm of risotto paradise.

Mushrooms provide the earthy wholeness grounding your senses; the creamy rice, perfectly cooked, warms you from the inside out; and the splash of dry white wine kicks off a spark of acidity that makes your palate soar.

But it was only the start of that night's festivities. Sarah had arranged for a small welcoming party for the both of us, where we passed wine as easily as we passed stories.

I had been a little nervous upon seeing a group already in her house. I thought of myself as an intruder, especially since most of the guests Sarah had invited are esteemed creators in their own right, and it took me a while to relax and enjoy myself. The wine (a dry red from Piedmont, hints of cherry, plum, and oak) might have helped.

The risotto was first on the menu, and I wish it hadn't been as delicious as it was, because I was already full by the time Fulvia produced the main course, Fiorentina. Steak! Rosemary and a little salt and pepper. No fuss, no rush. Perfectly rare and buttery, it melted in my mouth. Time is of no importance at the dinner table. It's something a lot of people forget, especially in the high-speed, breakneck rush of American culture. If you're eating, you're not working, and if you're not working, you're not valuable. This dinner exists in opposition to that mindset.

While Fulvia sliced the tiramisu for dessert, conversation was easy across the table.

[HD: Amelia inserts a picture of the group sitting around the table. Everyone is mid-laugh, as if she'd just told a joke, including Josh, squeezed between Alex Ciupa and Juro Pallares. It appears that everyone is at least a little buzzed, with the pink in their cheeks and the shine in their eyes.]

Grace Burke is also a travel YouTube creator. Like me, she is traveling Europe, though she's on an ambitious trek across the continent. Juro Pallares is the odd one out, though he fits right in. He specializes in video game streams, garnering millions of views on his videos. I admit, he pulls impressive numbers.

Alex Ciupa is a writer, like me. We bonded over our shared experiences with carpal tunnel syndrome, we're writing so much. He creates videos covering topics a lot of people don't like to talk about, particularly war and poverty in other countries. I imagine our line of work runs parallel to one another—his uncovering dirty secrets and harsh truths in the rubble of devastation abroad, mine finding inspiration and revelation in a culture's rich relationship with food, uncovering different kinds of secrets and truths.

I asked him where his favorite place to travel had been so far, and he said it was Sarajevo, which surprised me. Not many people claim Bosnia and Herzegovina to be their favorite destination, but he said that it was a place full to bursting with life, good people, good food, incredible architecture. He said he'd take me sometime, but Josh got a little jealous. I think Alex forgot I hadn't come alone.

One of my favorite things about my job is how food brings all of us together. A meal is one of the most intimate things you can share with someone. We learn about each other in ways we might never have before. Sometimes, all we really need is to take a lesson in patience and learn to eat a little more slowly, because then we might be better at hearing one another.

I want to hear, and I want to be heard.

CHAPTER THIRTEEN

JOSH

His lawyer, Peter Wilkinson, met Josh just outside the doors to the San Diego Police Department. The sun was bright and unforgiving that afternoon, and Josh already had a layer of sweat on his brow beneath his baseball cap. With everything else going wrong so far, he was sure the police would try to use his sweat as some sort of proof of guilt.

Mr. Wilkinson didn't recognize Josh on sight, so Josh had to be the one to come up to him and extend his hand. "Hello, Mr. Wilkinson. I'm Josh."

Mr. Wilkinson brightened when Josh introduced himself, smiling. Josh smiled back, somewhat relieved that Mr. Wilkinson had been so eager to help.

"Of course! Yes! Mr. Reuter, good to finally meet you in person."

"Yeah . . ." Josh wasn't sure there was anything really *good* in this situation, but he let it drop.

To Josh, he looked like a typical lawyer, standing out from the cops filing in and out of the double doors, with his pressed black suit-and-tie combo and his slicked-back gray hair. Josh had looked him up online, seeing what kinds of cases he'd worked on in the past. Peter Wilkinson was a partner at Young & Wilkinson Law in Los Angeles, specializing in criminal defense. At first, Josh got a lump in his throat reading those two words *criminal* and *defense*, but he reminded himself that he was innocent. It wasn't his fault that Amelia was missing. He reasoned that by getting a lawyer, the police could finally stop yanking him around, rule him out as a suspect.

Mr. Wilkinson had some success, the most high-profile being another missing persons case where the top suspect was charged with murder by an overeager police force despite a lack of physical evidence. The guy got off with no jail time. Netflix made a documentary about it, which Wilkinson had been interviewed for, something Amelia would have liked to watch.

When Josh called him, he had expected to reach an assistant or a secretary, but Mr. Wilkinson was the one who answered. Apparently Derek's dad had given him the heads-up. Mr. Wilkinson had just finished working on a case (which he'd won) and was looking for new clients and Josh was the perfect project. He hopped on a flight as soon as he could, especially when Josh had told him the police wanted to ask him some more questions regarding the blood in his suitcase; hence their meeting now.

Mr. Wilkinson said, "Nice handshake, Mr. Reuter. Strong. Means you're confident. That's good."

"Thanks for coming on such short notice."

"No problem at all." Mr. Wilkinson adjusted his tie while still holding his briefcase. All of Josh's notes were somewhere in there, no doubt.

Josh'd told him everything he could over the phone. "Anything else you want to tell me before we head in?"

Josh breathed deeply. "No," he said.

"The more you tell me, the more you're up-front with, the easier it is for me to help you."

"I didn't do anything wrong, Mr. Wilkinson. I just want Amelia found."

Mr. Wilkinson must have heard the lump in Josh's throat because he patted him firmly on the shoulder. "Don't you worry, Josh. You just take a breath, relax, and let me help you with this interview. They'll be asking you some questions, but there's nothing you need to hide from me, okay? I'm here to help."

"Sure, I'm just glad you believe me."

"Belief doesn't win cases, Mr. Reuter. But I do."

× × ×

Josh felt cramped sharing one side of the table with Mr. Wilkinson.

The officer who'd led them to the usual interview room had left them there for a few minutes and Josh watched the steam curling up from Mr. Wilkinson's untouched coffee. He was writing on a giant yellow legal pad, nodding his head every so often after pausing.

Josh's eyes flicked to the one-way mirror; seeing himself in the glass, he was disturbed by his reflection. He looked sick—heavy shadows under his eyes, hair pressed flat from his baseball cap, which now sat in his lap, skin unusually pale. He hoped the police would see a boyfriend desperate to find his girlfriend instead of a guilty man losing sleep over what he'd done.

The door to the room opened and Detective Hindmarsh entered. Wilkinson stood up and shook her hand. "Mr. Wilkinson, Mr. Reuter's representative."

"Ah, lawyered up I see, Josh! Good thing I'm familiar with your work, Mr. Wilkinson." She swaggered to the chair across the table and set down her own coffee and a pale folder with papers inside it as she took a seat. She still had on her signature headband, and looked amused by the situation in a way that forced Josh to push down a ripple of anger. What, was she excited for a challenge? This was his *life*.

Wilkinson said, "My client stands by his innocence. It's time that the San Diego Police Department move away from him as a suspect."

"Sure, but when we find blood in a suitcase, can you blame us for being a little concerned?"

"O-positive blood type is the most common blood type. It could be anyone's blood in that suitcase, not just Amelia's, and the fact that you're hanging your entire case on something as weak as that means you have nothing. There's no proof that she's dead, or that she's been injured in any way. You're merely working on assumptions."

Detective Hindmarsh's eyes flicked to Josh, who remained quiet in his seat next to Wilkinson. He had to physically force himself not to wring his hands around the brim of his baseball cap. He had known that getting a lawyer would make him look bad, especially in the public eye, now that most of the world was aware of Amelia's disappearance, but he had no other choice. And by the sound of things, his lawyer was starting off on the right track.

Detective Hindmarsh sighed. "Look, Josh. We're trying to find Amelia. You must understand that we're just going off of evidence, right? We just want to make sure she's okay. If you have any idea what might have happened—"

Wilkinson cut her off and answered for him. "My client has repeatedly said the last time he saw her was at Il Gusto hours before the flight. He has no idea where that blood came from, which—again, I must remind you—we have no proof is Amelia's in the first place. If this had happened down the block, would it take you this long to explore all other eyewitnesses who might be able to shed some light on the situation? This is lazy police work, detective."

Detective Hindmarsh pursed her lips. Apparently, she was holding back what she wanted to say. She let out a breath, then opened the folder in front of her. A series of printed photographs of Amelia stared back at Josh. Most were from her Instagram page, several of which had been taken by Josh himself. She posed for him, letting him capture her, but she'd been the one who chose what to upload, what to write for her captions, how to market herself. He had almost no involvement with her Instagram account, and he preferred it that way.

"Your lawyer is right, Josh," Hindmarsh said. "We don't have a lot here, even with blood in the suitcase. Without a body, there's just not a whole lot to it. Just questions, upon questions, upon questions, and we're sorting through the mess in front of us. That's the nature of missing persons cases—they're stuck in limbo, constantly facing the same questions until we're all running in circles. But we just wanted to clear some things up, get a more complete picture of the situation before we move on to other avenues."

"But I didn't do it. You can move on now," Josh said. Wilkinson put his hand on top of Josh's arm, a simple warning to keep his mouth shut. Josh bit his tongue.

"My client isn't being unreasonable," Wilkinson said. "The longer we waste our time looking at evidence that isn't there, the harder it gets to find Amelia, hopefully safe and sound."

Detective Hindmarsh tipped her head, placatingly. "The thing is, Mr. Wilkinson, we did exactly that. We started expanding our search efforts, reached out to the hotel and the restaurant, just to see if anyone else had anything to say. With help from the local PD, we started tracking down some people who could verify Josh's story. I assure you, Mr. Wilkinson, I just wanted to get Josh back here to see what he has to say about all of it."

"Sure, I have nothing to hide," Josh said.

Wilkinson flashed him a look, but Josh shrugged it off.

"Great, Josh. So we've compiled some photos that seemed to be of particular interest to us. Can you look these over for me?"

She slid three photos across the table surface toward Josh.

"My client doesn't need to answer—"

"It's fine," Josh said. "I took these photos. It's no secret. I like taking pictures for Amelia."

The three pictures were the last three she'd uploaded to Instagram during their trip. One was from Paris, when they went to the underground rave in the catacombs, another was in Sarah Speck's house of Amelia standing on the balcony overlooking the Tiber River, and the last was of her eating gelato—the original **WHERE IS AMELIA ASHLEY** picture that had been circulating around the internet nonstop for the past week.

Josh spoke around a lump in his throat. "I'm not sure what you want me to talk about." Seeing her again, even in photos, stirred up emotions he hadn't quite processed yet. If something really bad had happened to her, was this going to be all that was left? Photos? An Instagram account in memoriam? He slid the photos back toward Hindmarsh, but she stopped him by placing a hand on top of them.

"How about we start with that one?" she asked, pointing toward the one from the catacombs.

Amelia was posed in front of a wall of skulls reminiscent of a throne, perched over it like the John William Waterhouse painting of Circe offering a cup to Odysseus. She had worn her best black dress, a short, flowing, gossamer one, looking at Josh from around her mask, her face half-hidden but a clever smile shining through her eye. She looked mysterious, and all-knowing, and dangerous, and that made Josh's blood run hot. "What about it?" he asked.

"Just wanted to know if you noticed anything."

Josh stared at the photo. In any other circumstance, he would have said that she looked like something out of a movie. He remembered that night, the thrill of pulling her close in the noise of the club, watching her dance the night away with him, her body a hypnotic ghost against the dark. But in the austerity of the precinct he kept his beating heart in control. "She's beautiful. Everyone likes her. She's adventurous."

Detective Hindmarsh hummed and took the picture back. She pointed to the second one. "And this?"

"Sarah Speck's apartment. I think that was our second day in Rome." That guest room was bigger than his apartment with Derek. He'd be lying if he said he wasn't a little envious of Sarah's living situation, but he decided not to mention it.

"Yes, Sarah Speck. The beauty guru." Detective Hindmarsh said *beauty guru* with extra syllables. "What do you think about her?"

With a lurch, Josh realized something. "Do you think *she'd* hurt Amelia?"

Detective Hindmarsh kept her face neutral. "I want to know what you think about her."

Josh swallowed and looked at Wilkinson. Josh had already talked this much—he didn't stop him from continuing.

"She's fine. A little much for me."

"What do you mean by that?"

"I mean, she's a bit of a . . ." He needed to be tactful. "She's stuck-up."

Detective Hindmarsh slid the photo back toward herself. "With a house like that? I'm shocked."

Her attempt at a joke fell flat. Josh felt eyes on him, apart from the people in the room with him. His gaze flicked toward the mirror, then back at the photograph. What were they hoping to get out of this? He clenched his fists under the table, trying to calm his quickening heart, curling his baseball cap into a tighter circle.

"I'm sure by now you've heard that Sarah Speck told us about an incident at her house. How about you tell me about that."

Wilkinson interrupted, "Hearsay."

"Ms. Speck says she found a broken mirror and broken glass in her spare bathroom, the bathroom Josh and Amelia used when staying with her. She also said she'd heard Amelia yelling about something the night before you left, and then she heard something shatter."

Josh started to say, "We were—" But he caught himself. Both Wilkinson and Detective Hindmarsh stared at him. A flush rose in his cheeks and his breath hitched, but he had to say it. He couldn't keep secrets about this, even if it was embarrassing. "We were making out. Kissing. Nothing more than that. We knocked over a glass of water when I . . ." He remembered the way her lips crushed into his, the way she held onto his face, her breath hot and ragged against his cheek as he pushed her against the counter, locked in her embrace, wanting to be closer to her than ever before. Now he felt sick at the memory. He knew that, again, without Amelia here to confirm it, it was his story against Sarah's. All he could do was lay everything on the table. "We made out. That's all. It got a little . . . passionate. Amelia promised to pay her back for the mirror when we left. Ask Sarah."

What Sarah Speck had heard that night was a complete misunderstanding. She didn't know anything. She was lying. Amelia kissed him that night like she'd lose him. She loved him.

Detective Hindmarsh raised her eyebrows, but she didn't ask him about it anymore. Hopefully Josh's admission had her thinking about conducting another interview with Sarah. She moved on. "And this last photo." Detective Hindmarsh tapped her finger on it.

"Gelato," he said. "We ate ice cream outside."

"Before or after you shared a preflight meal?"

"Before. She wanted something sweet. I wanted to make her happy."

Detective Hindmarsh narrowed her eyes at him, as if trying to peer into his soul. He stared back. He didn't know what else she wanted to hear. He'd been honest with her about everything. All of it.

"And you don't see anything else?" she asked.

Josh looked at the photo again. There were people in the background, but Amelia was the star. He'd taken a short-focal-length photo, so that meant while Amelia was in the center of the frame, embracing the sunlight, a lot of people in the background were in focus too. He thought maybe Detective Hindmarsh wanted him to see if anyone in the background was worth paying attention to, but every face was a stranger to him. Amelia held her small wooden spoon up to her mouth, having just nipped the gelato from it, her expression a smile of pure joy. She was glowing.

"No," he said.

"Okay, Josh." Detective Hindmarsh slid the photo toward herself and tapped them all on the table into neat order.

"This runaround game isn't going to work for much longer," Wilkinson said. "You can keep reviewing the photos until the end of time and I doubt my client will have any other information for you. I'd start by comparing the blood in the suitcase with the missing person's DNA."

Detective Hindmarsh's eyes caught the light in a way that revealed a little more than she might have meant to. "Yes, indeed. We're working on that."

Josh's heart rabbited in his chest. They were hoping that he would confess and they could close the case. They were trying to pin him for something he didn't do, and he was going to die before he admitted to something like that. He was innocent—when were they finally going to believe him? Or would he forever be the One Who Got Away with It in their eyes?

Wilkinson was doing his best to rein in the situation. He too reviewed his own notes, looking over the account that Josh had provided both in writing and over the phone. "You have zero evidence that my client did anything wrong. Amelia Ashley attacked him, unprovoked at a restaurant, and walked away of her own accord. What more do you need?"

"One day she's kissing you, the next she's attacking you . . . Seems like you had a pretty tumultuous relationship, no?" she asked Josh, ignoring Wilkinson completely.

Josh kept his mouth shut. He didn't understand either.

"This is a waste of everyone's time," Wilkinson said.

Detective Hindmarsh leaned back in her chair and said, "My phone has been blowing up these past few days, mostly devoted fans of Amelia's who are obsessed with her case, some with claims that all the evidence we need is on Amelia's blog and her social media accounts, and that Josh should be our main suspect. We just wanted to clear the air, try to get a fresh take on anything, see if Josh recalled something he might have forgotten . . ." She let the sentence hang, implying that it was his last chance to suddenly remember some detail that would break the case wide open, that he could confess with the promise of a lighter sentence, or that they had one final bombshell revelation to drop before they'd haul him off to jail.

Josh only stared at the detective, quietly squeezing the cut in his palm so hard that the bandage started to feel wet.

"A bunch of fans' parasocial relationship with a missing woman is not exactly robust evidence, detective," Wilkinson said.

"It would be negligence if I didn't look into some of these claims. Rumors might have a grain of truth to them, even if we don't have the full picture yet. There have been some very concerning claims, even one theory that Amelia was younger than she let on—"

"That's ridiculous." Wilkinson laughed incredulously. "Theories? Is that what we call detective work? People are looking for cryptic messages and patterns that just aren't there. Pure speculation."

"I'm glad you brought that up," Detective Hindmarsh said. "I think it's very interesting that your client failed to notice the pattern of bruises on Amelia's wrists in the last photo she uploaded."

Josh's heart plummeted. "The what?"

"Bruises, Mr. Reuter. Would you like to take another look?"

She slid the gelato photo back toward him. There, he indeed spotted four rows of bruising around her wrists.

"Would you agree, Mr. Reuter, that those look like marks from a hand? Maybe a hand that grabbed her a little too hard, pushed a little too deep, didn't mean to take it that far?"

Had that happened when he grabbed her that night at Sarah's? When they kissed so deeply, so fiercely, almost as if it would kill them both if they stopped? "I have no idea how those got there."

Mr. Wilkinson jumped in. "Bruises can come from anything. To imply that bruises on a person's wrist are enough to charge abuse, let alone charge something more, is preposterous."

Josh could barely think. His blood rushed in his ears, drowning everything out. The edges of his vision tunneled, and he stared at

Amelia's face, at her smile. He'd never . . . The seriousness of the situation was closing in on him. The room had become very small, the chair too rigid, the air too thin.

"Go to her apartment!" he blurted out. "I'll bet you can find a hairbrush or something to compare the DNA from the suitcase!"

Detective Hindmarsh's eyes lit up. She knew something, and she wasn't telling. "Her apartment, you say . . . You've been there before?"

"Yes! Please! It'll help you see it's all just a huge misunderstanding." Josh's pulse was in his throat, choking him. "I swear, detective."

Wilkinson's shoulders got very stiff. He put a hand on top of the photograph, covering Amelia's face with his palm. "Quiet, Josh. Let me take it from here."

"But—"

"You've done enough talking for one day."

Josh clamped his mouth shut. He was going to puke.

Detective Hindmarsh looked victorious, a small smile curling her lips as she watched him.

Josh's whole face blazed hotter than the sun. Amelia attacked him! He should be considered a victim, not a suspect! She was the one who'd lunged over the table, grabbing at his throat and screaming about how much she hated him! And even then, he loved her. *Still* loved her. And they still didn't believe him. His palm was wet with blood.

"We have the witness testimony, Mr. Wilkinson. Several witnesses in fact. Not just Sarah Speck, but others staying in the house."

Alex Ciupa. The writer. Josh's grasp of the situation was slipping. He was losing control of the narrative. He'd thought a lawyer would help, but look where he was now.

The detective slid the legal pad over to him. "How about you start by writing down Amelia's address for us."

"Why?" Josh's mouth worked before his brain. He knew he shouldn't talk but he couldn't stop. "You should have it. You're the police."

Detective Hindmarsh's eyes narrowed ever so slightly. She looked like she was trying to peel the skin off his face with that stare. "Maybe you can help us cross some t's, dot some i's." Her favorite idiom, correct this time. What was so confusing about Amelia's address? What weren't they saying?

The cordial smile returned to her face as she leaned back once more in her chair, bringing some air back into the room. "I'll leave you two to decide what the best course of action is to take from here on out. We've got a lot of work ahead of us."

With that, Detective Hindmarsh stood and took the photos with her. She left the room, but it didn't make the drone in Josh's head go any quieter. Mr. Wilkinson rubbed his hand over his face and tapped the pen on the legal pad.

"Go ahead, Josh. You can do at least that much," Wilkinson said. "Get it over with. I'm in for a long night."

CHAPTER FOURTEEN

AmeliaAimlessly YouTube Channel

Uploaded on July 31

[HD: I hate this. I couldn't stop myself, but I had to dig deeper and what I found is making me feel all kinds of things right now. I don't know what to do with this information, but I need to save it. I need to keep it somewhere safe.

Amelia posted a video on July 31, a couple days into their stay with Sarah Speck, but she immediately made it private, maybe having second thoughts, or regretting letting the world see it, but I found it. I was able to hack into her account through a back door and found all her unlisted videos. I didn't want to get this deep into her account, but I couldn't help myself. My heart sank when I saw the title.]

I didn't want this

[HD: No punctuation, no snappy title. Just that. I have chills.

The video starts sloppily. It's unedited, raw. Amelia adjusts the camera and sits back heavily, her back pressed against the bed. She's sitting on the floor of their room at Sarah Speck's house, alone in the dark. I can't make out much of her face, but I can tell that she's crying or drunk, maybe both. Mascara is smeared on her eyes, and her hair is disheveled. This is not the Amelia Ashley everyone knows and loves. She sniffs and stares at the camera, shoulders slumped. After a long moment, she starts to speak through a thick layer of phlegm.]

Amelia: I want to go home. I know that's not exactly something you want to hear from me, because it's been my dream for so long, but . . . this has been the worst experience of my life. Everything leading up to today, it's all just hitting me how alone I am here. I don't know what to do, I don't know where to go. All I want to do is curl up in bed and forget about all of this. But I can't. Our flight doesn't leave for another few days. I'm so desperate, I want to get out of here. There was a huge fight and it's all a mess. I can't be here anymore. I can't be around him. He's . . . I don't know. I don't know what! I'm shaking, I can't stop.

[HD: When she tucks her hair behind her ear, you can see bruises on Amelia's forearms . . . She starts to cry again, burying her face in her hands.]

Amelia: I thought everything was going to be okay, but I feel like I'm losing control. I feel so cold, like I've been hollowed out, and I'm so scared. [Her voice cracks.] I should never have come here. It was all my fault, I was so eager to come.

But Josh, he . . . Oh God. I don't know what to do. I am so stupid.

I didn't know that Sarah would have friends over, and everyone hates each other, and it's all my fault. I blame myself.

And when I think about my parents . . . oh God. They won't survive this again.

CHAPTER FIFTEEN

HARPER

Harper Delgado's Private Journal

I knew it.

Something was off here.

I did some basic research on Amelia and . . . I can't believe it. I am documenting this in case I feel like I've officially gone crazy and I need to check myself into a psych ward but. No. I'm certain.

One of the first things I do when I'm helping a client of my own is get as much information as I can about a person—their age, their place of birth, their address, etc. It was only normal that I did some digging into Amelia Ashley and I had thought it would be a shoo-in job. The girl documented her whole life online, basically doxing herself, hardly trying to hide any personal details that might be found by someone with the slightest competence with computers. Like me.

She put her whole life on the internet for the world to see in YouTube videos and her blogs. Astrology chart readings with her birthplace and -date, documentary-style hometown visits, apartment tours including the exterior of her building, just short of showing off her passport for the camera. You'd think that someone who posted their entire life online would be easy to find but that's the thing . . .

I can't find any proof that she exists.

I figured with a name like Amelia Ashley that she was using some sort of pseudonym, maybe even using her middle name. A lot of famous influencers do that, to keep some measure of privacy, but even with that level of scrutiny, I cannot—for the life of me—find this girl. Anywhere.

In one of her astrology chart reading videos, she said her birthday was December 9. Sagittarius. 2002. And that she'd been born at Magnolia General Hospital in Wichita, Kansas.

No baby with her name was born on that day in that hospital. No baby had been born in that hospital on that day—period. The hospital had closed that week due to emergency flooding, so it wasn't even operational. I found a newspaper article about it, printed a week before her alleged birthday. So that got me thinking. Weird, but not totally unheard of. Maybe she really was trying to stay private while also providing content for her viewers. So I kept digging.

The town she said she grew up in? No record of anyone by the name Amelia anywhere. No high school yearbook photo of anyone named Amelia, or Amy, or even Ashley.

The house she said she grew up in is listed as being an empty lot, part of a cornfield in Google Maps. I've attached a screenshot, just so that I can have peace of mind for myself. The address is there.

1057 W. Palmer Street

Nothing. Empty. Emptier than empty—corn rows.

The house had been demolished five years ago. You'd think someone with her Content Brain would want to post a video about how her childhood home was being demolished. It would be perfect: nostalgic, tear-jerking reflection on growing up and how time passes . . . The last owner of the property died in the '90s. The house she claimed as her childhood home has been empty the whole time.

In one of her Q&As, she mentioned her elementary school: Lafayette Elementary. No such school exists in town.

One of these things, I might have been able to chalk up to coincidence. But . . . it's real. I mean, it's fake. It's real that she's fake.

Her parents' names, her date of birth, her name . . . All of it. Created. Manufactured. Phony. She doesn't even go to San Diego State, like Tori thought.

I don't know what to do with this information. I feel like maybe I'm really losing it and I've gone a step too far, stalking this poor girl who's gone missing, but at the same time, I feel like I've been T-boned by a semitruck. I don't know which way is up. My head is spinning.

I know I need to tell someone about this, someone who can help. If I reveal what I know, will I just be adding to the drama? I've seen what her community is doing, stirring up shit that's just making everything so confusing and emotional, and frantic. Would I be making it worse?

I want to do what I can to help but . . . this is too weird. I need to dig more, see what else I can find out before I go to the police. Maybe not the police anymore. This is FBI territory. But then would I be swept up in an investigation? If they find out I've essentially been stalking this person, they might start paying attention to me, to how I make my living. I can't have that on my family right now, not when they're relying on me. No, I need to think bigger, do more research.

I've come this far, so I might as well go all-in.

Would anyone believe me anyway?

The question everyone should be asking is . . .

WHO THE HELL IS AMELIA ASHLEY?

CHAPTER SIXTEEN

JOSH

"Go home, Josh," Wilkinson said, once they were outside the precinct. The air didn't feel any fresher now that they were outdoors. Josh still felt as if he were drowning, fighting to keep his mouth above the surface, while invisible hands were yanking him down into a deep, dark abyss.

"But what about Amelia?" Josh asked. "You still believe me?"

Wilkinson adjusted his tie and sighed. "Of course, I still believe you, but you need to keep your ego in check. The police are trying to get a reaction out of you, get you to do something stupid, so you need to relax and let me do my job from here on out. You need to go home and stay put, don't do anything, don't even *think* about anything until you hear from me, understood?"

Josh knew the police were using every tactic in their playbook to close the case, and he squeezed his fist to allow himself to focus on the pain in his hand.

"Fine," he said. "I'll go home, I don't know what else I'm supposed to do." He was powerless, and the feeling was not one Josh experienced a lot. He hated it.

"Until they can prove the blood is Amelia's, they can't arrest you. All they can do is keep an eye on you. I know it's not a fun feeling, but it's what you can expect. Maybe take one of those Xanax of yours," Wilkinson said, the corners of his lips turned down. "It'll help even you out until we can come at this again."

✕ ✕ ✕

When Josh got home, he found the apartment dark and empty. Derek and Tori nowhere to be found. It was a blessing, in Josh's opinion, because he wasn't in the mood to talk to or see another human being for a while. He wondered just exactly what Detective Hindmarsh was doing with Amelia's address. Why did they need him to write it down? The question troubled him as he hurried toward the bathroom and flicked on the light, stumbling to find his Xanax bottle in the medicine cabinet. When he did, he popped it open and took one of the pills, swallowing it dry. The medicine didn't work instantaneously, but it felt like it did. It calmed down his jackhammering heart long enough for him to feel like he could breathe again. He closed his eyes and inhaled deeply.

He needed to focus. He couldn't lose hope now. There was still a way he could sort all of this out. There was still time. Mr. Wilkinson was on his side, even if he'd let Detective Hindmarsh walk all over Josh, accusing him of purposefully ignoring the bruises on Amelia's wrists. He hadn't even noticed them. They were so faint, it could have been from anything, bumping into a taxicab door, or knocking into a table at dinner, or even something in her sleep. The police were focusing on the wrong details. Mr. Wilkinson could have easily stood up for him right then and there, said something that would change their minds, but instead he'd just sat there, doing nothing. Josh never should have gotten a lawyer. He was looking worse every day in the eyes of the police, the internet, everyone. He hated himself for trying.

But what else was Mr. Wilkinson supposed to do? He was his lawyer, but he couldn't protect Josh from himself and his big fat mouth.

He should have shut up, but his ego would not let him. It was his fatal flaw. He'd always known that. He always had to prove people wrong, or prove them right, never settling for the truth that he couldn't make everyone like him all the time. It was Amelia who'd pointed it out in the first place. She poked him in the side with her sharp fingernail and stuck her tongue out of the corner of her mouth as she smiled at him. "You just don't know when to stop, do you?" she'd said.

When Josh opened his eyes, he stared at himself in the mirror. In the harsh overhead light, he looked like he was going to throw up. The stress about Amelia's disappearance was manifesting on his face, making him look like he'd aged years in the span of a couple weeks. He gripped the edge of the sink and let out the breath he'd forced himself to hold. It hissed out between his front teeth, easing his shoulders.

He felt like a caged animal, pacing at the bars. He needed to do something, even if Mr. Wilkinson said otherwise.

Josh went to his room and grabbed his laptop from his desk. He kept the light off as he threw himself into bed and opened the screen, propping the laptop up on his bent knees. Sitting in the comfort of the dark, making it feel safer somehow, Josh pulled up his email. Already twenty-five unread emails about Amelia stared at him from the first page, even more on the next.

Everyone was talking about her now. Local media outlets, international news organizations, even the governor had made a statement. He couldn't escape her.

He opened each news article, scanning through every headline, seeing the same cheerful photo of her eating gelato in the sun as the Xanax counteracted his boiling blood.

Amateur journalists and amateur detectives alike were fixated on the bruises. No wonder Detective Hindmarsh had brought it up. People were hounding her about it, getting her to pay attention to details that she may have missed, but it only fueled Josh's desperation to prove that he was innocent.

If Amelia really had been spirited away by some kidnapper, they were going to nail him to the wall for it instead. And even if Mr. Wilkinson could somehow get them to see that he was innocent, they were never going to stop looking at him as a suspect. They couldn't throw him in jail for some blood and no body, but they'd forever watch his every move. See what he would do next, where he would go. He'd always have a tail, a shadow, waiting to see if he would slip up.

Munch jumped up on Josh's bed and curled at his feet, but Josh barely noticed.

His inner voice repeated her name over and over. *Amelia. Amelia. Amelia. Where are you?*

He opened all the unread emails he'd missed throughout the day, finding no answers, no kernel of hope in the lines. His eyes ached, dry and sore from staring at the screen in the dark, and the Xanax was making everything slow. Everything felt like it was moving at half-speed. It felt like Amelia was in the room with him. He couldn't stop thinking about her.

He was obsessed. He'd been for a while, but only now—sitting in the dark, his breathing stilted as he opened news articles with her face plastered under the bylines—did he realize it.

Every time he saw her name, he remembered her laugh, remembered the way she said his name, and as the hours ticked over from night into morning, he thought he started hearing her for real. Auditory hallucinations. She called his name from somewhere in the empty apartment, and he'd had to stop himself from following.

Josh . . .

But she was gone. She was missing. And he needed to find her.

He couldn't fight it anymore. The hours moved forward, the articles kept coming, but the Xanax won, dragging him down. Sleep took hold.

He dreamed.

× × ×

Josh . . .

Amelia's voice. He stood and turned around, walking right into the hallway of San Diego State. Abandoned. His footsteps the only sound. A snowstorm was roaring outside in the middle of Southern California. Total whiteout behind the glass windows.

There was a fountain at the end of the hallway. In the pool was a smear of red, red dye, no—red blood, oozing out of the eerie blue water. Trevi Fountain.

Whispers surrounded him, and Munch darted out from under his legs, chasing something or running from something.

More whispers. Josh turned around in circles. Only whispers, no people.

"Hello?" he called out but he hadn't moved his mouth. His voice worked on its own. No reply.

He walked forward, following his voice as it moved down the hall like smoke.

He was alone. Always alone.

Except for Amelia.

She met him around the corner, standing in front of him, wearing nothing but a bikini top and cutoff shorts, like she was going to the beach. She smiled at him, her dark red lipstick a stain on her white skin.

"Amelia."

She laughed and brought her hands to her stomach. They came away red. Red like her lipstick, like the fountain, like blood. Her blood.

His suitcase was now in her hand.

She laughed again, turned, and walked away, her ponytail swinging.

He moved to follow, but she was faster, just out of reach. She rounded the corner, the tip of her ponytail disappearing, and her laugh rolling through the hallway like an echo.

Josh followed, winding through the hall. Each corner folded over the next, impossible twists and turns, looping back in on one another, and still Amelia remained just out of his grasp. His hands clutched empty air.

He chased her, but she was gone. He was getting desperate, and ran, but she ran too. He sprinted, his legs moving like rubber bands, but Amelia moved ahead.

He tripped and fell through the floor, falling down, down. Amelia's laughter the last thing he heard before he hit the ground hard.

× × ×

The dream felt so real. He jerked awake, stunned by the bright sun pouring through the blinds of his bedroom, the laptop dark but still open beside him. Munch was pawing at his feet, pleading to be fed, but Josh stayed in bed, staring up at the ceiling. He could hear the garbage truck rumbling down the street, knowing that the undercover cop car was probably somewhere out there too, waiting for him to come out.

He had school, but he was going to call in sick. His body was slick with sweat, his muscles heavy and sore, as if he'd been running for real. He didn't know what to do; he was paralyzed with the weight of the day. It pressed down on him, pinning him like a butterfly trapped under a sheet of glass.

He checked his phone. He'd already missed his first lecture of the day. One text from Derek saying that he was staying at Tori's. No texts from Amelia. That laugh in his dream . . . He knew it was only a dream, but she'd sounded so alive.

The outfit she wore in the dream overcame his thoughts.

He pulled up Amelia's Instagram, viewing it as a guest, his account still deleted, and scrolled all the way to the bottom. He needed to start fresh, to see one of her earliest posts. The first she ever uploaded was a selfie, taken from the floor of her apartment. She was wearing that bikini and shorts outfit. It was a favorite of his. He'd checked out her profile before they officially started dating, an attempt to get to know her a little better, and that outfit had done its job—it caught his attention. No wonder he dreamed of it.

She hadn't changed a bit, except for the length of her hair. She was smiling at the camera, her chin propped up by her fist, grinning like she had a secret she wanted to tell. No, it was more like she was grinning at *him*.

The caption read: **Well hello there.** No hashtags, no tagged accounts. Just a greeting. *Hello, Amelia.* The straight edge of her nose, the way her blue eyes sparkled, the gentle twist of her lips as she smirked. It ensnared Josh.

The second oldest photo next, a mirror selfie, Amelia wearing a farmhouse dress and boots. He stared at her wrists, only covered by loose bracelets. Her skin was unmarked, unblemished. No bruises. His stomach lurched at the memory of Detective Hindmarsh's scrutinizing gaze. She thought he was an abuser, she thought he was hiding it.

If he had bruised her, he hadn't meant to. He loved touching her, loved how soft her skin was, the tickle of her hair against his shoulder when she leaned on him, how easily her fingers interlaced into his own. When he touched her, she felt like something magnetic; he couldn't let her go.

This one had a caption: **Just new boots** followed by three emojis. A lasso, a cowboy hat, and a target.

She was always terrible with captions. She'd gotten better at it the more she worked at her Instagram photos. If he'd been in a better mood, he might have smiled at the idea. Amelia wasn't always so perfect.

Munch stared at him, demanding food. His unblinking gaze penetrating Josh's forehead. "I know, Munch," he said. Munch didn't even acknowledge him. He only stared.

Josh needed to keep looking. He'd convinced himself that if he looked at Amelia's photos long enough, he could manifest her. He could make her finally reach out to him, finally let him know that she was okay. But as he stared at her photos, he couldn't shake the feeling that he was missing something.

The photo was old, so the comments were old too, and mostly spam.

Great pic! Promo on _@beauty-girls-IG_!

Get more followers now! _@followers4u_

Are you looking for someone?

Love it! Send to _@hotgirlpics_

He went to the next photo, the third earliest. She was on the beach, her arms spread wide in the wind. She either had help taking the photo or had the camera set up on a timer and tripod. The photo had been rotated by ninety degrees so it looked like she was standing on the side of the frame. The blue waves of the Pacific stretched out behind her, the horizon lining up perfectly with the angle of her head. It looked like it was beheading her.

The fourth, Amelia sitting at the fish market at Tuna Harbor. She was grinning over a plate of whole halibut, cooked with perfect grill marks, its lifeless eyes staring at the camera.

The fifth, Amelia with her head thrown back, about to eat a blackberry at a local farm stand.

In every photo, she looked beautiful. Not a hair out of place, makeup flawless, composition perfect, lighting immaculate. She knew how to work the camera, how to draw the eye, how to attract attention.

Each photo got more and more likes. As he went through her photos, he watched her audience grow. More likes, more comments, more attention.

Everyone loved her. Everyone still loved her.

He kept scrolling, flipping through photo after photo, a blur of Amelia's face filling up his vision, until all he could see were her eyes. She looked familiar somehow. But he couldn't place it. She haunted his dreams, his every waking moment, he felt like he was seeing her face everywhere, in every girl who passed by him on the street, or stared at him across the classroom.

But then something occurred to him. He went back to the first photo, that first picture of her knowing smile. There was nothing else remarkable about that photo. Nothing that stood out to him. So he moved on to the next, and then the next, reading each caption, and then the comments . . . It was like someone flipped a light switch on in his brain.

Are you looking for someone?

The comment was recent, and appeared over and over in her photos, all from the same anonymous account: Zm9lbmQgeW91.

At first, it looked like a spam account trying to lure desperate people into a scam, only to bleed them dry of their life savings. It shouldn't have bothered him, but it did. Was it really a bot? Or was it something else? He stared at the question on the screen.

He *was* looking for someone.

This was right up Amelia's alley. A treasure hunt, like geocaching. Digital hide-and-seek in the real world. And she was good with computers, studied computer science, and loved codes and ciphers. Adventure was her second nature. She was clever and sharp, like a knife's edge. And that's what made Josh pause.

It could be nothing, or it could be everything.

Curiously, he googled a decoder-conversion site and pasted in the jumble of letters from the end of the user's name.

Zm91bmQgeW91

Decimal, hex, binary, none of it worked, except for Base64.

The moment he hit ENTER, he pushed the laptop away from him. He felt like he was truly losing it, he had to be going mad. There had to be a better explanation, a better reason. It must be a coincidence. It couldn't be real.

The code was only two words:

found you

CHAPTER SEVENTEEN

JOSH

Josh had to go. Somewhere. Anywhere. He was losing his mind. No way. This was too crazy.

Found you? What was what? Was it some sort of threat?

He hadn't even noticed when he got up from bed, pacing around his bedroom. Munch watched him patiently from his disheveled sheets as Josh walked back and forth across his wooden floor. He rubbed the stubble on his chin and ruffled his hair, searching for some sort of reasonable explanation, but he couldn't find one.

He heard the front door of the apartment open. Derek was home. Josh could identify the sound of him anywhere, noisy and obvious.

"Josh! You home?"

"Of course I'm home," he said, emerging to find Derek standing in the entryway, kicking his shoes off, still wearing his dark sunglasses. "I have nowhere else to go, not with them watching me all the time." He was starting to sound like a person who actually believed in conspiracies. Paranoid.

"What's the matter?" Derek asked. "You look terrible. Did they find Amelia?"

"No."

He propped his sunglasses on top of his head, revealing concerned eyes. "How'd it go with the lawyer?"

The noise Josh made was a cross between a groan and a growl. He didn't even want to think about any of that. He held his phone out to Derek, nudging it toward him. "I need you to look at something and tell me I'm not losing my mind, okay?"

Hesitantly, Derek said, "Okay," as if he wondered whether Josh was going to do something unhinged like jump out the window or shave his eyebrows. He was feeling like he just might at this point.

Josh pulled up a photo of Amelia from her Instagram, one with the anonymous comment, and handed the phone to Derek. Wordlessly, Derek looked at the phone, then at Josh, then back at the phone.

"Scroll," Josh said. He started pacing again.

Derek scrolled. "Um . . . okay. What exactly am I looking for?"

"Look closer. Look at the comments."

"Josh . . ."

"Do it." He didn't mean for it to come out like a bark, but it did. His cool, calm, collected demeanor was getting harder to maintain. "What do you see?"

Derek's lips disappeared as he sucked them together, watching Josh for a long while with a knit brow. He caved, and looked back at the phone. "I see spam bots."

"*Are you looking for someone?*" Josh said, his voice hoarse with desperation.

"Tori gets those kinds of comments all the time on her Insta. Sugar-daddy scams and stuff."

"Exactly like this? From this account?"

"I don't know. Maybe? But . . . dude. Have you slept yet? When's the last time you ate?"

Josh didn't have a good answer for either of those questions. While he knew he'd slept, it didn't feel like it. And he couldn't remember the last time he'd eaten; it might have been yesterday morning before his disaster of a day.

Derek must have sensed the growing disturbance swirling in Josh's brain because he patted the air with his hands, as if tamping the space between them. "How about you take a seat, take a breath. I'll make you something to eat that doesn't come from a box. Does that sound good?"

Josh threw himself onto the couch and held his head in his hands. Amelia had driven him completely mad. He listened to the sounds of Derek moving around in the kitchen, softly setting down the cutting board on the counter, gently removing a chef's knife from the block, attempting not to make too much noise, in case it would spook Josh. It almost made him laugh. Maybe he really was one microwave beep away from a full-on meltdown.

Was it really just a spambot? Or was it something else?

Derek was right. He wasn't a computer expert like Amelia, he couldn't even begin to understand how Base64 worked. For all he knew, this was coincidence.

Previous psychology classes he'd taken had talked about Carl Jung's synchronicity, the concept of coincidence in causality, like seeing the same number throughout the day or thinking about a song and then hearing it on the radio.

He'd dreamed of Amelia. She had invaded his every waking thought; now she had invaded his sleeping ones. Of course he'd try to find patterns where there were none. Coincidence was only meaningful when the observer made it so.

But what were the chances? A random string of letters that just happened to hide the words *found you* . . .

Was this some sort of game? Like some messed up version of hide-and-seek? Would it be out of the realm of possibility, truly?

Josh made himself breathe, forced air into his lungs as he had on the flight home, attempting to quell his galloping heart. His fingers felt numb as he unlocked his phone again, Amelia's beautiful face smiling up at him once more. He swallowed thickly and clicked on the anonymous account. There was no way of knowing when it had been created. The account had two followers, more spam profiles, and followed no one.

Only one picture had been uploaded to the grid. It was a stock photo of one of those plaques you might find at a home-goods store, the kind with kitschy, shallow, motivational word art in looping cursive, saying, *Live Laugh Love* or *Believe*. This one said, *Where the Heart Is*. It had been uploaded the same day Amelia left him.

What were the chances?

Josh's thoughts swirled, as if circling the drain, leading back to the interrogation last night. Why did the police ask for Amelia's apartment address? What were they having trouble finding?

Home. That's where the heart is.

His own heart pounded, as if knocking on a door. He had to see for himself.

He needed to go. Everything felt too real, too close. He needed to move or else he might explode.

Josh leaped off the couch and grabbed his baseball hat and keys.

"Where are you going?" Derek asked. Something was frying in the skillet. The smell of onions would have made his stomach growl if it wasn't churning with anxiety.

Josh didn't answer immediately. He peered out the front window blinds, pushing them apart ever so slightly. The unmarked cop car was still out there, a shapeless figure sitting in the driver's seat. He couldn't go out the front.

He pulled on his shoes and pocketed his phone. "I have to check on something," Josh said. "If anyone asks where I am, just say I'm in the shower."

"But—"

Before Derek could finish, Josh had already moved to his bedroom. Munch had given up angling for food and had posted up near Josh's pillow, curled in on himself. He barely roused himself when Josh stepped up onto his bed, opened his bedroom window, and pushed himself through. Being on the bottom floor, he only had to drop to the back alley pavement.

The afternoon was bright and balmy, perfect for a barbecue, and Josh looked both ways up and down the alley to make sure there weren't any pedestrians enjoying the weather, taking shortcuts or walking their dog. The coast was clear, so he hurried down the lane. Josh pressed himself up against the building and pulled up his hood just before darting between the gaps between buildings in clear view of the street.

His heart raced as he tried to walk as calmly as possible down the sidewalk, perpendicular to his street, waiting for the sound of tires on pavement to follow behind, but he spared a glance over his shoulder. No one was following him. The unmarked cop car was nowhere to be seen.

They didn't know he'd left. He'd escaped. But he needed to be fast. They would know soon enough.

✕ ✕ ✕

Josh waited until sundown, watching the window to Amelia's apartment from the shadows of the building across the street. He'd needed to make sure that the police weren't milling around, and based on the darkness of Amelia's apartment, they weren't there either. He would bet a million bucks that the cops had already visited earlier in the day.

Her apartment was in one of the few high-rise complexes in North Park. It was a nice apartment, even though it was small for a studio, but she filmed all her YouTube videos there. It was a quick walk to the nearest pizza place, called Artie's Pizza, where he and Amelia would catch up after they'd finished their classes for the day. They didn't share any of the same ones. He ached to have that life back. Now it felt like it was gone forever, since the moment Amelia vanished.

The building was a little shabby, with several of the units already lit up in the quickly darkening evening, but Amelia's unit remained unlit. The last time he'd been here, it had been a week before their trip abroad. He knew he looked like a pervert, staring up at the window of a woman's apartment, but this was different. He couldn't help the rush of fear, or maybe excitement, that vibrated through his body seeing her apartment now after she was gone. He felt like he was nearing the end of this nightmare.

It was time to finally get to the bottom of this. Whatever game Amelia was playing, it needed to be over.

He crossed the street and pulled out the keys to her place. He remembered when Amelia had presented them to him after they'd started dating, and she'd put them in a small box, the kind usually used for engagement rings, right after they'd finished eating at Artie's. She'd made a big deal about it too, making it seem like this was a moment to be remembered.

"A girl giving a guy the keys to her apartment means she trusts him," she'd said, her eyes sparkling in the candlelight. "So. If you accept, does it mean you trust me too?"

Josh opened the door to the main entrance. It always smelled like carpet cleaner and standing water on the lower floor, and he ascended the stairs to her fourth-floor apartment. He could hear people in their own units moving around, smell the dinners they were making, hear the television shows they were watching, the conversations they were having. He tried not to make too much noise as he went up, but the building was old, and the stairs creaked. He hoped no one would come out. Amelia had always talked about how she'd made friends with her neighbors, especially when they were cooking. She'd said that food was the best way to get to know a person. No doubt if anyone saw him now, ascending the stairs toward his missing girlfriend's apartment, they would call the police.

Fortunately, he made it to her floor without incident, not seeing a single soul, and walked down the hall to her apartment, 4B. His heartbeat thumped in his throat.

With shaking fingers, Josh inserted the key to her door and unlocked it. When he swung it wide, the light from the hallway only caught the bare wood floor. The air smelled stagnant. He waited.

Visions of finding her flooded his thoughts. Amelia, dead on the floor, pill bottle in her hand. Amelia, hanging from her neck in the bathroom. Amelia, sitting on the lounger with her feet kicked up, a grin on her beautiful face.

He called into the dark. "Amelia?"

When he flipped on the lights, his stomach dropped.

His first thought was that she'd been robbed.

His second thought was that the police had cataloged everything for evidence.

The third thought was that he was still stuck in a nightmare.

Amelia's apartment was empty.

All the furniture, gone.

All her kitchenware, gone.

Television. Gone.

Wall art. Gone.

Rugs.

Books.

Plants.

Gone.

He stepped into the apartment, stunned, taking in the view of nothing as the reality of what he was seeing finally took hold of his insides, like frozen claws.

It was as if she'd never lived here in the first place. This was the right apartment, he'd had the right address. His key opened this door. He'd been here dozens of times, recording YouTube videos with her, shared meals with her on the couch, stared out that exact window watching the cars amble down the street below.

"No," he mumbled. "No, no no. *Nonono.*" He rushed into the bathroom, hoping this was a huge prank, but he found it spotless, not even a water stain on the kitchen sink.

"Amelia!" he shouted to nothing but thin air.

His phone pinged in his back pocket. He whipped it out and stared at the screen.

NEW TEXT FROM UNKNOWN NUMBER

Do you believe in ghosts?

Josh had to read the message over a few times before the shock had finally worn off for him to understand the question. It was a strange one. Ever since Amelia's disappearance, people had messaged him, demanding answers. Normally he blocked anyone who crossed a line. This question, though, was too strange to ignore. Something in his gut told him to reply.

No, he typed out and hit SEND.

He stared at the conversation before a new text appeared almost instantly.

You should, joshreuter. You should.

Joshreuter. The only person who called him that was . . . Amelia.

She was alive. It was her. He gripped his phone so tightly, he could have cracked the screen. Thousands of questions stormed in his head: *Where are you? Why are you doing this? What happened? What is going on?* They layered upon one another until it was just a chaotic tornado of rage and shame and frustration.

Could this be Derek or Tori messing with him? They knew Amelia well enough to have picked up her mannerisms. But they weren't the types to play cruel jokes.

Who else would know his phone number? He didn't have any other friends. He hadn't posted his number anywhere on his socials, he'd been so good about keeping everything contained, never shared more than he was supposed to online. He kept everything in a neat little package, giving the world exactly what it needed for him to be just like everyone else without giving too much away in turn. He was a private person, keeping himself safe, keeping to the sidelines, keeping his head low.

That habit of hers, calling him by his full name all the time, like it was one word. He'd thought it was cute, that it made her unique. Now he hated her.

None of this made any sense. He wanted to throw his phone through the wall, to scream, to pull his hair out. He'd been under the cops' thumb this whole time and she was really alive. No one believed him, and the truth was right there, in his hand. He could run to Detective Hindmarsh now, show her some proof, and maybe she'd take him seriously. Most likely, she'd think he'd truly lost his mind.

Amelia was alive, and she was talking to him.

Was it all one big game? Had she really been the one who'd posted that anonymous comment? *Are you looking for someone? Found you?* Had she set this whole thing up?

He'd never done anything to her. He'd never hurt her. He loved her with every atom of his being, and this was how she repaid him? She was torturing him, like it was fun. He could barely type out the next message. **Why are you doing this?**

The reply came shortly after, with a blushing smiling emoji.

One more clue. What else do you say when you've found something, Archimedes?

Josh's thoughts raced above the roar of blood rushing in his head. He closed his eyes and focused on his history knowledge.

Archimedes. The ancient Greek scholar. The first to understand the concept of displacement.

Then it hit him.

Oh.

Oh.

Eureka.

His confusion turned into something else as he got very still. His shoulders dropped and a simmering rage settled on his face as he uttered two words.

"You bitch."

PART 4

GIRL, GONE

Five Years Earlier . . .

CHAPTER EIGHTEEN

MIGNON

Confidential and Personal Diaries of Mignon Lee

Date 3-7

I know my family hates me. They don't try to hide it. I can see it in their eyes whenever they look at me. I'm a disappointment. Trouble. Work that they need to take care of.

I don't blame them. Really. I get it. I've been me my whole life. I know what it's like to live with myself.

They can't take me anywhere without me having some sort of meltdown. I can't help that my brain sometimes feels like a nuclear reactor and I'm going to explode.

That's why I'm running away. I'm writing this for my family, just so they know I'm okay. For my sister at least. She won't have to worry.

I've already packed my bag. Headphones. Extra clothes. It's raining right now, but I can't find my raincoat. (I'm going to use a garbage bag and punch holes in the sides for my head and arms.) Twenty dollars, that'll be enough to get me at least to Sacramento. I've already memorized the bus schedule. I should be going.

If my parents accidentally throw this out, and this note winds up somewhere in the trash, carried away by the wind on its way to the dump, then let me introduce myself. I'm Mignon. I'm fourteen years old. And I don't want to be found.

× × ×

Date 3-8

Well, they found me.

I only made it halfway down Elk River Road before the car pulled over on the shoulder and the police officer got out, asking my name. I hadn't thought about giving him a fake one, so I panicked.

I tried to run into the woods, but he was faster. He grabbed me by my backpack and hauled me back to the car where I sat, still dripping wet from the rain, while he called it in on the radio up front. Apparently, my parents had been looking for me. I'm surprised I made it this far.

I almost didn't recognize him at first, but it was Officer Kennedy, the same one who'd picked me up last year. I've lost count of how many times I've tried to run away. (I could probably go back through this diary and see, but I'm tired. My medicine is kicking in—it's making me sleepy.)

Officer Kennedy asked me what I was doing out here, in the middle of the night, in the pouring rain, and I told him to let me go, but he ignored me. He just turned on the engine and drove me home, all the way back to Eureka. I'd walked almost four miles by the time he found me. My sneakers were already soaked through, so I guess maybe I could plan better next time for unexpected rain, maybe bring some boots, especially if I'm going to have to cut through one of the national parks. I can't get very far with lakes in my shoes.

He didn't even turn on the radio for us to listen to music as he drove. It was so quiet. And it smelled like armpit in the back seat. There was sand on the cracked vinyl, and it made everything so itchy. Someone must have been picked up from the beach and then my wet clothes picked up the sand, and I couldn't sit still.

Officer Kennedy kept looking at me through the rearview mirror. I couldn't really see the rest of his face, but his eyebrows were narrow and he looked at me like I was annoying him or something. By the time he pulled up to my house, the rain had mostly stopped, but he had to let me out from the back. (The door was locked. I'd already tried it.) He watched me as I climbed out of the car.

Mom and Dad weren't waiting for me on the porch as usual whenever this happens, which meant they were inside. I could see the kitchen light on. Dad's car was gone from the drive—I figured maybe to look for me—but Mom's old Jeep was parked in the street. Officer Kennedy kept watching me as I trudged up the driveway, as if he thought I might try to make a break for it again, but my shoes were making *squish-squish-squish* noises as I walked, and he followed close behind me so I wouldn't have made it far anyway.

He stood behind me as I opened the front door and went in. I kicked my shoes off and tried to hang my sopping socks on the radiator. They were limp, like wet noodles, and slapped the floor when they slipped off.

I heard Mom moving in the kitchen, but she wasn't making dinner. I only heard the soft *dink* the wineglass made as it was set down on the table.

Officer Kennedy watched me from the other side of the door, his hands looped on his belt.

He asked, *Can I talk to someone?*

I called to Mom and she came shuffling out in her scrubs. Her soft blond hair was falling from a messy bun, and she massaged her face as she walked toward the front door. Officer Kennedy introduced himself and said where he'd found me.

Up past Humboldt Hill.

Mom sighed a *thank-you*, said I wasn't going to be trouble again.

We can't keep doing this, he said. Then he said that he might call child services if Mom or Dad couldn't keep watch over me. The specific words he used were *child endangerment.*

Mom apologized, pleading for him not to do that, that we were all working on it and that he didn't need to call anyone. Officer Kennedy said he hoped not. The police couldn't keep wasting resources like this forever. Mom apologized again.

I couldn't look at either of them because I knew both of them were looking at me, so I turned my attention elsewhere. From the shadows on the stairs, my sister was sitting halfway up the steps, her fingernails painted bright green as she gripped the posts of the railing, peering at me through the gaps.

Mom thanked Officer Kennedy, ending the conversation, and watched him leave before she closed the door. She didn't even look at me. She just turned around and went back to the kitchen, and I knew to follow.

I shivered in the cold. The rain made my clothes stick to me like gum. My trash bag poncho idea hadn't worked out the way I pictured. I ripped it off myself and it fell in shiny black pieces to the floor. I toed at them with my bare feet and gathered them in a pile while Mom took her spot at the kitchen table, handling her mostly full wineglass with one hand while she held her forehead with the other.

I asked where Dad was and she paused a moment, taking me in with her steady gaze, before she said he was out. Looking for me. Like I'd thought.

She asked me why I was doing this again. She thought we'd been over this, that I couldn't run away like that. And I didn't have a good answer. No one really gets me. I doubt they ever will.

I didn't have the heart to tell her I never really meant to leave forever. I always mean to come back. I don't think it'd be a satisfying answer for someone like her, someone who is happy rooted exactly where she is. Sometimes I get these urges to run, to be somewhere else, and I can't help it. It's like I'm possessed, and I need to move or else I'm going to die. Literally die, heart stopped, on the floor. She doesn't understand. She never inherited whatever mental problems Grandma had, but I did. Lucky me.

Except when Grandma had her problems, the medicine hadn't been created for it yet. Plus most people didn't believe a housewife could ever be unhappy. You just didn't talk about that kind of stuff. It wasn't good manners.

But when Mom looked at me over the kitchen table, with tired eyes after working a double at the hospital, asking me *why* again, I didn't know. I still don't.

Sometimes I wonder what it would be like if I wasn't around anymore, if I'd never been born. I think about someday finding people who might understand me. That's why I leave, so I can find a place to rest my head where it doesn't feel like I'm trouble.

Mom didn't say anything else, just covered her eyes with her delicate hand, blocking me out of sight. So I left her alone.

I climbed the stairs, squeezed past Sis, palmed her head for balance, and took a bath. The sand from the police car fell off my skin and gathered at the bottom of the tub. I heard Dad come home. He slammed the front door behind him. I knew he wasn't mad. When he's scared, it can come off as mad. The door just happened to be the best thing to let out his feelings on. I used my foot like a squeegee to push the sand down the drain. I couldn't get rid of it all. It's kind of like me and my impulses. I can try to push them down, but sometimes a little bit remains and piles up and before I know it, there's a beach in my bathtub of a brain.

As I unpacked all my things in my room, I heard Mom and Dad talking downstairs. I knew it was about me. I heard my name a few times. I didn't care. At least they weren't yelling.

All my clothes were wet, my headphones totally busted, and I'd completely forgotten to put the Nokia in a plastic baggie, so it dripped out water when I tipped it over. No phone, no music, square one.

Everyone knows I'm going to run away again. It's only a matter of time. I think maybe I won't for a while though. I took my medicine and things are quieter. I can lie on my bed and stare up at my ceiling, at the glow-in-the-dark stars we put up there, and think about all the places I could go, dreaming about someday . . .

×××

Date 7-30

I learned a new word today. It was in a book called *Travels of a Forgotten Voyager.* I found it in the attic when we were cleaning it out for the garage sale.

Wanderlust: noun

A longing to wander

Do you think a lot of people have it? Or do you think it affects only a few? It's kind of nice knowing that other people feel what I'm feeling and put a name to it.

It's like I'm part of a club.

CHAPTER NINETEEN

MIGNON

Date 1-11

Mom and I went to the mall today. I needed new shoes since I'd worn holes in the toes of my old ones. I was happy to go. I wanted to spend some time with her, really. Just hanging out.

Lots of people were at the mall, and she kept me close as she stopped and said hi to some of my classmates' moms, all of them wearing leggings and carrying water bottles. Later, Mom would tell me apparently it's a group that gets together and walks for miles in the mall. Mall walkers. I don't really understand it. They just walk in circles, pumping their arms, and chatting. Around and around in circles they go, where do they stop? Nobody knows. Don't they feel like hamsters in a cage? Nightmare.

The other moms looked at me while Mom tried to strike up a conversation, but I knew I was a subject of the mall walkers' gossip. My classmates know all about my outbursts, and how I'm a "distraction" when teachers are trying to teach (thanks, Mrs. T).

Because I look Chinese, like Dad, people always think I should be good at school for some reason. They've said so to my face—teachers, counselors, even the vice principal last year. They all think I should be a "model student." (I'm not the smart one in the family. I already have enough going for me. Can't have it all! Ha!) They don't say the quiet part out loud, that they think all Asians are overachievers with perfect grades, but I get the message loud and clear. And when I call them out on it, they say not to take it so personally, that it's actually a compliment, that they can't be racist for assuming something good. Fun fact: It's still racist! And me saying so just makes them angry and it gets me in more trouble.

So I wasn't really surprised when the mall-walk moms smiled at me, but the smiles only went halfway up their faces, which let their eyes tell the real truth: They want to know why I'm not quiet, demure, or obedient like they expect.

I don't really remember what they talked about, but Mom waved as they left, then looked at me and rolled her eyes, smiling. She said those ladies were nothing but gossips and we laughed as we went the opposite way. Mom never liked them, and I asked why she bothers being nice and she said because it was the adult thing to do. *More adult than mall walking?* I asked, and she laughed, and it felt good.

Things have been better between me and Mom. It's been almost a year since I ran away last, and I have no intention of doing it again. It's like we're friends again.

We got to the discount shoe outlet and Mom bought me boring white sneakers. At least she let me wear them out of the store. I know my parents have some money, but they don't buy us fancy things. Maybe because they know I'll just ruin anything they get me. I have a tendency to doodle on things, gives me something to work on, and soon these white shoes will be totally covered in ink. My jeans, my hands and arms, sometimes my legs. I'll draw on myself until I'm blue—literally. Why buy me expensive jeans if I'm just going to make a mess of them anyway?

I got to break in my new shoes as we walked all the way to the other side of the mall to Claire's. They always have the best jewelry for kids my age, sparkly earrings and bracelets. Sis and I got our ears pierced here when we were really little. My ears closed up though, because I didn't wear a lot of earrings. The doctors told Mom and Dad I shouldn't have sharp and pointy things.

Mom had to pick up a new phone case for Sissy, so I made a lap, like the mall walkers, through the aisles. I didn't have any money, but that was okay. I just wanted to see some of the shiny things and think about what I would do if I had a million dollars. I'd buy everything!

I came upon a display tower full of necklaces that had names on them. I can never, ever find my name on anything. Do you think I could change my name someday? Maybe I would be able to find my name on a necklace then. I couldn't even find one with Sissy's name. Bogus.

But I did find some necklaces that didn't have any names on them. One was actually two-in-one, a matching pair with compass pendants, exactly my style.

FOR YOU AND YOUR BESTIE! the label said. I already had someone in mind.

But it cost twenty dollars. I didn't have twenty dollars. I heard Mom talking with a clerk on the other side of the store, under the blaring pop music, and I knew she'd say no if I asked her for money. Knowing me, I'd lose it almost immediately. Dad jokes that when I set things down, it's like they disappear into a parallel dimension, never to be seen again.

But these necklaces looked like real silver and I wanted them so bad. If I had one, I'd never take it off.

I knew I shouldn't have done it, I didn't need it, but I felt itchy all over again, and a part of me said to do it. It wasn't hurting anyone. I knew Mom would be mad if she found out, but it's not like I was running away again. I wanted to have something for myself, a secret. Everyone knows everything about me all the time anyway, so I might as well have something just for me that no one else knows about.

Mom called my name, she was ready to go home.

She never even saw me slip the necklaces in my pocket.

Date 7-9

I've got mosquito bites all over.

Me and Sis stayed out too long in the tree house again, way after dark, and the bugs went to town on our arms and legs. I've been making little Xs on them since coming inside, but they're already red and itchy, and now they just have X-shaped indents in them from my fingernail. It's supposed to stop the bite from itching, but I think it just makes me look like a map now, with tons of X-marks-the-spots all over.

After dinner, Sis and I went to play in the yard. It's one of the few times Mom and Dad let me go anywhere alone, when I'm with her. She wanted to show me how many cartwheels she could do, and I showed her how all the blood rushed to my head when I stood on my hands. I can't ever do it for very long so I fell over, and we laughed until we were both red in the face.

After it got too dark, we went up into the tree house Dad built for us when we first moved in. Easily, the coolest place ever. We go up there to count falling stars and share secrets. I thought about making it my room someday, moving my bed up there and trying to live on my own. Sis says that's stupid, but what does she know? She's only thirteen. I could do it if I really wanted to, I'd just have to try.

We sat up there with the lantern and went through all of the travel books I found in the attic when we were cleaning it out last month. I even found an old map that I nailed to the wall, and we could trace our fingers on the lines, measuring how far it would take to go from one destination to another. Three fingers long to Seattle. Five and a half to Vegas. Too many to Mexico. We've spent hours up there, talking about all the places we could go, all the things we could see and do. I can't wait until I'm old enough to go by myself. I could wake up and choose anyplace to be and then I would be there. Simple.

Australia had its own book, all by itself. There are tons of pictures of the deadliest animals on the planet in there. I guess Australia has the most kinds that can kill people, like the whole continent is designed to scare people away. I think it's awesome. Imagine having a touch that hurts, that can kill, like the box jellyfish. It floats around, not really having a brain, going wherever the current takes it, and it catches its prey and stings it to death, and then keeps on floating. Not tied down by anything at all.

The ocean scares me though. It's so deep. I'm too afraid to go, even when we make trips to the beach.

I've got a whole list of all the places I'd like to go:

- ❑ Iceland—ice and volcanos!
- ❑ France—to fall in love
- ❑ Antarctica—the "loneliest" place in the world, but I think it'd be peaceful
- ❑ Japan—visit one of those hot springs outdoors
- ❑ Italy—it's where all the best food is; Mom inherited all Grandma's recipes
- ❑ Galápagos Islands—I want to see one of those giant tortoises, just once! I could die happy.

Sis hates flying—she's scared of it—but I told her it's one of the safest ways to travel. She could see the world, born at the right time, when only a few generations behind us, people still had to spend weeks on a boat or train to get them where they wanted to go. Now all we have to do is go to an airport and take a nap and we're in a new city. She's still scared, but at least I got her to smile. I knew what else would make her smile. She's so smart, and sometimes I forget that she's still young. She's got a lot to learn about the world.

I had the necklaces that I'd been saving in my pocket, and I showed them to her. The silver glinted in the lantern light and Sis's eyes got as big as the moon. They're big and round like Mom's.

She asked me where I got them and I said it wasn't important. I tore up the little cardboard backing and gave one to her.

She cried. Even though I think she's too old for it now, she cries easily, but this time I understood why. She thought I was leaving again, that this was a parting gift. She hates it when I run away.

I told her I wasn't going anywhere! I said I want to leave all the time, but I always want to come back. I can't stay away from her too long. She's my other half.

She said I hurt her feelings whenever I go, because she feels like it's her fault, that she's not good enough for me to stick around, but I told her that as long as she's got her necklace, I'm always with her. She didn't believe me. She pouted, like a little kid, which made me laugh.

To make her feel better, I let her set up tracking on my "Find My" app, a way for her to check on me "just in case."

I think she's lonely. It's tough being a kid genius, homeschooled most of her life and already taking college classes online. It's kind of scary how smart she is. Most kids her age are intimidated by her, and most of her college classmates don't want to hang out with her.

Watching her set up my phone, my heart broke a little for her. I wish there was more I could do, but when I go to college, she'll be on her own.

I think I'm her only friend. I'd never do anything to jeopardize that.

I told her that we had too much traveling together to do still, I wasn't going to leave her behind.

CHAPTER TWENTY

MIGNON

Date 9-15

It's been a while since I've last written in my diary. A lot's been going on. School is keeping me busy, and I've barely had time to even think about it. Maybe that's a good sign? I don't feel like I need to seek solace here. Writing in this diary is one of the only places I can really spill my guts without any judgment. It's helped me so much, and it's crazy to look back at how far I've come. I can finally breathe.

But I have to spill: There's a new boy at school.

His name is Bennet and he moved here from Colorado. I've always wanted to go to Colorado! Add "climbing a mountain" to my bucket list. Bennet said he'd take me sometime, but I think he was just joking. When he smiles, my stomach flips.

I really like him. Really, *really* like him. I've had crushes on people before, but this feels different.

I told Mom about him this morning when she was packing my lunch in a brown paper bag. I love paper bag lunches. The food she packs in them tastes different, I don't know how. Different and better. Mom has never skipped a day to pack lunch for me, even though she's got a long shift at the hospital ahead of her. She always knows my favorite foods: peanut butter and jelly sandwich cut diagonal, baby carrots, pretzels, sliced radishes, and a fruity yogurt (no sliced radishes for Sis—such a picky eater. More for me!). It's not a five-course meal, but it might just be. Dad used to make my lunches before he got the fancy job. My favorite is his stinky tofu, exactly how his mom does it in China, but I can't eat it at school anymore. Too many kids made fun of the smell, saying I was eating rotten garbage for lunch. I know Dad was heartbroken when I told him I couldn't bring it anymore, but he didn't say so.

I don't care that I'm already sixteen and I still let Mom pack lunch for me. It's her way of telling me she cares.

I think she's noticed that I've been feeling better too. It wasn't overnight, but ever since they got me on new medication, I've been sleeping better, and it's made life a little easier. My moods don't swing as bad as they used to. I'm not cured, but that's not the point.

Mom and I have been getting along better. I think me talking about my crush with her proves it. And she smiles when she writes my name on the bag, flourishing it with a stroke of her Sharpie.

Is this what love is? Making things?

Mom packing me lunch, Dad making spring rolls, playing hide-and-seek with Sissy outside? Maybe. I'll have to do some more research.

Love in the movies looks different. Time stops and the love interest walks in slow motion. Stopping time would be a cool superpower. It kind of happened like that when I saw him and I couldn't look away. It was like everything got still and I saw my whole future ahead of me.

I'm going to ask him out. Maybe I'll show him the tree house. I hope he says yes. I'll have to find the North America travel guide. It's around here somewhere.

Mignon + Bennet = ❤

CHAPTER TWENTY-ONE

MIGNON

Date 6-11

It's wild that Bennet and I are official. It's only been a few months, but it feels like a lifetime ago when I asked him out in the tree house. I didn't think he'd say yes, but he did. He saw something in me he liked, and I wanted to chase that feeling. I'm still not quite sure what he sees in me. I know I don't have a very high opinion of myself. Sis likes him too, although she's too shy to hang out with us when he comes over.

I want to be loved. I really do. But sometimes I wonder if I deserve it. I know I haven't earned it.

Things have gotten better though. Really. My doctor says my medication is doing its job and he wants me to stay on it. My grades are up, I get along with Mom and Dad better than ever, I even have more friends. Jenna Johnson invited me to her birthday party next month. A year ago she wouldn't have even acknowledged my existence.

It was tough going for a while, I see the proof in this diary. I've been reading through it because this one's almost all used up. There are only a few blank pages left. I get to add it to my collection when it's done. Rereading what I wrote, even just a couple of years ago, it's hard for me to believe we're the same person. I wonder how much better it'll get next year and the year after that.

Last weekend, Bennet brought me up to his family's cabin at Shasta Lake. His uncle has a boat, and snorkels, and mopeds and other fun stuff to do. I'd never been before, but it's beautiful, a glassy lake surrounded on all sides by lush evergreens. When we took a hike up through the woods to the cliffs, we got a bird's-eye view of the lake. It was like an ink splotch, this craggy blue hole in the world. It actually reminded me of a fork of lightning streaking across the sky. We lounged on the beach, and we talked, and soaked up the sun, and ate so much barbecue I could have burst. My mouth is still watering!

Bennet let me talk about all the places I'd want to go next. I probably talked for hours about Guam, and Kenya, and Turkey, and Iceland. I think he likes listening to me talk, and I don't think it's just because he wants to hear me go on and on about volcanos in Iceland forever. Maybe he can see himself going to those places too.

I didn't bring my diary with me. I barely had time to write anyway. All I want is to be with Bennet.

Date 6-30

I know it's corny, but I think I love him.

Bennet. Even seeing his name here makes me all fluttery, like the butterflies in my stomach are going to carry me away. When he kisses me, I'm pretty sure I could fly.

He took me for a drive in his dad's car out to Samoa Beach and we watched the sunset, sitting on the sand, and we made out for hours, taking breaks to count the stars. I haven't done that with anyone but Sis before. He brought a blanket, candles, and some champagne. (Not the real kind from France though. Not that I care.)

His hand was warm and strong as he stroked my hair. His hand feels so good in my hair.

Look at you, he whispered, his breath warm on my cheek as he touched my necklace. I am blushing just remembering it. He brushed his thumb across my lower lip and kissed me there. He traced his lips down my jaw, down my neck, sighing, and my head swam. Sand got stuck between my toes as they curled with pleasure.

We were going to stay there longer, maybe do some other stuff, but a beach patrol came by and shined flashlights on us, and we ran away laughing. He brought me home and we kissed some more before I had to go.

He makes me feel so good, inside and out. I might really know what love feels like. But I know it's not perfect.

I've never said it to his face, but sometimes he can be a little controlling. He tries to tell me what to wear, how to do my hair, that I'm too loud sometimes. But when he says it, he says it like a joke, or like he's helping me, and I don't really know how to tell him it hurts my feelings. I want him to like me for me. I know I'm not perfect either, so . . . who am I to judge? I guess it's just one of those things about relationships.

I know we're still young and there's plenty of time for us, but it's nice being able to tell the truth in this diary.

One day I'll get my words out there. I'm glad no one else gets to read what I wrote in here though. I'm so embarrassed. If Bennet ever found my diary, I think he'd break up with me on the spot. I am so cringy. I can't help it though. I have a lot of feelings and I don't know how else to get them out. If I can't write, I might die.

I'll finish writing my book soon, my travel book, and then I'll be a real writer. I want to get it published. I'll call it something like *A Runaway's Guide to Travel*. (I'm still working on the title. It'll be better, I promise.)

I want to do so many things. I want to write about people, and places, and food until I'm six feet under. My dream is so close, I can almost taste it. I want to go to college to get my degree in travel writing. Then I'll be unstoppable.

PART 5

FAULT LINES

CHAPTER TWENTY-TWO

AMELIA

Two Weeks Later . . .

Amelia was putting the finishing touches on a binary grid puzzle when Mignon burst into her room and threw herself onto her bed. She was always doing that, suddenly entering Amelia's dimmed bedroom like morning sunlight.

"Can I help you?" Amelia asked, looking at Mignon from the corner of her eye as she kept typing. "I'm busy."

Mignon's smile was bright and infectious. "What are you doing?"

"Making a geocache puzzle. It's a scavenger hunt if people know the cipher—"

"For fun?" Mignon interrupted. "Come on. It's summer. You're too pretty to be sitting inside all day being a computer nerd. You're pale enough as it is."

Amelia gave her sister a withering look and returned to her work.

"I have a favor to ask," Mignon said. "A tiny little favor."

Amelia groaned and spun around in her chair. "What? Do you want to swap chores again? I'm tired of doing dishes."

"Not that. I was hoping you could keep a secret."

"A secret?"

Mignon's warm, brown eyes sparkled, and her lips curled, holding back a mischievous smile. Even though they were sisters, she and Amelia looked almost nothing alike. Amelia always admired the way Mignon's presence could brighten any room. Mignon was her own stylist, artfully cutting and shaving her shiny black hair so she looked even more like a rock star, and doodled on her arms in pen like temporary tattoos, and tore holes in her jeans to add even more personality to her wardrobe. She was wild, and free, and it made her beautiful. Amelia never felt brave enough to do any of that.

When people looked at Amelia, they saw a white girl—light hair, light eyes, not quite blue, not quite gray. When they went to visit their dad's side of the family in Beijing two years ago, they accepted Mignon at face value alone. They admired her big eyes and her pointy nose, and aunties would grab her by the chin, saying she was blessed with a "first love face." It didn't matter that Amelia was fluent in Mandarin and could code as well as a first-year at Peking University, she was still treated like her mother: as an interloper.

"I'm going away with Bennet this weekend, to his cabin at Shasta Lake. He invited me up there, alone, and I don't want Mom or Dad to know, so I need your help."

"You mean, you want me to lie."

"It's not really a lie. It's just . . . I'm going to tell them I'm sleeping over at a friend's house. That's not exactly a lie, is it?"

"Yeah, it is."

Mignon rolled her eyes and slid off Amelia's bed. She went over and grabbed Amelia around the wrists, tugging on them like she used to when she wanted Amelia to go outside with her to play. She was the only person who could pull Amelia away from her computer. "Come on, *Sissy*."

"Don't call me that," Amelia groaned, nudging her glasses up her nose. She hated that nickname.

Mignon's laugh was like a ringing bell. "Just this once? I owe you big-time."

Amelia knew Mignon wasn't going to let it go. Once she had her mind set on something, she was going to do it. There was no use putting up a fight.

Amelia thought about it a moment. She was a terrible liar. But when Mignon flashed those sparkling brown eyes at her, she couldn't resist. She smiled back at her sister—it was the one feature they had in common, people always said: They had the same smile. "Fine. Don't forget that you owe me."

Mignon whooped with victory. "You're the best, Sissy."

✕ ✕ ✕

Amelia turned the page of her vintage mystery novel, pausing to wipe a drip of red-flavored Popsicle from the paperback. She'd figured out who the killer was ages ago, but it hadn't spoiled the experience. Part of the fun was getting to the end to see it all come together. She liked reading outside, sprawled under the clothes hanging on the line, drying in the heat of the sun.

She bit off the last half of her Popsicle as her phone rang from a number she didn't recognize. She let it go to voice mail and returned to the story.

Her parents were out, Mom at a shift at the hospital, and Dad on a business trip in Hawaii, and with Mignon away with her boyfriend all weekend, Amelia had the entire house to herself. She'd done laundry, tidied her room, and vacuumed the floors. Amelia even made lunch for herself, a relatively healthy one that consisted of avocado and tomato, which made her feel doubly grown-up. Her parents always said she was mature, independent, could take care of herself, they didn't need to worry about her. Not like Mignon, who would be heading to college soon, something that had her parents both nervous and hopeful. Amelia dreaded Mignon leaving, but privately thought their worries were overblown. It had been years since Mignon had run away or had a manic episode.

While Amelia waited for her clothes to dry, and licked the melting Popsicle juice from between her fingers, enraptured by the story unfolding in her novel, her phone went off again. It was the same number.

She had half a mind to shut her phone off. She barely answered the phone as it was, but for some reason, something prickled at the back of her mind.

When she picked up, she heard her mother's voice on the other end.

"Amelia, has Mignon called?"

"No," she said, chomping on the wooden stick that had been her Popsicle. She felt like an outlaw in an old Western movie, a quick-draw with a score to settle. She pointed her fingers at the sun, like a gun, and pulled the trigger. "Why didn't you call me on your cell?"

"My phone ran out of battery. I can't find a charger cable anywhere. I don't know where it is—"

Something in her mom's tone made the skin on Amelia's neck tight. She sounded frantic, haggard, and she only sounded like that when Mignon was in trouble. "What's wrong?"

"Mignon didn't text me and she's not picking up her phone. I'm just worried she's—"

"Maybe she forgot?" Amelia asked, though she herself sensed that it was out of character. She hadn't gotten any texts from Mignon either, no annoying series of emojis describing something adorable Bennet had said or done. "Or maybe Jenna's house has bad reception." She'd sold the lie that Mignon had stayed over at Jenna Johnson's house over the weekend, as Mignon had asked her to. "I can call her for you."

"I've tried calling her. Her phone keeps going to voice mail."

Hi! This is Mignon. You know what to do. BEEP.

Amelia knew that voice-mail message so well, she could imitate it perfectly. And she often had, just to bug Mignon. "Maybe she ran out of battery too, Mom. Don't worry!" Amelia tried to calm her mother down, but she could hear the panic bubbling between every word. She hooked her thumb around her compass necklace and raked the pendant across the chain, finding comfort in the way it vibrated against the metal grooves.

Her mother took a shaky breath. "Please call this number back if you hear from her. I'm calling Jenna's parents now."

"Just take it easy. I'm sure it'll be fine."

Mom didn't sign off, she just hung up. Amelia stared at her phone, her book forgotten. In a few minutes, Mom would find out that Mignon had never gone to Jenna's in the first place. Her gut coiled with nerves.

Mignon had a tendency to disappear, but this time felt different.

A year ago, Mignon let her set up her "Find My" app to track her phone, so when Amelia opened it up, she located Mignon's little phone icon and tapped on the profile.

MIGNON'S IPHONE

OFFLINE

PLAY SOUND

LOST MODE

The "Last Known Location" was a giant circle around a green and blue map of Shasta Lake. Since it was turned off, it needed to use GPS data of its last known ping to guess where it could be. Amelia tried to stop her heart from hammering, but she couldn't help it.

Had she really run away again? Amelia swallowed the guilt building in her throat and desperately grasped for any other explanation. She could be having such a good time with Bennet, maybe she lost track of the days. The sweetness of her Popsicle had turned sour as she stared at her phone with ever-growing dread.

"What happened, Min?" she asked, under her breath.

CHAPTER TWENTY-THREE

AMELIA

"And do you have any reason to believe that your daughter is in danger?" Officer Kennedy asked, bored, as if he were reciting his line in a play. He'd grayed out over at his temples since Amelia had seen him dropping Mignon off after the last time she'd run away, but he was still the same dick who used to stare between Amelia, Mignon, and their parents as if their very existence was offensive.

Amelia and her mom had gone straight to the Eureka police station once night washed across the sky and there was still no word from Mignon or Bennet.

"She was with her boyfriend this weekend," Mom said. Her eyes flicked toward Amelia for a split second before they went back to Officer Kennedy. Mignon might be mad at her, but Amelia thought it was worth it. "At Shasta Lake. We can't get hold of either of them. Or his parents."

Mom desperately clung to her purse, leaning forward on the counter, as if it were helping her stand up. In the harsh fluorescent lights of the police department, Amelia noticed how much older her mom looked.

Officer Kennedy typed into his computer, the screen obscured, but he didn't seem to be in any rush. Amelia watched his fingers move, but his face remained impassive.

"Mignon Lee," he said, as he typed it out.

"Yes," Mom said, breathily.

"This is the one who's run away before, correct?"

Mom's lips pressed into a thin line. "Yes."

"The one with bipolar disorder?"

"Yes."

"And the drug problem."

Amelia clenched her fists at her sides.

"Mignon is on *medication*," Mom said, the word coming out sideways. Despair was rolling out of her, Amelia could practically feel it in the air.

Amelia forced herself to speak calmly even though her blood was boiling. "None of that other stuff matters," she said. "My sister is missing. Can you send someone out to look for her and Bennet?"

Officer Kennedy barely looked at Amelia, but when he did, he did a double take. When people learned that she and Mignon were sisters, most of the time they assumed Mignon was adopted. It was offensive, to say the least. And Amelia hated it. She frowned at Officer Kennedy, who resumed typing. "You say she was last in . . ."

"Shasta Lake," Mom said. "How many times do I have to—"

"I'm just getting all the facts, ma'am. Bear with me."

Mom glanced at Amelia, perhaps looking for assurance, and Amelia tried to give it to her with a small smile, but already Amelia felt like they were up against a brick wall.

She'd had to defend Mignon her entire life. When she was younger, she'd get angry at her sister for the way she was. She didn't know what *bipolar* meant; she'd heard other kids at school use it when they were being dramatic and trying to explain their mood swings. Her parents hadn't explained it to her until she was old enough to understand, and Amelia had felt guilty for the way she'd thought of her sister. Having bipolar disorder meant that Mignon's moods would swing from extreme manic episodes to extreme depressive episodes. Amelia had ugly memories of crying in her room because Mignon had "spoiled" her birthday due to an episode of mania that made her stay awake for days. Those memories embarrassed her, but she worked hard helping Mignon once she realized what was going on. Being mad at Mignon for her illness was like being mad at the sun for rising and setting every day. It was a cycle, one to plan for and manage. Amelia knew a lot of other people weren't going to be so understanding, and if Mignon didn't have her family to back her up, no one would.

Officer Kennedy seemed as uninterested as possible. "It sounds like it's only been a few hours since you last heard from her. And you said she's seventeen?"

"She always calls," Amelia said, taking over for Mom, who haggardly ran her fingers through her blond hair. "She would never let it get this far."

Mom shouted, "She's a kid! Please."

Officer Kennedy said, "I'm sure it'll all work out, ma'am."

"I'm begging you," Mom said. "Help us."

Amelia lifted her head and stared furiously at Officer Kennedy until he finally looked away, muttering something about filing a report.

× × ×

The detective assigned to the case came over to the house the following morning. His badge said his last name was Foster. He was a balding white man in his sixties, rather unremarkable appearance-wise, and all Amelia truly remembered about him was that he smelled like cigarette smoke. He took a look around Mignon's room, giving it a once-over, before he sat with them in the living room, his tea untouched on the coffee table, as he took notes about Mignon.

"We're so grateful someone is taking this seriously," Mom said, a little breathless. "Thank you for coming over so quickly."

"Our daughter, she's a good girl," Dad said to the detective. He'd taken a red-eye flight from Hawaii, cutting short his business trip and landing in Sacramento only hours before and driving through the morning to make it home. He held onto Mom's shoulders, tracing his thumbs against her biceps to calm her down. Shadows hovered under his eyes, weighing him down even more. "We don't know what else to do."

"I've been informed of your daughter's previous history with running away. Can you tell me more about that?" the detective asked.

"Mignon's had some difficulties with her mental health, but that shouldn't be an issue. She's been doing better. She hasn't shown any indication that she would run off again. We're still not able to reach her."

The detective nodded. "And Mignon, is that an anglicized version of another name? A, um—one that might be harder to pronounce?" He didn't want to ask if she had a Chinese name.

"No, her legal name is Mignon. Just like her sister is named Amelia," Dad said, trying to keep his tone level.

A spike of annoyance made Amelia's lip twitch and she swallowed the acid creeping up her throat. Mignon wasn't anglicized anyway; it was obviously French. But she didn't dare open her mouth to say anything about it. This guy was supposed to be smart enough to find a missing person?

Mom shook her head, her eyes welling up with unshed tears. She must have sensed the tension in the air. The detective was latching onto the wrong things. Amelia could barely take it, seeing her parents like this, so she stared at her hands pinned between her knees. All she wanted to do was sink into the couch. It had been her fault. If she hadn't covered for Mignon, lied for her, then maybe they wouldn't be in this situation.

Detective Foster's lips pressed into a tense, flat line. "Unfortunately, we don't have a lot to work with. I went to Bennet's home and interviewed him before coming here."

Mom's knuckles went white as she clutched onto Dad's hand and Amelia's heart thumped hard against her rib cage. She felt like it was going to explode.

Dad asked, bewildered, "You spoke with him?"

"He said Mignon left on her own. Do you have any idea why?"

Mom and Dad looked like they'd been struck over the head. "No . . . He's— He's home? Already? Why didn't he call us?"

Amelia stared, slack-jawed. Bennet was home, right now, curled up on his own couch, with his own family, and Mignon was . . . The outer edges of her vision closed in, tunneling. How could he have just left her?

"Bennet's a good kid," Detective Foster said. "I spoke with him at length. He's a little confused right now. He confirmed that he took your daughter to Shasta Lake, and he was planning to drive her home on

Sunday, but she left very suddenly. His uncle confirmed it, said she took all her things and ran away. It's my understanding that she did this a lot."

"She used to," Dad said. "We had a hard time with her outbursts for a while but she . . . She hasn't called us. She always calls us. She knows how this hurts all of us."

Detective Foster didn't seem convinced. He leaned back, tapping his pen on the notebook. "When's the last time you heard from her?"

"She called me before bed last night."

"She didn't sound distressed? Or . . . unlike herself?"

"No."

"Forgive my asking, but have you noticed Mignon having money lately? Money that you're not sure where it came from?"

"No."

Amelia didn't want to think about what he was implying.

"Is there any place she might have gone? Anywhere she might have spent the night? With anyone?"

"No! We don't— We don't have anything that way, any other place she might go. It's just forest out there and Bennet was the one who drove. She only took her medicine for the weekend. We thought she was sleeping over at a friend's house." Mom's face had gotten paler the longer she spoke. She looked like she was going to pass out.

"Take a breath, Mrs. Lee," Detective Foster said, leaning forward now. He smiled, encouragingly. "We see cases like this all the time. Just last week we had a missing persons report turn out to be a simple one-day adventure. A kid, no older than Mignon, decided to take his parents' car for a joyride and was too afraid to come home after he'd crashed it. He was fine, but it was all over nothing! I'm sure that wherever she went, she'll come home when she runs out of money." He licked his lips. "I've been a detective for over twenty years. Sometimes the answer is the simplest one."

Mom and Dad looked stunned. Amelia couldn't believe her ears.

"You don't know our daughter," Dad said, his eyes sharp. "And I don't think you're getting the whole truth from Bennet's family. You need to get to the bottom of it, or we will."

Detective Foster cleared his throat and dropped his gaze to his notes. "Let me be very clear about something: From here on out, you should not contact Bennet and his family in any way. It only complicates things and will make it harder for us to find your daughter. You wouldn't want to do anything to interfere with our investigation, would you?"

To Amelia, it sounded like a threat. Mom and Dad too looked startled.

"We only want to find Mignon," Mom said.

"I understand that. But I can't do my job unless I have the space to do it." Detective Foster stood up. "I'll be in touch. If you have any more questions, please let me know." The conversation was over.

Even after he saw himself out, no one moved. Mom and Dad sat on the couch together. Dad taking deep, calming breaths; Mom's shoulders rising and falling with silent shudders. Amelia felt disoriented, like she'd been spun around in circles, blindfolded, and left alone in the desert. She had no idea which way was north.

Amelia turned inward, completely lost all sense of time or place, shrinking in to focus on the feeling of her compass pendant pinched between her fingers. She hadn't even realized she was holding it in the first place.

CHAPTER TWENTY-FOUR

AMELIA

Amelia had just finished making Mignon's MISSING PERSONS Facebook page when she heard shouting downstairs and went to find her father standing in the kitchen screaming into his phone, her mother at the dining table with her head in her hands.

"I'm not *accusing* your son of anything!" Dad said, his face flushed red. "I don't care what Detective Foster said, I want to know what your son knows. I want to know what happened that weekend."

Amelia heard the voice on the other line, tinny and small but angry all the same, and Dad paced, grinding his teeth and clenching his fist.

Amelia took a seat next to Mom and whispered, "What's going on?"

"He's talking to Bennet's father. Don't worry, sweetheart. Everything is okay," Mom said, trying and failing to smile. She held Amelia's hand and her fingers were cold.

Dad continued. "I don't have to talk to Bennet. I don't even want to talk to your lawyer. I just want answers. I need—" He cut himself off as the voice on the other line grew louder. "How is this harassment?

I want to know what happened to Mignon. I'm only asking questions . . . I am calm!"

Amelia glanced at Mom, who squeezed her hand, sensing her fear. Seeing her dad this way scared her more than she wanted to admit. The wariness in his eyes made them distant and far away.

Dad's voice picked up an octave. "Really? A restraining order? Against *me*? Are you insane?" More harsh words on the other line. Frustration and anger burrowed into Dad's brow. "Fine. Get a restraining order. I don't care."

"Go back upstairs," Mom said to Amelia, but Amelia didn't move.

"I'll go to your brother's cabin whether you want me to or not. I'm not giving up." The voice on the other line started screaming obscenities and Dad shouted them back before he stared at the phone in shock. They'd hung up on him. He swore again, once, loudly, and collapsed into the other chair next to Mom. They held each other and Amelia went back upstairs. She couldn't bear to listen to her father sobbing.

✗ ✗ ✗

Detective Foster didn't bother telling them that Bennet had been brought in for questioning. The next morning, they found out for themselves in the local newspaper, the *Eureka Post*:

PERSON OF INTEREST QUESTIONED IN MISSING GIRL'S CASE

"'Person of Interest,' it says. Not 'suspect.'" Amelia pointed to the headline and glanced at her parents over the table. "Shouldn't it say 'suspect'?"

Mom and Dad both looked grim. Mom took the newspaper out of Amelia's hands, folded it up, and shoved it in the trash. She called the police station and found out that Bennet had been released shortly after questioning.

Amelia hated feeling this helpless.

At least Bennet's name was out there for the whole city to see and everyone was talking about it. But the community was split. The reporter who wrote the article had interviewed Mignon's classmates, neighbors, teachers, and most people had a lot of nice things to say about her, but some thought Bennet was innocent. Despite the fact that he was the last person to see her, people had reason to doubt any foul play.

He's a good kid.

What a terrible thing to go through.

There's no evidence Bennet did anything. That girl ran away. Simple.

✕ ✕ ✕

Weeks passed, still no Mignon. All that remained was the life she'd left behind.

Amelia stood in the doorway to Mignon's room, taking it all in: Mignon's flower duvet cover, her Clairo poster, her stuffed animals— Mr. Pig, her favorite. All of it untouched. The room had a musty smell— it surrounded Amelia's head like a cloud. Some fresh air would help, but then it wouldn't smell like Mignon anymore.

All Amelia wanted to do was bury her face into Mignon's back as she hugged her so tightly, Mignon would complain and make a fuss.

She wanted to ask her where she'd gone, what she'd been up to, why she hadn't called. She wanted to hear her voice again, even if she only said one word. One word would have been enough.

She didn't even remember the last thing she'd said to her sister. Was it "Have fun"? Or "Did you steal my headphones"? Maybe "Be safe"? Mignon leaving for the weekend had been so mundane, so ordinary, forgettable, Amelia hadn't cemented it in her memory. Not knowing where she was or what happened to her was the worst. She liked to think she'd been a good sister, that she hadn't annoyed Mignon too much, especially as they got older. What would she give to sit outside when night fell, bundled up in blankets in the tree house, counting and wishing on falling stars with her again?

Amelia sat on Mignon's bed and picked up Mr. Pig, tracing her fingers over his little top hat.

She often went to Mignon's room, especially when the noise got too loud in her head, from all the blood rushing in her ears after yet another news station declined to report on the story. They didn't say it outright, but Mignon simply didn't lead, wasn't a story people cared about. She wasn't like the missing girls on the nightly news with bright smiles and brighter futures.

She put Mr. Pig back on Mignon's bed. There were too many memories of Mignon lying there, her legs a pretzel as she wrote in her diary, Mr. Pig her proofreader. She was always writing, a pen never not in her hand, scrawling notes on napkins, and on the back of receipts she used as bookmarks, and even on her own body. Thoughts and ideas poured out of her like a cup overflowing.

For a guilty second, Amelia thought, *Is the diary here somewhere?*

Reading it would be a major invasion of her privacy, but Amelia missed her too much to care. She wanted to know what her sister had been doing, what she really thought about, how she really felt. It would be a way to get a fraction of her back, even if it was just a voice echoing in Amelia's head while reading her words. But they were her words.

Despite a little voice in the back of her head telling her not to do it, Amelia first looked in the dresser, an obvious place to stash a diary, but she figured getting through the obvious places was a good start. All the drawers served their purpose, filled with clothes, no diary. She checked the closet next, then under her bed, then Mignon's bookcase, stacked with uneven piles of books she'd devoured well into the night. Nothing. She flipped through Mignon's favorite copy of *Peter Pan*. She'd marked the pages with underlines and notes near her favorite lines.

Amelia wondered if Mignon had taken the diary with her—

Amelia.

She whipped around, thinking she'd been caught snooping, but the doorway was empty. No one was there.

It took a moment for her heart to dislodge from her throat. She was so tired, staying up late, staring at Mignon's dedicated MISSING PERSONS page. The stress was wearing on her. She put her hands to the side of her face and took a slow, steadying breath. It wasn't Mignon.

Amelia didn't want to believe she was dead. She couldn't believe she was dead, she couldn't give up. It was not an option. She was going to find Mignon.

She moved to leave, but when she stepped down, the floorboard felt different than the others. She stepped back, then forward again, testing the pressure. Normally the wood gave way slightly, but this part felt solid as stone.

Amelia kneeled down, hands splayed on the floor. Sure enough, part of the paneling was different than the rest. She ran her fingernails through a deeper groove in the slat and the wood came away, revealing a hidden compartment. There were crystals and rocks, shiny things Mignon had picked up on walks, like a magpie stealing treasures. There was a romance novel with a half-naked man on the cover that surely Mom and Dad would freak out about if they knew Mignon had it, a couple of twenties wrapped around a pack of gum, and—Amelia reached inside—Mignon's personal diary.

The velvety purple cover glistened in the light and an ache twisted in her gut. She knew she was crossing a line, but she needed to do this. She needed to know.

CHAPTER TWENTY-FIVE

MIGNON

Diary Entry
7-15

I don't know if I've changed, or he has. Maybe both of us have. But I think I need to break up with Bennet.

No, not I think. I *need* to break up with Bennet.

Ugh! I need to stop doing that. *I think, I think, I think.* As if I'm always so unsure about everything. I know how I feel and even then it's like I'm not sure. Sometimes I feel so happy being with him, and other times . . .

It doesn't make sense, I know. I'm not sure I even know why I feel this way. There's so much to like about Bennet and he's so sweet, but at the same time, I wonder if this is how it's supposed to be. He's so thoughtful, and remembers the littlest things about me, it's like he thinks about me all the time, and I'd be lying if I said I wasn't flattered but at the same time I feel like I'm suffocating.

He says he loves me, so then why am I not happy? I thought if someone says that they love you, that it's one of the best things in the world. I really thought I was happy, honestly. But I feel like we're not meant for each other. I can't picture myself being with him anymore.

But I feel like the more I try to push away, the tighter he holds on.

I'll wait until after the weekend trip with him—one last hurrah. He's been looking forward to it, I don't want to hurt his feelings, but I know it's inevitable.

After this weekend, we're done.

CHAPTER TWENTY-SIX

AMELIA

"Amelia! Where are you?" Dad's voice carried up the stairs. It nearly gave her a heart attack.

She rushed downstairs, Mignon's diary in hand, to find her parents had come home. Their cheeks were pink, wind-chapped and sunburned, having been out all day putting up Mignon's missing persons posters at Shasta Lake. "Is Mignon . . . ?" Mom asked, hopeful.

Amelia held out Mignon's diary. At first, her parents looked confused, but Amelia's heart jackhammered in her chest, racing with worry and dismay. It was their first lead.

✕ ✕ ✕

Without delay, her parents handed Mignon's diary over to Detective Foster at the precinct, but they made Amelia wait in the hallway. Amelia knew they were trying to protect her, but she felt even more useless as she sat on a lumpy office chair alone. Based on the volume of their conversation, it was not going well. She could hear Mom's desperation through the closed door, and see Dad's rigid silhouette through the frosted glass of Detective Foster's office door.

Amelia stared at her feet. Even though she had hoped otherwise, she thought something like this would happen.

Mignon's final diary entry didn't mean anything. What they claimed had happened afterward was pure speculation. It was still likely that she ran away.

Without physical evidence, Bennet's story was stronger. It was clear what happened. The uncle backed him up. They'd believed Bennet's family over her own. One word against another. What good were the police for anyway if they weren't going to help?

But Amelia knew, deep in her bones, that Bennet had hurt her sister. It couldn't be a coincidence.

She needed to prove it.

✕ ✕ ✕

A bitter rage formed inside Amelia that felt like an amorphous, slithering eldritch beast. Venomous, with sharp teeth and bloodlust.

Sometimes it came out when Amelia was alone, and she'd smash things in her room and scream and cry, and other times it sat nestled cozily in her gut, as if napping, readying itself for another round. Amelia fed it, reading and rereading Mignon's diary, until she heard Mignon's voice again, and she had the pages memorized.

Reading let her hate, and hate was one of the only things she could feel most days. It kept her going. She could hate that Mignon was gone, hate that no one cared, hate that the world wasn't fair. The more she read, the more she felt.

Every time she thought of Bennet, the beast grew stronger.

One day, she saw him in the grocery store. She'd been sent to pick up food for dinner, having run out of casseroles from sympathetic neighbors, and she almost collided with him in the frozen food section. He didn't look up from reading the back of a frozen pizza box. Amelia had to scramble back the way she came so he couldn't see her.

She slumped against the shelves in the snack aisle and crumpled to the floor, panic rising in her chest and darkness taking over.

The police had questioned Bennet again about the diary entry, asking whether Mignon had broken up with him, but he stuck to his story: She had run away without warning. Everyone took Bennet at his word. It was like his voice had simply drowned out Mignon's. Like she was silent and invisible, the way people had always expected her to be, even though Mignon had never conformed to their stereotypes, had always been loud and impossible to ignore. Until now.

Amelia felt like a predator, peering around the corner, watching silently as Bennet closed the freezer door and headed away from her, pizza box in his cart. A couple of elderly women from church recognized him at the end and smiled, patting him kindly on the hand and offering words of encouragement. Even from afar, she could hear one of them say, "It must be terrible what you're going through." Fury made everything white-hot.

She imagined what it would be like if she charged and tackled Bennet, pummeling her fists into his face, demanding to know what he'd done to Mignon, hearing the shrieks of shocked onlookers, feeling the sickly, warm, sticky blood of his mouth coating her knuckles. But reality snapped back into focus and she looked down to see that her palm was slick with her own blood, her fingernails having dug so deep that there were little red crescent moons there. She wiped her hands on her jeans.

She didn't know anything about Bennet. They'd barely even been in the same room together. He never paid attention to her. He barely even knew her name. Besides, who would want to hang out with his girlfriend's younger sister? He was older, cooler, carried himself with a confidence only older boys could. Amelia was just background noise.

The beast inside her gnashed its teeth and foamed at the mouth. She saw nothing but red.

No one could prove that Bennet had anything to do with Mignon's disappearance, not when he was so well-liked in the community, so handsome and thoughtful. He had anyone he wanted wrapped around his finger, and he could play the part of a concerned, worried boyfriend who was still trying to find Mignon. Mignon could be out there somewhere and he knew her last whereabouts.

Without a body, she would be forever missing.

✕ ✕ ✕

Hope was like a wound, and, if not properly cared for, it festered. It turned sour and acrid.

The Lee family was not immune. After a certain amount of time, never-ending hope had turned into finger-pointing, missing persons posters faded and torn from telephone poles, a Facebook page that stopped getting updates. Calls to police and news stations weren't worth it anymore.

Mignon had been gone for a year. No sign of her, not even a cryptic message in the mail.

Mignon was never coming back.

The reality had been hard to swallow. Amelia didn't want to give up. She refused—but it wasn't because she was stronger than anyone else, or more desperate to find Mignon; it was because she was fueled by something else entirely, the beast in her soul, a spark of darkness that, she worried, if left unchecked, would consume her entirely.

The family fractured like ice.

Dad was the first to go.

One day Amelia came home to find him packing the suitcase that he usually took on business trips.

"Going somewhere?" Amelia asked.

He jumped, as if he hadn't heard her, and stared, like he'd been caught. "Oh, Amelia. Sweetheart. Uh, yeah. I'm going away for a while." He folded up one of his white dress shirts and laid it on top of the rest.

"Where?"

"Uh . . ." He held out his hand, frozen, thinking as if on pause, and then said, "Beijing."

"Why?"

Dad smiled, obviously finding it amusing that Amelia was asking questions like she had when she was little, but his smile was more sad than anything. "I need to take care of my mother. She's not doing well."

"What about us?" Amelia asked.

Dad continued folding his clothes. "It'll be okay. It's just for a little while."

She knew, in that moment, that he was lying, but she didn't have the strength to say so.

He blamed himself the most. Amelia heard him crying in the bathroom a lot, whispering Mignon's name under his breath over and over again, with running water to muffle the sound. She cried herself to sleep after hearing that.

Now she watched him pack up the rest of his things, taking in his every movement, the way his hands carefully folded his clothes, the hunch of his shoulders as he leaned over his suitcase, the shine of his black hair in the soft light of the master bedroom. She didn't cry, or reach out to him, or try to stop him. She'd already lost him a long time ago.

Before he left, he put his hand on top of her head, just as Mignon used to do, and looked down at her, smiling, though his smile was shaky and unstable. She knew every time he looked at her, he was looking at Mignon.

"Bye, Sissy," he said.

The last memory she had of her father was his back as he walked out the door.

× × ×

Mom was never the same.

She continued to go to work at the hospital, but every day she'd come home looking more tired and haggard, shoulders slumped and eyes vacant. Dad deposited money in their account to cover their expenses, and she didn't need to work anymore, but she still did. Amelia guessed it was because it gave her something else to put her energy into, while also constantly worrying about Mignon. She never gave up looking for her. She joined support groups for parents of missing children so when she wasn't working or calling private detectives asking for help, she spent nights with other grieving parents who were going through the same anguish she was feeling. It was like Amelia barely existed anymore.

Mom stopped watching the news. Every time a report aired about another missing child or the tragic death of a teenager in an accident, it reminded her of how the news media had barely covered Mignon's disappearance. She quit going on social media, as recommended by her support group. In-person community was best for healing, and online spaces led to downward spirals.

Amelia was on her own most of the time. She learned how to cook, how to clean, but most of all, she learned how to lie. She learned how to avoid tough questions, how to convince everyone that she didn't need help, how to put on a smile and pretend that everything was fine.

She couldn't move on.

"Mom," Amelia said, finding her mother sitting in the kitchen among a stack of bills. "I got in." She handed over her acceptance letter to UCLA. She'd gotten into the graduate program for computer science, one of the best in the country, and at sixteen, she would be one of the youngest students in her year.

Her mother's eyes shined when she looked at the letter, but Amelia felt hollow on the inside. She didn't have the heart to tell her mom that she wasn't planning to attend. What was the point of anything anymore?

Mom hugged her tight, and told her she was proud of her, and Amelia went through the motions. "Thank you. Will you be okay here?" Amelia asked, looking at the stack of papers on the table. Mom's hair had turned gray since Mignon vanished. She looked smaller, and frail, sitting in a kitchen that now seemed too big for her alone.

Mom smiled, silver lining her eyes, and she said, "Of course." Her voice was thick with a sob sitting heavy in the back of her throat. "You need to live your life. Don't let anything hold you back."

Amelia wanted to believe that, but she felt guilty all the same. "I'll call, and email," she said. "Every day." And she meant it. But Amelia needed to move out. The house reminded her too much of Mignon. Her ghost was everywhere. She could feel her wherever she went, hear her, sometimes see her. Her raven black hair, her warm eyes, her laugh. Amelia never told her mother—it would only break her heart. She was sure Mignon haunted her too.

Amelia knew she should do what her mother said, try to move on. And still, even though she had a healthy allowance, and independence, and a chance to start over . . . she couldn't. She'd become obsessed with the life she'd lost. She was unraveling at the seams.

And she only had one person to blame.

PART 6

REVENGE

CHAPTER TWENTY-SEVEN

HARPER

Harper hadn't meant to get this deep into Amelia Ashley's disappearance. She'd only meant to poke around, lift up some rocks as they say, root around in the cellar for skeletons. But the more she learned about Amelia Ashley—or, rather, the more she learned about this fake persona—the harder it was to look away.

Harper had ignored her side hustles writing code and doing homework for lazy classmates in favor of research into Amelia's background.

Lucy came into her room one day to find Harper wrapping red yarn around thumbtacks and pinning documents and pictures to her wall.

"Um . . . ," Lucy said, staring. "Okay, so you've got a crazy-person wall now. Great. That's . . . great."

"Is it so crazy?" Harper asked.

"When you have a missing girl's face plastered all over your bedroom, yeah!"

Harper did not appreciate the sentiment. She noticed that Lucy had brought her dinner, a steaming hot bowl of pasta. She had completely forgotten to eat today and practically lunged at it. Lucy shoved it into her chest as she walked farther into Harper's room, looking at the meticulous organization and documentation she'd done over the past few days.

"What exactly are you trying to accomplish?" she asked, staring at Harper with her eyebrows so twisted, she almost looked like a cartoon.

Harper practically inhaled dinner and said, around a mouthful of penne, "Basically, I don't think Amelia Ashley is real."

"But people have reported her missing. Her friends and stuff."

"No, I know! A girl is missing. I just think Amelia Ashley is a construct. She's an invention, a character, created by this one." She pointed her fork at Amelia's pretty face, her smile that could light up any room.

"What do you mean?"

"I mean," Harper said, a little annoyed that she still had to spell it out. She hadn't told anyone about it yet, not even Tori. She didn't quite know how to break it to her. "Everything about this girl is fake. Literally everything. Usually folks who get really famous online have entire webpages dedicated to them, like where they grew up, their birthday . . . Everything the internet has on her is all fiction. Almost like she made it that way."

"So like a real-life lonelygirl?"

"Not quite. I think it's bigger than that." Harper chewed and swallowed, then put down the now-empty bowl on her desk. "No. I think she really is missing. She's gone totally dark, I can't find her using any of her social accounts, passport, or her credit cards—"

"Okay, stalker."

"Not funny. I only took a peek. A small glance at her charge history. No big deal."

Lucy frowned. "Harper, that *is* a big deal. That's the definition of a big deal. What if you got caught?"

"I won't get caught. I'm good at this."

Lucy didn't seem to share that opinion. She crossed her arms over her chest and stared at the wall. "It would take an awful lot of work for all this, to make up a whole new person," she said. "So what's the point then? Why do all of this?"

"That's the real question, isn't it," said Harper. "So I dug a little deeper. That's when I found this."

She opened her laptop and found the file of Amelia Ashley's confessional. "This is the last video she ever uploaded," Harper said. She had it saved as a file on her desktop and she played it for Lucy.

They watched Amelia's tear-streaked face in a dark room, her barely muffled sobs, and her small, quiet voice say:

"And when I think about my parents . . . oh God. They won't survive this again."

Lucy shivered. "That's so creepy, turn it off." Harper did and closed the laptop. She too thought it was creepy, but she'd watched that video so many times, it had lost its effect on her. "What does Amelia mean by 'again' though?"

Harper's eyes sparkled and she held up a finger. "Exactly my question. So I started digging, and I started with Josh Reuter." She pointed to his photo on the wall.

"The concerned boyfriend."

"Come on, you really believe that?" Harper asked, incredulously.

"No, I'm just quoting the papers."

Harper cracked a smile. "Anyway, it got me thinking, if there was nothing real about Amelia Ashley, then the best place to find some answers was Josh Reuter. And guess what?"

"Let me guess, he's fake too."

"Ha. Not quite." She pulled a sheet of paper down from the wall and handed it to Lucy.

As Lucy read it over, her eyes got wider. "Where'd you find this?" she asked.

"Suddenly you don't disapprove of my methods?"

"Harper, come on. A background check is bound to draw some attention."

"Luckily, I wasn't the one who did it. The San Diego Police did it for me. I just happened to intercept and make a copy on its way. No one is any the wiser. People notice when things go missing, people don't notice when it's just a copy."

Lucy made a noise like she wanted to sound impressed, but she still wanted to be the voice of reason in this situation. "You went through all that for this?"

"It was worth it to verify some rumors. It started as a few rumblings, got lost in the fervor and the flood of hashtags, but that background check proves it. A few people on Twitter said they recognized him, but he'd been going by a different name before he moved to San Diego."

Lucy looked at the copy of the background check, her eyebrows pinched in thought. "Okay, so Josh Reuter isn't his name. Big deal. Lots of people change their names."

"Not when they've been previously tied to another missing persons case."

CHAPTER TWENTY-EIGHT

AMELIA

One Year Earlier

"There you are, Bennet," Amelia said, staring at her computer screen with a small, hungry smile. "Huh, I guess you do look like a Josh. Josh *Reuter . . .*" She said the name with an upswing, the way you might call someone "big shot" or "hot stuff." His last name had remained the same, but according to the San Diego State freshmen photography portfolio exhibit, he'd started going by his middle name, Joshua.

"Are you sure you want to do this?" Mignon asked.

Ever since Amelia moved out, Mignon had come with her.

She watched Amelia from a corner of her bedroom in her new apartment. She filled in the emptiness of every space, coming and going in Amelia's mind when she was feeling particularly lonely, or needed someone to talk to. It was better than talking to the nothing around her, even if she wasn't real.

"Call me curious," Amelia said.

It had taken her a long time to find Bennet, no—Josh. He was good at hiding, practically a shape-shifter. A wolf in sheep's clothing. He was free to walk around, live his life, go to college, perhaps waiting to take another girl up to his family's cabin only for her never to be seen again. A couple months had gone by since she'd last seen him, but he hadn't changed all that much. He was eighteen now. Mignon should be eighteen now too. He was in college. Mignon should be in college now. He was alive. Mignon should be . . .

A part of Amelia wanted to believe that Mignon was alive and out there somewhere, that she really had run away to pursue her dream of traveling the world, but a realistic part of her knew that wasn't true. Mignon was dead. She'd died that weekend in Shasta Lake. Amelia might have known it that first day when she didn't come home, but it hadn't felt real until she'd sat with Mignon's absence for so long, and the hole she'd left behind had become septic.

Amelia clicked on his profile. He'd taken a self-portrait, capturing his elegant face, his wavy hair, his charming smile, leaning casually against a brick wall. His biography read:

Josh Reuter is an award-winning portrait photographer specializing in human form and movement. He uses classic techniques with the eye of baroque artists to create imagery that appeals to the tension between light and dark, the duality of man and nature, of motion and stillness. Click here for Josh's social media.

All his photos in the exhibit were of pretty women, mostly young women, posed wearing flowing gowns and flower crowns.

She clicked on each photo, looking at the faces of his models, and seeing Mignon staring back.

The Mignon in the corner of her room somewhere behind her looked at his photos too. "He's good," she said.

"He's reductive," Amelia said. But Josh did have an eye for composition, she'd give him that. He'd won a scholarship, according to the website, paving his way for a bright future in photography. "How many pictures did he take of you?" she asked her sister's ghost.

Mignon couldn't say, because Amelia didn't know. Mignon only knew as much as Amelia did. She was a ghost, a memory.

Amelia clicked on more photos. Each model looked like Mignon to her. The same energy in the angle of their bodies, a soul in their eyes. She saw them as Josh saw them, through his eyes, his lens, and her skin crawled at the thought of being Josh. What went through his head? Did he dream of Mignon? Did he remember her?

Did he feel guilty about what he'd done? Did he have nightmares? Did he panic every time a police car so much as pulled up beside him on the road? She hoped he did. She hoped he couldn't ever rest.

More photos. More models. Had any of these women gone missing too? Amelia considered starting a search.

"Amelia, you're exhausted. You should rest."

"I'm not tired." Her eyes ached. She'd been stalking Josh Reuter's online footprints all day. She had completely forgotten to eat, to drink, to stand up, and her joints ached from sitting hunched over her keyboard, until her voice cracked and the words felt hard on her tongue. "Why does Josh get to live when you don't?" she asked.

Mignon didn't answer. She was back in her corner, peering at Amelia through the fringe of her dark bangs.

Josh was free. And Mignon was dead. The injustice of it was an open wound, seeping into her gut like acid, the beast feeding on it.

"What are you going to do?" Mignon asked.

Amelia hadn't realized she was planning anything, not until that moment. She hadn't even noticed the plan taking shape in her mind, the edges of it becoming a solid thing she could grab onto.

To catch a monster, she had to become one.

CHAPTER TWENTY-NINE

AMELIA

For Amelia Ashley to be born, Amelia Lee had to die.

Amelia Lee was a dirty blonde. Amelia Ashley had hair like sunshine. Amelia Lee wore glasses. Amelia Ashley was blessed with perfect vision. Amelia Lee never smiled, not anymore. Amelia Ashley smiled like she had a secret she wanted to tell. Amelia Lee was forgettable, a girl in the shadows, no one looked at her twice. But everyone looked at Amelia Ashley. It helped that Amelia looked more like her mother's side of the family, and it was startling to see how easy it was to pass.

No one from her old life would recognize her. She didn't have close friends, and she'd scrubbed her entire existence off the internet. Who would be looking for her anyway?

She waited around the corner of the laundromat in downtown Eureka just as a light rain started to fall, misting her down and making her feel like she'd broken into a cold sweat.

Her guy was late. She didn't know his name. It had been on purpose, just in case either of them decided to start talking to the police. But she regretted not having his phone number so she could call him. Her feet ached and her jacket didn't stop the trickle of rain that had dripped down the back of her neck as she hunched in the cold Northern California fall. Cars rumbled by, unaware of the girl standing in the shadows out of sight of the streetlights. Still no sign of her contact.

His services were pricey too. She had spent a few thousand dollars, half of what he'd asked for, up front as insurance, and she was starting to think it had all been a scam. She silently cursed herself and her stupidity before a black sedan pulled up and rolled down the window.

"You got the money?" a voice inside asked. He was in shadow, and she couldn't see his face except for the glint in his eye from the cell phone store across the street. She knew he was in his twenties, with stringy blond hair and pockmarks all over his temples, but other than that, she didn't know anything about him.

She asked, "You got my stuff?"

There was another shadow in the passenger's seat. Amelia hadn't expected a second person. She couldn't help that her heart skipped in her chest, perhaps as a warning. She was new to this kind of thing, trading money in exchange for illegal documents like some sort of spy operation, but she was aware enough to understand that changes like these, including unexpected hangers-on, were something to worry about, especially since it meant that someone else would see her face.

The driver pulled out an envelope from the middle console. It was full to bursting. "Money first."

Amelia's eyes had adjusted to the dark and she could see his passenger now. It was another guy, roughly around the same age, with dark hair. He wouldn't look her way, purposefully keeping his face turned toward the passenger's side window, his hand covering the bottom half of his face. He kept fidgeting with the zipper on his hoodie.

Amelia tried to quiet her pounding heart and took out the last remaining thousand from her waistband.

They traded easily enough and Amelia glanced a peek inside the envelope. There was her new passport, driver's license, and Social Security card. Everything she needed to start a new life.

Automatically, she said, "Thank you" but the driver pulled away before the words had finished leaving her mouth.

She took a step back and watched the car as it drove off down the road, and she was about to leave when the brake lights flared and the car screeched to a halt. Shadows moved inside the car, and Amelia took another step back. Every instinct told her to run. But the passenger's side door flew open and the dark-haired guy scampered off into the mist, running full tilt on flailing legs into the night.

Amelia stared, dumbstruck, and the driver's side door opened. The blond guy emerged, clutching his hand to his face. Even from that far away, she could see blood dripping between his fingers. She knew she should run, but she stood, rooted to the ground, and stared.

"He stole my money!" he shouted, his words muffled through a layer of blood. The other guy was already long gone.

Amelia could barely think. She had never seen anything like it before, and she didn't know what to do. She had frozen like a deer in the headlights.

The blond guy spotted her. "You—come back here!" He marched forward and Amelia stood frozen, brain on lockdown. Once he was right in front of her, he tried to grab the envelope from her hands but she pulled back.

"Give it back," he said. He sounded congested. His nose looked broken, it was smashed flat against his face.

"No," she said.

He tried to grab it again, and she stumbled back. He snarled and lashed out, grabbing her by the front of her raincoat and yanking her toward him. No one had ever touched her like that before. Not even when boys on the playground in elementary school got too rough, a move everyone said was because they liked the girl. She wanted to scream, but she couldn't.

"I need more money!" He shook her again and put his hand around her throat and squeezed. The edge of her vision went dark. She gasped, but no air came into her lungs. Panic set in. She thought she was going to die.

White-hot fear made her feel too big for her skin. She held on as tightly as she could to the envelope. He shook her again, his fingers squeezing around her neck, and she lashed out. She struck out at his face, the heel of her palm connecting with his already broken nose, and he let out a horrendous scream as she broke free and sprinted in the opposite direction.

His screams echoed after her as she ran, legs pumping, as far away as she could before her legs gave out and her throat tasted like hot copper. She collapsed behind a 7-Eleven, startling a creature that had been digging around in the garbage, and she let out a hoarse, "Oh shit." She was safe, but she didn't feel like it. She let herself cry for a moment.

She only calmed down when she realized the guy wouldn't report what had happened to the police. He'd be crazy to say that he'd been mugged after selling fake IDs.

Mignon watched her from atop the dumpster, knees to her chest, her head tilted to one side as Amelia caught her breath. She had never been that scared before. She'd had no idea what she was getting herself into. There were dangerous people in the world, and she was dancing among them, tempting fate. If she wasn't careful, it would all be for nothing. And she would fail Mignon again.

She cried more, just thinking about it, and bit on her fist to stop herself from making too much noise.

Mignon watched with her warm, dark eyes. If she were real, she would have reached out and tucked the loose hair around Amelia's face behind her ear. But she wasn't real. She wasn't real and Amelia was alone.

"You don't have to do this," she said.

"I do," Amelia cried to the dark. "I have to do this. I have to. I need to."

It took Amelia a long while, panting and crying against the dumpster, to feel like she was safe enough to walk home.

✕✕✕

The flight to Los Angeles was the first test using her new ID. It worked like a charm.

She was headed to CreatorCon, a YouTube convention for creators like herself. To be invited was the internet's version of the Met Gala. Everyone who was anyone was there.

For months, Amelia had worked tirelessly building her brand as a travel writer, just as Mignon would have done. She was meticulous, and worked long into every night, scraping and scrounging for every last view, every last comment, every last follower, faking her way through her travels, using Google Maps in order to write believably, imagining herself standing on a street corner and selling the story from the comfort of her bed.

She hated flying. But Amelia Ashley loved it. It was her job, after all.

Every week, she sent messages to her parents with a fake UCLA email account, checked in to make sure her mom was okay, that her dad was doing better, making sure they were none the wiser that their daughter was leading a double life. Her parents would never agree to this. She was on her own.

But as she worked, she came to genuinely care about the online life she had made for herself. She was doing something only a few could dream about. She was a full-time content creator. She scoffed at the term initially, but a part of her soul had emptied out into Amelia Ashley. It made her real.

And it paid off.

Through the crowd, Amelia spotted Sarah Speck among a small group of other beautiful women in the middle of the convention hall floor, most of them filming vlogs for their own YouTube channels, showing the world just how much fun they were having. Sarah noticed Amelia as she approached and waved her arm over her head. "Amelia!"

She and Sarah Speck had connected online through Amelia's travel blog. Sarah was moving to Rome to start her new fashion line and she'd been on the lookout for travel tips. They hit it off immediately. Sarah couldn't run out of nice things to say about Amelia and her work. Amelia's cross-promotion with Sarah was already boosting her blog.

Amelia genuinely liked Sarah, but there was a gaping canyon between them that only Amelia knew existed. The lonely part of her wanted to confide in someone—that someone being a bubbly, if not a little gossipy, internet celebrity—but she knew it was impossible. Maybe in another life she and Sarah could have been friends for real.

Amelia put on a wide smile and waved back to Sarah. Seeing her in person after having chatted for so long online sent a nervous thrill down her spine, but Amelia Ashley wouldn't be so meek. Amelia Ashley was a creator; she belonged here. Sarah stepped away from her group to greet Amelia, sweeping her up into a big hug.

"You are officially a Big Deal," Sarah said, gesturing to the vendor booths and swarm of con-goers.

Out of the corner of Amelia's eye Mignon melted into the sea of people, but Amelia asked, "Really?"

Casually, Sarah said, "Haven't you seen your line for the meet and greet? It's a mile long."

Amelia couldn't believe actual real-life people had shown up to meet her. Her hard work was paying off, even if it should have belonged to Mignon. It was surreal to even think about. Sarah took a lock of

Amelia's recently dyed blond hair and clicked her tongue. "You look exhausted, like you just got off the plane. I'll help you put on your face. You're a perfect test subject."

Before Amelia could take it as an insult and process what was happening, Sarah whisked her away to her hotel room connected to the convention center.

✕ ✕ ✕

When Sarah Speck told her to open her eyes, Amelia lost her breath as she looked at her reflection.

"Witchcraft," Amelia gasped.

Sarah beamed, proud of herself. "Isn't it incredible what a little contour can do to change a face?"

Amelia leaned forward in the makeup chair, getting closer to the mirror. She looked so different, but Sarah made it look natural. She'd given her a full makeover, the effect totally changing the face Amelia had seen looking back at her for seventeen years. The makeup made her pale blue eyes pop; she almost looked otherworldly.

"Teach me, please," Amelia said.

Sarah laughed. "Okay. A natural beauty like yourself should have a few tools in her back pocket. With my help, any person who so much as looks at you will fall deeply, *madly* in love with you." She grinned at Amelia.

Amelia smiled back, hungry as a wolf. "Perfect. I have just the person in mind."

Sarah laughed like Amelia had told the funniest joke she'd ever heard.

Mignon sat on the empty hotel bed, twirling a lock of her hair around her finger, as if she were bored. If she were really here, would she recognize Amelia now? Amelia didn't even recognize herself.

CHAPTER THIRTY

AMELIA

Amelia looked out the window, taking in her new view. Wind rattled the windowpanes. It was a blustery summer day, the gusts making a tree branch scratch at the glass like fingernails. San Diego was a much larger city than Eureka, and the size of it somehow made her feel more anonymous, like she could be swallowed up by it. The air smelled dusty in her new apartment, a studio in North Park.

"What do you think?" The landlord, a wiry man named Ed with a bald spot and the face of a bulldog, stood just inside the apartment. He lingered by the door, watching Amelia take in her surroundings, hopeful that he wouldn't have to sit on an empty apartment in his database any longer. He sounded as if he wanted to be anywhere else but there; he had other business to attend to. But Amelia took her time.

"It's perfect," she said. There were dead flies on the windowsill, even more dried husks pinched in the windowpane rail, crushed to dust from countless openings and closings to let in the chewable San Diego air. She didn't care.

"Where'd you say you were from again?" Ed asked.

"I didn't." Ed was either trying to flirt with her or he was nosy. Both options were annoying.

"And you said you're nineteen?"

"Why do you ask?"

"You don't look nineteen."

A chill raked down her spine. She hated the way he looked at her. She planned on changing the locks as soon as she could.

"Will you take cash?" she asked, turning to him.

"Can't argue with that."

She paid six months up front. His eyes widened when he was handed the wad of cash.

"Here's your keys to your door and to your mailbox," he said, handing them over, looking her up and down.

Mignon stood behind Ed and peered over his shoulder. "You know he's ogling you, Amelia."

"Nothing I can't handle," she said.

"What was that?" Ed asked, eyebrows pushed together like fighting caterpillars. Mignon had taken up an invisible spot in the opposite corner of the room.

"Nothing," Amelia said, putting on her best smile, one she'd practiced in the mirror for hours on end. It disarmed, but she wielded it like a knife, precise and shiny.

Fortunately, Ed didn't bother checking her credit (if he had, he'd have found it was perfect). Amelia didn't plan on being a problematic tenant anyway. Once she got what she came for, she'd be gone before anyone was any the wiser. If anything, no one would even notice she was there.

When he left, still counting the six months' rent in his hand, Amelia stood in the middle of her empty apartment for a long while, taking in the subtle sounds and smells it had to offer.

She thought of this place as a set, like on a television show, and planned to furnish it with things that Amelia Ashley would like: fairy lights, and baubles, and aesthetically pleasing patterns on fabrics and pillows. Amelia Ashley liked bold but tasteful colors, sensible clothes like flats and leggings, so she could move and breathe, but she knew how to present herself as if she were always waiting for a camera to be pointed her way.

But she also needed to furnish it with things she liked, things that reminded her of home, and the only thing she allowed herself to include were pictures from Mignon's travel books. She couldn't afford to bring anything else from her home life into this place; it was too risky. She needed to start over to be Amelia Ashley, and she couldn't bring her mom's CDs or her dad's books. She couldn't even bring her stuffed animals, even though all she wanted to do was curl up in bed with Mr. Peanut—her stuffed elephant—and never leave.

But she had work to do.

The only thing she brought with her to the apartment was her backpack. All it had inside was a change of clothes, Mignon's copy of *Peter Pan*, and her wallet, and she tossed it to the wall, where it thumped to the floor. She took a seat next to it, her back pressed up against the cool brick, and pulled out her phone. She'd hired a publicist, and she had a few emails waiting to be answered about getting her name out into the public, specifically collaboration work with other creators to boost her own audience, and Amelia made a note to respond to them later. She had other business to attend to; first of all to set her roots deep into the city.

From her backpack, she pulled out her credit cards and IDs, bound together in a stack with a hair tie. She unwound the hair tie and used it to pull back her new golden locks, then sorted through the evidence of her new identity. Amelia Ashley existed purely in these little plastic cards. It was surreal to think in this day and age, a person could be a ghost on the street without these things.

"Going out?" Mignon asked.

"I have to use my credit cards. That makes me look real," she said.

Mignon said, smiling, "But you are real."

"Not in ways that matter."

The first place on her stop was the athletic store. She bought a yoga mat, a foam roller, a marathon running GPS chip inserted into shoes to track mileage, some weights, and most of all clothes, including new running shoes. Amelia Ashley cared for comfortable but chic athleisure—signaling that she had means, but she could afford not to try so hard. She was building a history for Amelia, a legacy. Amelia's style would reflect that. Leggings, flowing cotton tops, sporty but cozy at the same time. As she tried on each outfit, Mignon stood behind her in the mirror, giving a thumbs-up or thumbs-down. Amelia's subconscious was awfully picky.

Eventually, Amelia found a few outfits she liked and could use for a while until she got more settled in her apartment and gathered everything up at the front.

At the cashier, she arranged for everything to be delivered to her apartment except for one thing. She held up the marathon tracking chip. "I'm taking this with me," she said. "Going to test it out."

"Sure," the cashier said, using a smile designed for customers only. "Your total today will be one thousand eight hundred and two dollars and seventy cents." She could have balked. Creating a new life cost more than she thought, but she couldn't let it show.

Amelia held up her new Visa card and casually swiped it. On the outside, she looked calm and collected, but on the inside, her heart was hammering. This was the moment of truth. A second ticked by, but it felt like an eternity. Either her fake identity had been flagged and her accounts had been terminated, or . . . Sure enough, the credit card reader turned green.

THANK YOU! COME AGAIN!

Amelia Lee was dead, but Amelia Ashley was living her best life.

✕ ✕ ✕

Amelia waited for just the right moment, timing it carefully, and then she dashed out from around the corner, slamming right into her target.

"Oh!" Tori tipped almost her whole iced coffee on Amelia's shirt, a dramatic collision, and Amelia dropped to the ground. "Oh my God! I'm so sorry!"

Amelia shivered. The ice from the cup shocked her almost senseless and she shook out her hands, now drenched in pale coffee and cream. But she'd come here to play a part, and so had Tori, even though she didn't know it. Amelia said, "I'm such a klutz! I didn't watch where I was going! Oh no, I'm such an idiot."

"No! It was my fault! I totally didn't see you! It's like you came out of nowhere."

Amelia had been keeping an eye on Tori for weeks.

While she had started building her online profile, grinding and clawing through Instagram hashtags and thousands of selfies to find the perfect one, she'd also been keeping tabs on her primary target: Josh and his inner circle. The best way to get to him was through one of them. Tori was a marketing major at San Diego State with Josh, currently dating Josh's roommate Derek. She and Josh had been tagged by Derek in one of his Instagram stories on a night out after midterms and naturally Amelia followed the trail. She needed an "in" into Josh's world without making it obvious. She needed to get close to him, to circle him like a hawk, and Tori was her key.

It was easy to track her down. Tori had tagged this coffee shop several times on her Instagram feed, and all Amelia had to do was wait for her to show up eventually.

From her spot on the ground, Amelia slowly got up, and made a show of the scrapes on her hands. Blood had already bloomed on her pale skin and it stood out against the dirt and small pebbles that stuck to the cuts.

"Your shirt is totally ruined!" Tori exclaimed. "And you're bleeding!" Her hands hovered over Amelia's wet T-shirt, frantic, as if unsure of what to do.

"It's fine, I'm okay, really." Amelia winced, toeing the line between acting and hamming it up. She needed to sell it, but still make Tori want to help, make her feel like it was a wrong that needed to be made right.

"Here, please, let me help you clean up," Tori said, gesturing to the coffee shop's front door. "They've got napkins inside. This is all my fault. I feel awful." Amelia let Tori take her by the elbow into the coffee shop. She told the barista behind the counter, "Ralph, I need the keys to the bathroom."

The bathroom only had one toilet and Tori planted Amelia on top of it while Tori wet some napkins she'd taken from the cafe with the sink water and dabbed at the scrapes on Amelia's palms. She clucked like a hen when she saw the damage.

Amelia watched her as Tori winced, cringing at the blood, and wet some more napkins. A part of her felt bad for using Tori in this way—it wasn't Tori's fault that she was friends with a killer. But another part of her, a cold and dead part, said it was necessary. Tori had a role to play in all of this; it was for the greater good.

"You're bleeding a lot," Tori said. "Sorry if it stings." She was a good person; Amelia was not.

How would she react if Amelia told her, right then and there, what Josh had done? A complete stranger, sitting on a closed toilet seat, claiming that her boyfriend's roommate had disappeared a girl her age only a year ago. Preposterous.

Mignon watched, crouched on top of the sink, looking like an amused gargoyle. "Really oversold the injuries there, Sissy. Did you dig in some dirt for good measure?"

Amelia ignored her. It was a necessary step. She would have thrown herself into traffic if it would guarantee that Tori would help her.

"Thank you so much. I would have figured San Diego folks wouldn't care," Amelia said.

"Are you from out of town?" Tori glanced up at her, making small talk.

"I just moved here, actually," she said, wincing as Tori dragged a dry napkin across her raw skin.

"I'd say welcome to the city, but I guess I don't do too well with warm welcomes." Her smile was rueful. "I promise, not everyone knocks folks new to town to the ground."

"It's not a problem, really. I'm Amelia, by the way."

"Tori." She smiled, though warmer this time. "What brings you here?"

"School. Just transferred." Amelia had a fake San Diego State ID in her pocket, but she couldn't fake her way into being a real student. When most people asked for an ID, they took a school ID at face value. It got her halfway through the door. Thankfully, Tori didn't ask to see it. She wasn't as paranoid as Amelia would have been.

"What school?"

"San Diego State."

"Crazy! Me too!"

Amelia smiled. "How fun! Maybe we'll have some classes together. I've always wanted to move to the West Coast."

"Oh, where are you from?"

"Nowhere really. Middle of nowhere, USA."

"I'm sure it's not nowhere. Where you grow up is always special. Coming here should be like a second home. And there I went, barging right into you like a bull, ruining everything. Again, I'm so sorry."

"Seriously, no worries. I live nearby actually. I'll go home and change. It's just up on Morrison."

"Oh, no way! I live on Campbell. We're practically neighbors."

Of course Amelia knew that. She had entire folders on her laptop dedicated to Josh and his friends. She smiled. "It's nice to know that there are some good people in the city."

Tori smiled back and for a split second, Amelia almost thought she saw Mignon in her eyes. Her heart hurt and she swallowed a thick bubble of emotion that had started moving up her throat. She hated using someone as nice as Tori as a pawn, but she had come too far to turn back now. This girl deserved to be free of Josh, just as much as Mignon had, didn't she?

"I don't know anyone here. Do you know of any place to hang out? Meet people?" she asked.

Tori threw away the used napkins and put her hands on her hips. "It just so happens that me and my boyfriend are going out to celebrate a friend's birthday. You should come, get a feel for everything. You seem pretty cool, not like an axe murderer."

"Ha, yeah," Amelia said, smiling. She knew whose birthday it was. Josh's. He was turning nineteen. She'd had everything about him permanently seared into her brain. Her heart pounded. She couldn't believe this was happening. She was already so close, and she'd only had to give up everything to do it. "Sounds fun."

CHAPTER THIRTY-ONE
AMELIA

Tori and Amelia exchanged numbers after their literal run-in at the coffee shop and Tori told Amelia to meet them at a club called the Inferno.

Amelia dressed up for the occasion. She did her hair, her makeup, put on her favorite black dress and heels. Armor. Inside, she was shuddering with anticipation, but on the outside she was Amelia Ashley, shoulders thrown back with confidence only gained through perseverance.

When she got to the club, she lost herself in the drone of music and bodies. She moved with the crowd, slithering through bodies, peering into faces looking for familiarity.

"What will you do when you see him?" Mignon asked, appearing in Amelia's way. Amelia skirted around her. She wasn't sure. "You need to be careful," Mignon said, manifesting between gaps in the crowd.

"I will."

She had imagined this moment several times. What would she feel the second she saw Josh's face? Panic? Rage? Satisfaction that she'd finally found him? Grief? Insanity? She wouldn't know until it happened, but she'd imagined every scenario in her head. She could see a version of herself flinging toward him, claws out, ready to tear into his eyes, hit him in the face until he choked on blood and teeth and bile, all while screaming about what he'd done to Mignon.

"Amelia!" Tori had spotted her across the room. She was sitting in a small nook with a round table on the edge of the dance floor. Five others were with her, leaning into one another, deep in conversation.

Amelia smiled, just as she'd practiced, and went over.

Tori got to her feet and grabbed Amelia's hand, like she was already a friend. "Guys, this is the girl I was talking about—Amelia. Amelia, this is everyone."

As if drawn by a string, her eyes went to the person sitting at the edge of the seating area and the whole world dissolved into white noise. There he was.

~~Bennet.~~

Josh.

He looked at her, an easy smile on his lips as he took her in, seeing exactly what she wanted him to see: *Her*—the perfect girl. He had only grown more handsome since moving away to college. Tall, dark-haired, striking with a strong brow that shaded his eyes like a brooding, Byronic hero. She smiled wider, despite the beating panic rising in her bloodstream.

Time seemed to stand still as she looked at him, his hands, his mouth, his eyes. What was the last part of him Mignon saw as she died? Did he hit her from behind like a coward? Or had he been facing her, determined to see the light go out in her eyes?

Tori went through everyone's names, but Amelia hadn't been paying attention. Her whole focus had been on Josh, and he too couldn't take his eyes off her.

Tori waved her hands. "Josh, scoot over. Make some room."

He did and Amelia slipped into the space next to him. His body heat had left a ghost on the leather seat. Amelia almost drowned in his cologne—woodsmoke and musk. She wanted to be closer to him, only so she could wrap her hand around his throat and dig her fingers into his neck.

"So you must be the birthday boy," she said, grinning. She felt like she had sprung fangs.

"I am," he said. His eyes glittered in the dark. "I'm Josh." He held out his hand.

He didn't recognize her, not one bit. He didn't even blink at hearing her name. She figured. He was one of those guys who didn't pay attention to anyone who didn't matter, and she didn't matter, not back then. But now Amelia was going to ruin him.

He was the one who'd made her this way. He'd turned her into this person sitting next to him, a beast with venom in her veins. She was forced to sharpen her edges into needle points because of him.

And she was going to make him pay.

She took his hand and shook it. His handshake was strong, and warm, and confident. "Amelia," she said, smooth as a knife. "But you can call me whatever you like."

Amelia settled in nicely among Tori's friends, fit herself into the group, morphing into a person who filled in the gaps between others.

Meanwhile, she'd posted a few hundred photos of herself over the past few months, slowly gathering followers and creating her own brand of relatability. She bought a few hundred thousand followers from some Chinese site. It worked. Now she had a million—give or take a few (or very many) fake ones.

She had to admit, she liked being Amelia Ashley. Most things she said in her videos were true and came from her own heart. That much was real. One of the highlights of her day was responding to user comments and messages, connecting with people who cared, finding solidarity and inspiration in her content. Planning posts, taking polls, doing collaborations with other creators . . . it was a break from reality. Her online community was more real than the one she'd known growing up in Eureka. Most of her life, she'd been isolated and now she felt like she was finally making friends in the real world too, even if it was all pretense. She could have tricked herself into believing her own lies.

Still, it was exhausting being authentic while lying through her teeth every day, every hour, minute, second. Being Amelia Ashley was a full-time job.

If only it could have been Mignon's life. She was the one who deserved to have it.

Everywhere she went, she brought Mignon with her, a constant reminder of what she was doing, what all of this was for, even when Tori invited Amelia to the local independent bookstore, Verbatim, one sweltering afternoon.

"Ooh, this is a classic," Tori cooed, making a beeline toward the mystery section. She pulled out a Hercule Poirot book and flipped through it, letting the breeze from the pages blow across her face. It was nice getting out of the So-Cal heat to browse in the comfort of an air-conditioned bookstore. "Have you read it?"

"Five Little Pigs? Of course," Amelia said, beaming. She didn't have to pretend as much when Tori was around, but her guard was up all the time. "I love crime fiction. It's nice seeing the bad guys always get their comeuppance."

Tori smiled. "If only life were that fair."

Just as Amelia took another Poirot book from the shelf and read the back cover, Mignon pointed at Amelia's pocket. "You got a notification," she said.

Amelia put the book back on the shelf and pulled out her phone. A small thrill of excitement coursed through her body like an electric shock. "Hello, Josh Reuter," she said, seeing his name. He'd started following her Instagram account, liking twenty of her photos in a row.

Tori noticed Amelia smiling at her phone and asked, "What's up?"

Amelia turned the phone toward her and Tori's lips curled knowingly.

"He is so predictable," she said. "Typical boy. I knew he'd like you." She pulled an old copy of Agatha Christie's *Murder on the Orient Express* and flipped through it idly.

All the pain Amelia had endured, in her body and mind, felt worth it.

"Do you think I should say something?" Amelia asked.

Mignon leaned against a bookcase, her arms folded over her chest. "You can still back out. You don't have to do this."

"Of course, slide into his DMs," Tori said, speaking over Mignon. "Only if you like him though. Do you like him?"

The look in Amelia's eye could have been mistaken for excitement. She licked her lips. "He's perfect."

× × ×

The first time Josh Reuter kissed her had been in his apartment. She'd come over with the pretense of watching a movie and eating some take-out, but it quickly turned into something more. In the closeness of the dark, he slipped his hand against her thigh. She let him, feeling like she was outside of her body, looking through someone else's eyes. His lips grazing hers, his breath hot and sweet against her skin, his hands roaming across her hips and her back.

She imagined biting down hard, clamping like a vise with her front teeth on his pillowy lips, tasting his blood as it poured into her open mouth and he struggled against her and tried to pull away, crying out in pain and shock and horror. Fantasizing about how she could hurt him was all she could do to play his game. Amelia separated herself from reality, retreated to the smallest part of her mind, and watched herself move. She kissed him back, fiercely, turning her rage into a falsehood of passion. She could feel the smile on her lips as she breathed him in, consuming him. She was going to devour him, steal everything he cared about.

She sensed Mignon behind her, watching, warning, and she pushed her out of her mind.

The second time she kissed him, it had been after a dinner date at Artie's Pizza. He brought her to her apartment and they kissed on the stoop, under the soft light cast from her building's lobby. She was an actress, performing for an audience of one, and the way he touched her let her know she was enchanting.

The third time she kissed him, he told her he loved her, whispered in the dark as they cuddled in his bed, clothes on. Even she couldn't bring herself that far. Being in his bed made her skin crawl. She wanted to scream, to explode, to throw something, but instead she smiled and answered with another kiss planted on his lips. She was going to steal the breath right out of his lungs.

✕ ✕ ✕

Amelia transplanted herself into Josh's life, easily slipping into the role of girlfriend, even if the thought made her stomach churn. Every friend he introduced her to, she wore the mask of sincerity. None of these people knew who Josh was, not really. They didn't realize how much danger they were in.

Once, at a frat party Josh invited her to, she saw it firsthand. She nursed a bottle of beer, barely having any of it, and let Josh have fun. When he went to the bathroom, she went to get some air on the back porch, the loud music and smell of bodies suffocating her, but she was intercepted in the hallway by a gentle touch on her shoulder.

"You're Amelia, right?" He was handsome, with caramel-colored curls and an easy smile. A lot of people smiled easily when Amelia was around.

"Uh, yeah," she said, barely above the noise of the music and the party-goers. She looked over her shoulder, aware that Josh could appear at any moment. She hated parties. She'd never been to one before, especially not a college party, and she constantly felt in the way, especially as people moved past her to get from one part of the house to the other.

"I've got you," he said, grabbing her around the elbow, guiding her to the side of the hallway and out of traffic. "I'm Reece, by the way. Reece Sanchez. This is my frat house. We're kind of known for this stuff around here."

Amelia wanted to do anything else but have this conversation. "Oh yeah?"

Reece propped himself up on the wall, stretching his arm out. The sweat stains in his armpit blocked her exit and she put the beer bottle to her lips while looking for another way out.

"You come here alone?" he asked.

"Nope." She didn't want to know what Josh would do if he saw her talking to another guy. She needed to be as blunt and short as possible, but Reece was already a few beers in and either didn't get the message or ignored it entirely. "So I really should be going, Reece," she said.

Reece only smiled. "Can I get you another beer? Looks like you're almost empty."

Amelia's eyes darted up and down the hall. "I'm good, really. You shouldn't be talking to me."

Reece laughed, confused. "What?" Then a hand grabbed him by the shoulder and ripped him backward. Josh.

Fear cut through Amelia like a hot knife. She didn't want Reece to get hurt.

"Hey, man. Easy there!" Reece said, his eyes soft and dazed. Josh looked downright scary. She'd never seen anything like it before, like a wolf standing over his recent kill. But if Josh was a wolf, Reece was a golden retriever. He wasn't looking for a fight. Like the flip of a switch, Josh held up his hands, placatingly, and smiled, his entire face changing in an instant. There was the handsome, charming guy everyone knew.

"This your girl?" Reece asked.

"Yeah, she is." Even though his expression had softened, Josh's eyes were still hard.

Amelia swooped in. She put on a smile, took Josh by the hand, smiled at him. "Let's go." She glanced at Reece, a warning in her eyes. "Nice meeting you, Reece Sanchez." Then she led Josh away.

"My prince charming," she said, putting a sparkle in her eye. "Here to save the day."

Josh seemed to like that. He grinned at her, and she grinned back.

CHAPTER THIRTY-TWO

AMELIA

Amelia's plan centered around lying and spying. The only way she could keep track of Josh's movements was to secretly watch his phone. She highly doubted he would keep evidence of what he'd done to Mignon on there, but it was a huge part of her plan moving forward. If she ever wanted to get to the truth, she needed to play by different rules.

She got an opportunity to install spyware she'd developed when he was in the shower one bright Saturday afternoon. They'd just gotten back from the zoo on a double date with Tori and Derek, and both of them had already taken up spots on the couch in the living room after being on their feet all day.

"Should we order some pizza?" Tori asked. "I'm too tired to move."

"You read my mind," Derek said.

Josh stretched his arms over his head. "You guys order whatever you want, I need to take a shower."

Amelia waited, not paying attention as Derek placed the call, instead listening for the shower running.

Quickly, she got up and hurried to Josh's room. Munch was the only creature there, curled up near his pillow, and she picked up his phone from his nightstand and sat at the edge of his bed. The shower was still going, but she had only a few minutes.

She tapped in his code to unlock his phone and then she installed the executable, her heart in her throat the entire time. She was good at this, she'd been coding for years, and still she wondered if it would work. The software would hide in plain sight, active only when she opened the app on her end, recording everything he did so she could watch in real time. In any other circumstance, it was a huge violation of privacy. But nothing about this was ordinary. If Tori did something like this on Derek's phone, it would be grounds for a breakup. If Josh found out, he might kill her, and then all of this, everything she'd done, would be for nothing.

The app took a while to download, and she watched the little circle fill up with bated breath.

"What are you doing?"

She jolted at Josh's voice. He was standing in the doorway with only a towel covering his lower half, looking at her with a curious knit in his brow. She'd been too focused on the download; she hadn't heard the water shut off.

"I didn't mean—" She put the phone facedown on his bed. It needed more time to install.

"I know what it looks like."

Her heart hammered as he stepped into his room, the smell of his musky shower gel overwhelming her. She looked at him with doleful eyes, under her lashes as she'd practiced so many times before. "I'm sorry," she said. "I couldn't stop myself."

"Do you think I'm cheating on you?" he asked.

"I don't want to lose you," she said, going with a lie of his own creation.

He padded toward her, surrounded by a cloud of steam and shaving cream, and took his phone from the bed. She watched with wide eyes, her heart hammering painfully, but he looked at the screen and then at her, smiling, amused, patronizing. He set his phone on his nightstand, screen up. From her spot on the bed, she could see that the app had finished downloading. Everything looked normal, as it should.

"How can I prove to you that you're the only one I care about?" he asked, lowering himself toward her. He towered over her, his playful smile filling up her entire vision.

"I don't know, *joshreuter*," she said, slipping into a smile of her own, matching his. If she could drool venom, she would. "Would you ever lie to me?"

Josh chuckled at that and stepped away. He went to his closet, where he picked out a zip-up to put on. "Never," he said, and winked.

Liar. Liar liar liar liar! She smirked. "How did I get so lucky? What did I do to deserve such karma?"

He smiled at her again.

"You're right. This is all my fault. I'm so paranoid. I need a vacation . . . Hey, I have an idea. Let's take a trip together, you and me. We can film a real travel vlog for the channel while finally going someplace new, together."

"You know how I feel being on camera . . ."

"Afraid, are we?" She used his pride against him.

"Not in the slightest. But a vacation doesn't sound like a bad idea. Especially if I have you all to myself."

Amelia's spine went stiff.

He leaned in, swooping down for a kiss, and she let him. When they broke apart, he smiled at her again. "Where do you want to go?" His gaze fixated on her lips, then bounced back up to her eyes.

He liked the mystery of her, an allure of unknowability, and it worked like bait.

She pretended to think for a moment, tapping her finger on her lip. "Someplace magical, someplace romantic, someplace unforgettable. Rome."

PART 7

GHOSTS

CHAPTER THIRTY-THREE

AMELIA

Amelia left her stomach on the ground as the plane took off. She was almost certain she was going to puke, but she was Amelia Ashley, and Amelia Ashley wasn't afraid of flying. Just as Mignon wasn't. Traveling to Paris and Rome had been Mignon's dream. And now Amelia was living it. She swallowed her fear down and closed her eyes, counting backward by seven from a thousand.

On the outside, she had a veneer of tranquility. Josh sat on one side, Mignon's ghost on the other. "Don't do this," Mignon whispered in her ear.

"There's no turning back," she murmured.

Josh thought she was talking to him and he turned to smile at her. "That's right. What's the *Peter Pan* line you always quote?"

"Second star to the right and straight on 'til morning," she said. Fourteen days to go.

Mignon followed her to the catacombs, standing among the skulls and bones of the underground cathedral, watching Amelia dance the night away with Josh. "I'm dead, Amelia. You're not. It's not too late."

Amelia twirled round and round in Josh's arms, his skull mask bone-white in the pulsing lights. Ten days to go.

✕✕✕

Sarah Speck's house was bigger than she ever imagined. She felt a slight pang of guilt to be using her this way, but it needed to be done, like squeezing pus from a wound. It would hurt, but it was necessary.

"Do we really have to stay here?" Josh asked. "Can't we just go to the hotel early?"

"It's a free place to sleep, no complaining."

Josh sighed, and rolled his eyes. Pouting was an ugly look on him. She grabbed him by the front of the shirt and pulled him in close. "You'll have me all to yourself later." She raised an eyebrow and smiled, then shoved him back, a playful push. "Now hold the camera. I want to vlog." Five days to go.

✕✕✕

Dinner at Sarah's was loud and fun, which was normally the case when someone like Sarah Speck was involved. Amelia partook of the wine that was served with dinner, almost forgetting what she was there for. Almost.

She could feel Josh's eyes on her, watching from across the table, as Alex Ciupa reached over and grabbed the bread basket from in front of her plate.

"Pardon my reach," he said, flashing her a charming grin.

"Reach away," she said. Her face felt hot, and her smile came naturally. It wasn't Amelia Ashley's smile, but hers now. Alex was someone she would have liked to know in her real life. If that even existed anymore. The wine was making her lose focus. She was doing this for Mignon, not for anyone else, and she tricked herself into thinking she was having fun for real. Guilt bled into her gut.

Josh took a long sip of his wine, his eyes glassy but his gaze sharp as it lingered on the charismatic journalist.

She'd almost gone the whole day without seeing Mignon, but she appeared now, standing behind him, shaking her head.

She'd been foolish to think she could ever escape the way Josh looked at her. Four days to go.

CHAPTER THIRTY-FOUR

AMELIA

After dinner, Amelia returned to their guest room and went to the bathroom to get a glass of water. She downed half of it in one gulp, washing the taste of wine away, and water dribbled out of the corners of her mouth. She had never had wine before, and she hoped no one had noticed. It had gone to her head so quickly and she wanted to go to bed, but she couldn't.

She turned on the faucet in the tub and let the running water drown out the thoughts rushing through her head. This whole trip had unfolded exactly as she'd planned, with the exception of the guests at Sarah's house. Alex Ciupa and company were eyewitnesses that she needed, but the more time she spent with Josh the more doubt started to creep in.

In the mirror, Mignon stood next to her, her back pressed up against the wall, same as Amelia, her gaze locked on Amelia's own.

"You might be wrong about Josh," Mignon said. "You don't know if he killed me. Or if I'm even dead."

"No," Amelia said. "I know he did it. He's guilty." She braced herself on the sink, head bowed low. Her head felt too light from the wine, and it made the rest of her body feel too heavy.

Mignon shook her head. "You don't know anything. You don't have any proof."

Here was the face of the person she trusted most in the whole world, and she was saying things that Amelia didn't even want to consider. She'd been so focused on her plan, she couldn't make room for any hesitation. Hesitation would mean failure, and she could not fail. It was not an option.

"You have nothing," Mignon said.

Doubt was a nasty sensation. It made the bathroom collapse around her, growing smaller with each passing second, and the more she breathed, the closer the walls got.

"Josh is the obvious suspect," Amelia said, eyes narrowing. "He did it. He was the last one to see you alive."

"What if you're ensnaring an innocent person? What if I went for a walk and fell? What if I was kidnapped by a stranger? What if I really did run off, and what if I never loved you enough to come back? What if I killed myself—"

"Shut up!" Amelia yelled and smashed her fist into the mirror.

The glass fractured, like a spiderweb, and Amelia stared at it, shocked. She cradled her hand to her chest and let out a gasp; the pain finally arced across her knuckles and her eyes watered. She wished she'd bled—maybe it would feel like purging venom. Now her hand throbbed and Mignon had vanished.

There came a knock at the door. Amelia whipped around, pressing herself against the sink, as Josh opened the door a crack.

"Ams? I heard a—" His eyes went to the broken mirror. "Are you okay?"

"I . . . I slipped and . . ." Amelia blinked back tears and she smiled through it. "I'm so clumsy!"

Josh let himself in, closing the door behind him. His cheeks were flush, the wine making him practically glow. "What happened?"

"Nothing."

"Did Alex Ciupa say something to you earlier? You left in a hurry."

"Wh-what? No. This isn't about . . ." Her hand pulsed with pain and it was all she could think about. She tried to think of something, anything, to get out of there, but Josh blocked the door.

A shadow crossed Josh's face. He closed the gap between them and she drowned in the smell of red wine. "I saw the way he looked at you. Were you flirting with him?"

"No," she said, for once speaking the truth. It spilled out of her when she said it. This was Reece Sanchez all over again. Her heart pounded.

Josh got so close, he took up her whole world. He reached over and shut off the faucet on the tub. Droplets fell in a steady rhythm, *tap*, *tap*, *tap*.

"Don't lie," he whispered.

"I'm not lying. Nothing happened. Nothing will happen."

Josh towered over her. His eyes scanned her face, looking for something. His long lashes brushed the tops of his cheeks as he looked down at her. Her heart palpitated in her throat, echoed in the throb of her hand. She looked away but he grabbed her just below her jaw, his fingers wrapping around her neck, forcing her head up.

"Look at me," he said. His fingers were solid and strong. His thumb pressed against her throat and she knew all he had to do was squeeze.

She froze. The memory of the man who'd made her fake IDs attacking her surged into the forefront of her mind. Just like before, her skin felt too tight, her lungs unable to fill up with air.

So this was the real Josh: obsessive, possessive, controlling.

"Josh," she gasped, her breath shallow and quick. She didn't want to panic, not now.

The shadow lifted from Josh's face and he looked at his hand on the side of her neck, as if noticing it was there. He released his grasp, holding his hand up, as if unloading it, and air rushed into her lungs, making the light in the bathroom brighter than it really was.

"I'm sorry," he said, a little breathless. "You know I'm crazy about you. I just get so protective. I don't want to lose you. Too many people in my life leave me."

Like Mignon? Amelia thought.

He asked, "You won't leave me, will you?"

The ghost of Josh's hand on her neck was still warm on her skin. Amelia wanted to put that same fear into him. She wanted to make him taste his mortality.

"I will never leave you," she said, making her words smooth as silk, like a spider's web. "Not ever."

Amelia pressed her lips to Josh's, hard and swift, kissing him to sell her lie. She clutched the sides of his face, making sure he couldn't pull away. He didn't fight her, instead he leaned toward her, a small moan escaping his throat. She nipped his lower lip, wondering what it would be like to make him bleed, make him feel pain, make him afraid. She broke away to remember to breathe, and Josh smiled.

"You love me, don't you?" she asked.

"Yes," he breathed.

He yanked her closer, and her elbow knocked over a glass of water on the counter and it shattered on the floor, making the voices in the dining room falter, but neither of them cared. Josh grabbed her by the wrists, pinning them above her head as he pressed her into the wall, kissing her again, squeezing them until it hurt, until she almost cried out. She kissed him back instead.

He sighed against her, his hands clutching her sides, gripping her tightly, his nails digging in just hard enough to pinch. He couldn't let her go, even if he wanted to.

She was certain now that she was destined to ruin him. No more doubt.

CHAPTER THIRTY-FIVE

HARPER

Harper didn't even hear when her mom and Lucy came home from a track and field meet that evening. She had been holed up in her bedroom, eyes aching from staring at her computer screen, all day and well past sunset.

"Harper!" Her mom's voice carried down the hall. "Dinner!"

She could smell the garlic bread already. They must have stopped at Nino's, their favorite Italian restaurant. But still, Harper didn't get up. She couldn't stop staring at the Facebook page. Everything clicked together, like the last piece of the puzzle missing from the box had been found under the couch. She just had to shine a light to see it.

Amelia Ashley was playing a game no one could understand, not unless they were paying attention, and Josh Reuter was her endgame.

Revenge. That was all it was.

And it had all started in Eureka, the place that missing girl Mignon Lee was from. The word itself wouldn't have been significant, but context gave it meaning.

Josh's background check had blown everything wide open, but it had only been the start. Now she knew everything.

She'd spent all day, ever since she found out about Josh's past with a previous missing persons case, finding out any information she could about Mignon Lee. She was a seventeen-year-old girl in a relationship with a guy named Bennet Reuter when she went missing two years ago, leaving behind a family who mourned her, desperately searching for answers in the dark, with no one to help. There were only two newspaper articles about him, one when he was questioned and one when he was cleared of all suspicion. Everyone decided that Mignon had run away.

Mignon had, as they said, "slipped through the cracks." As if it couldn't have been helped, as if there were nowhere to lay the blame. No, the system ignored girls like Mignon every day. She hadn't slipped through the cracks, she had been pushed. The police never gave her a second look, newspapers made half-hearted attempts to run her story, and her name didn't trend on social media.

Harper wasn't surprised that it took this long for the truth to come out about Josh. Police were hard-pressed to share cases outside their jurisdiction. If they had, maybe the cops in San Diego would have been able to figure it out by now.

No one cared about Mignon Lee. No one except Amelia Ashley.

And now Harper.

She stared at Mignon Lee's abandoned missing persons page, a page created by a familiar face.

It was hard to believe.

Lucy barged into Harper's room. "Mom told me to come get you," she said, annoyed by the task.

Harper leapt up from her chair and grabbed Lucy into the tightest hug she could muster.

"Harper!" Lucy huffed and struggled, pushing against her. "What are you doing?"

Harper grabbed Lucy by the arms to look at her and her scrunched-up face.

"You're being weird," said Lucy.

"She's her sister."

"What?"

"Amelia Ashley is Mignon's sister—the other missing girl Josh Reuter was tied to." Tears swam in her vision.

"What?" Lucy said again, this time shocked rather than confused.

Harper explained, "Mignon's family was devastated. She had a younger sister, Amelia. I found the page Amelia made for her after she went missing. It took me too long to find it because she tried to erase everything else, but she couldn't scrub this one thing from the internet because she needed to keep Mignon's page active. Maybe she couldn't let it go. It's the one part of Amelia Lee that still exists—this Facebook page. I accessed archives of her profile and found old pictures she'd uploaded. It's her. That's Amelia Ashley." She pulled up the photos to prove it, photos of a smiling family before tragedy.

Lucy blinked, stunned. "Oh my God. You're right. She looks so different. Wait! Hold on, Amelia Ashley's . . . Asian?"

"Half. She's half Chinese," said Harper. "Like her sister."

"But she was passing for white." Lucy squinted. "You can tell she's half Asian if you know, but . . . I'm not sure I would've noticed otherwise."

"Yeah."

"But why though? Why pass for white?"

Harper shrugged. "She wanted to get people's attention. It worked. And she wants revenge. She thinks Josh hurt Mignon."

"Really?" Lucy asked, the garlic bread and pesto long forgotten. "That's . . . a lot for someone to do."

"Is it?" Harper asked. "I would do it for you."

Lucy looked at her, dark eyes shining, then looked back at Harper's computer, taking everything in. Pictures of the sisters stared back, one of them smiling wide in a tree house, another of them eating a huge Thanksgiving dinner, one with their arms thrown over each other's shoulders and laughing. How many photos did Harper have like that too?

Harper scooped her up into a hug again, and this time Lucy didn't fight it. Lucy wrapped her own arms around Harper's rib cage and squeezed.

"Do you think she's alive? Amelia? Do you think she's out there?" Lucy asked.

Harper pulled back and wiped her eyes with the back of her wrists. "Yeah," she said. "I do. I think she wants to see Josh pay. She might be watching from afar, but I think it's only a matter of time before it all comes out."

"Are you going to tell someone?" Lucy asked.

"I should, right? I mean, it's probably the biggest break in the case. The cops have been so confused about Amelia, running in circles trying to find this girl. As long as she stays gone, she's just a ghost."

"Then you should say something. Get Mignon's name out there, help Amelia. It's the right thing to do." And with that, Lucy left, headed for the kitchen.

Harper remained staring at her computer for a few minutes. One question remained:

What were you planning, Amelia Ashley?

CHAPTER THIRTY-SIX

AMELIA

In their room at Hotel Artemide, Amelia used a straight razor to make a small incision right above her eyebrow. The mirror helped her see what she was doing. She needed to be precise to make the cut as invisible as possible, blending in with the shape of the hairs in her brow. To plant the evidence, she needed to bleed a lot, but not enough that the cut would leave a visible mark or make it so deep that she needed to get stitches. She knew that there were a lot of blood vessels in the head. There had to be enough blood that when police inevitably searched his suitcase, they would find it.

As soon as she dragged the metal edge across her skin, crimson bloomed above her eye. She didn't even flinch.

She used his T-shirt as a wrap, catching as much of her blood as it flowed freely, and ate a granola bar while she waited. She had never been bothered by blood. It was a fact of nature, more of an inconvenience than anything.

She needed physical evidence that something had happened. Without it, she would just be missing. She needed to plant clues, show her hand, just a little bit, even if she kept a loaded deck in her back pocket. If the police couldn't prove it right away with DNA, they would know the blood type from her blood donation vlog, and it would be enough to put Josh in their crosshairs. As a bonus, some of her hair might be mixed in with the blood. Two-for-one special.

She and Josh had already packed for their trip home. Amelia had offered to do it for him while Josh checked out at the reception desk downstairs. She was the dutiful, doting girlfriend, so thoughtful and conscientious. It gave her plenty of time to work.

She never planned to get on the plane with him.

He would never check his suitcase. She knew him too well. He would be too lazy to open it and unpack everything by the time he got home, opting to pull any clean clothes he had left out one by one as he needed to use them, and by then the damage would be done.

Mignon watched from the bed in their hotel, eyes vacant and dull, just like Amelia's, as she waited for the cut to stop bleeding on its own.

"There's still time to stop," Mignon said, softly. "If you go through with this, there's no turning back."

"I'm beyond that point now," Amelia said. She checked the cut. It had mostly clotted, and Josh's T-shirt was more than thoroughly smeared with red. She wadded up the shirt and shoved it in his suitcase, haphazardly, as if he'd put it there in a panic, not in the right state of mind to think to throw it out.

Satisfied, she closed and locked his suitcase, wiping any remaining blood with tissues. By this time tomorrow, she would be as good as dead. She glanced at Mignon, sprawled on the bed, and smiled. But Mignon's expression was flat, disapproving.

"This won't work," Mignon said. She stared up at the ceiling. "He'll get away with it again."

"I planned everything. This can't go wrong. It won't. Everyone will see what he's done, even if it's all been a lie from me."

"It's not your story."

"You're right, it's yours."

Everything Amelia had posted online had been a lie, yes. The relatable, inspirational, authentic girl had been a fraud all along. Josh had been too swept up in his own narrative to realize it had been Mignon's spirit she was mirroring back to him.

"You're making a mess," Mignon said. She gestured to the bloodied tissues in the trash can. Amelia would need to hide those too. She picked up the tissues and shoved them into her jean pockets. She would throw them out in the public trash can in the lobby on the way out to her own death.

"Revenge is messy," she said.

By the time Amelia looked at the bed again, Mignon had vanished.

"Fine," Amelia said. "Be that way."

She looked at herself in the mirror again, checking the cut above her eyebrow. Imperceptible. No one would ever notice, and even if they did, she had a thousand excuses lined up and ready.

"I'm going to find you, Mignon."

She tucked her compass necklace beneath her shirt, its usual hiding place. Amelia too would disappear in the chaos.

CHAPTER THIRTY-SEVEN

HARPER

"Yeah, hi," Harper said, stepping up to the San Diego police precinct counter to a bored-looking officer in the midst of writing something on a piece of paper. He looked up at her, eyes half-lidded. "I'm here to talk to someone about Amelia Ashley."

The precinct was, for all intents and purposes, popping off. Dozens of officers were milling around, processing handcuffed perpetrators in a waiting area; a handful of other civilians mingled in a separate waiting area, where someone was trying to get a bag of chips that had gotten stuck out of the vending machine; a queue of people were lined up at a telephone waiting their turn to make a call. Their cell phones must have been confiscated. It was just past four in the afternoon and Harper had skipped class to come with the evidence she'd gathered about Josh Reuter. She'd worked all night pulling any information she could about Mignon Lee and the inadequate investigation into her case. She'd compiled everything on a flash drive, ready to hand it over to someone who could actually use it to help find Amelia.

The officer—the name tag read Porter—actually rolled his eyes. "Oh yeah? Let me guess, a psychic who claims to know where her body is?"

"What? No. Not at all." She was shocked by the accusation at first, but realized that she should have thought about how many phonies were trying to jump on the bandwagon of Amelia Ashley's disappearance. Countless hacks and grifters were no doubt trying to claim some sort of fame or fortune from taking wild guesses about the biggest true crime story in years. "Is there a detective in charge or . . . ?"

Officer Porter sighed and brought out a form. It was filled with boxes for her to fill in. "You can put your name, contact information, reason for visit . . ." Harper licked her lips.

"Listen, I just need to talk to someone," she said. "This won't take long. I have everything I need with me." She gestured to the messenger bag at her hip.

"Don't know if you can tell, but we're a little swamped as it is. You're not the first person today to come in saying you want to help find Amelia Ashley."

Now that she was looking at a badge, Harper's confidence had vanished. She couldn't tell them she was a hacker. The things she did to get info on Josh Reuter were technically illegal, but then again, she'd found information that she was almost certain the San Diego Police Department didn't have, like Amelia Ashley's real identity. They would no doubt be upset about how she'd found it, having broken about a dozen laws in the process, and would probably charge her with something. She was not about to go to jail because she wanted to be a Good Samaritan.

"Officer Porter," she said, cautiously, "is there a way I can do this . . . anonymously?"

Officer Porter's eyes narrowed. "Why?"

"Nothing important. I just don't want to get any blowback or whatever. Retaliation."

Officer Porter looked at her, but he didn't ask anything more.

Harper knew that the best chance she had at helping Amelia was putting her name down, so she picked up a pen from the cluster in a cup on the counter and clicked it. She put her name down, trying to ignore the voice in her head telling her that this was a waste of time. She wanted to believe that the police could help Amelia here, but Harper was the only one who knew that this was bigger than they realized. She knew that Amelia was planning something, that she was doing this for a reason. She'd planted those clues in her background, maybe on the off chance that someone like Harper would come along and pick up the bread crumbs.

Her pen hovered over the form.

It was crazy to think, but Harper had a gut feeling that this was all part of a grand plan. Amelia wanted someone like her to see that something was wrong and be unable to resist the mystery. Amelia Ashley was clever, and vengeful, and manipulative, but she was doing something that mattered, and Harper could help in a better way.

"No, you know what?" She crumpled up the paper and shoved it into her messenger bag with her laptop. "Just forget it. Never mind."

Officer Porter didn't seem to care one way or the other. He threw up his hands and exhaled sharply just as the phone on his desk rang again. Harper took that as an opportunity to leave, returning to the out-doors and escaping the dank smell of the precinct.

She hurried down the street, her heart pounding with what she was about to do.

She was going to do this the old-fashioned way. She was going to the press.

CHAPTER THIRTY-EIGHT

AMELIA

Amelia checked in at the Leonardo da Vinci International Airport for her red-eye flight home. She stepped up to the counter as a new girl. Amelia Ashley had vanished. Glasses back on. No more golden hair. Makeup wiped clean. All that was left behind was a brunette in sneakers, leggings, and an oversized cardigan. Plain, forgettable, invisible, exactly as she wanted. She was almost unrecognizable, but more importantly she matched her new passport and travel documents. You really can get everything from the internet.

Amelia couldn't stay in Italy forever, but lying low had been all part of the plan. She'd seen the beginnings of Josh's downfall start from the comfort of an Airbnb she'd rented near Ponte Milvio to watch the chaos unfold as Instagram exploded with questions about her. *WHERE IS AMELIA ASHLEY?* At the time, she'd been kneeling by the clawfoot bathtub, dying her hair brown while she watched a true crime channel's YouTube video about herself. Josh looked so helpless, and confused, and truly baffled in all the photos covering her disappearance. His selling of the poor boyfriend role was Oscar-worthy. She'd applauded him as her brown hair drip-dried into the tub.

She meant every word she'd said when she attacked him.

"I hate you so much . . ."

Iceland. He was already thinking about the next trip with her, a place Mignon had always wanted to go. *Iceland.* Did he remember? Or was it unconscious? His expression was so open and hopeful, and something inside her snapped.

She hadn't planned it that way, lunging over the table at Il Gusto and scratching his arms so deeply she pulled skin out from under her nails as she walked away. She didn't care about the broken glass, or the shocked tourists. It was like she was possessed. She could still hear the confusion and hurt in his voice as she left.

She'd meant to leave an impression, make a scene, leave signs of a struggle, forcing him to choose between telling the police an unbelievable truth or a believable lie after she was gone. Funny, she'd only meant to pretend.

But when he said *Iceland*, the beast gnawing on her insides woke up, and Josh had set her plan in motion for her.

It was all Josh's fault. He had no one to blame but himself.

She had a narrow window of time to get back to America, before too many people started paying attention to an international story and right after she'd been deemed missing. She'd tried making her confessional video private, a video filmed in a moment of weakness after Josh kissed her in the bathroom, but she knew it was too late. If someone looked hard enough, they'd find it, and she needed to be ready.

She slid her ticket and passport over to the front desk at the airline, and the pretty woman typed her information into the system. "Wendy

Tesoro," she said, her Italian accent bright and cheerful despite the late hour. Amelia smiled politely. "Nonstop to New York, yes? Packing light, I see. Are you checking any bags?"

Amelia only had her carry-on with her. She'd thrown everything else away, everything except Mignon's copy of *Peter Pan*. "No. I have all I need here," she said. She had to be placid, and unassuming. No one would bother glancing her way.

"Excellent. There you go then." The attendant slipped the ticket to Amelia and never once gave her a second look.

× × ×

Try as she might to start a new life on the East Coast, Amelia was haunted.

She found a rental house by the sea, practically a shack, on the Jersey Shore. It had internet, a bed, and a small refrigerator, and that was all she needed to keep tabs on Josh.

She sent a long-overdue email to her mother. She hoped her mother was still keeping off social media and avoiding the news, as her support group had advised.

Things might get a little crazy soon, she wrote from her fake UCLA email address. All her lies would come tumbling down eventually. **I miss you. Stay strong.**

She hit SEND. She didn't quite know it would happen so fast.

It was the television in Amelia's room that broke the news, drawing her attention away from her computer at the sound of his name.

The anchor Hugh Brittle spoke to the camera. "An anonymous hacker has released information to us here at USN about Josh Reuter—the primary suspect in the missing persons case of his girlfriend Amelia Ashley—who was at the center of another missing persons case two years ago. The hacker revealed that Josh Reuter, then going by the name Bennet Reuter when he was seventeen, had been dating a girl by the name of Mignon Lee when she disappeared after spending a weekend at the family home near Shasta Lake in California."

Mignon's smiling face from her Facebook page, the picture Amelia had picked out over a year ago, flashed on the screen. Amelia's heart thundered like a drum line as she watched, tearing her eyes away from her laptop.

"Mignon Lee's body was never recovered, leading police at the time to suspect she had run away, since she had previously run away from home. But as new questions circulate around Josh Reuter in connection with Amelia Ashley's disappearance, investigators can't help but wonder about the San Diego State sophomore. Mignon Lee's cold case has led current investigators to consider it a murder investigation. Amelia Ashley's whereabouts are still unknown, but investigators are starting to believe this is only the beginning. We go now live to our correspondent in San Diego, Faye Cavendish, for more. Faye?"

Amelia danced on her bed.

She flailed her arms, and screamed, and cried, and laughed, a whirlwind of emotion spewing out of her like a waterfall, and she couldn't stop, she didn't want to stop. She was high on vengeance.

Mignon watched her silently from a corner of the room, wedged between the vertices where the walls met, and said nothing. Mignon's ghost never could fit in the spaces Amelia's mind had made for her, like she was simultaneously too big and too small, not quite right with the world that had forgotten her.

"They see you, Mignon! They see you!" Amelia cried.

She expected a phone call from her parents any time now, telling her Mignon's case was being looked at again, asking her to come home. She was too thrilled to feel guilty for keeping her secret from them. It was all worth it in the end.

But Mignon didn't react; she just stared at Amelia. Her eyes were an empty void, and Amelia wanted to fill it with something, make her smile, make her laugh, make her proud. Mignon just looked at Amelia with those dark eyes of hers, shadowed by her fringe bangs, and Amelia didn't know why.

"What?" Amelia asked, still buzzing with joy. "I did it! I made them pay attention to you! Josh can't hide anymore. Everyone knows—or at least suspects—what he's done. I got him! I did it! Someone found him for what he is!"

"At what cost?" Mignon asked.

Amelia didn't know what she was talking about. "I thought you'd be happy. I did this for you."

"There's still time."

"For what?"

Mignon stepped out of the corner, filling up the shack, surrounding Amelia on all sides. Amelia's grasp on reality was tipping sideways, as rickety as the shack she lived in. "You can confess. You can tell the world you're not missing, that you're alive. You're not a vigilante."

"My plan was perfect. Better than perfect. Everything happened the way I wanted it to. I *will* find you."

Mignon shook her head. "This is not a story. There is no happy ending."

Amelia's smile fell and she dropped to the bed, making the springs squeak. Mignon didn't have the imagination she did. She couldn't see the big picture. Rage made her bitter. "I don't care what happens to me."

"Well, I care!" Mignon snapped. "I care what happens to my little sister."

"What about you? You're dead! What do you care about anything?"

Amelia blinked and Mignon vanished.

She was ready to finish this, see it through to the end, finally accomplish what she came here to do. Josh was going to pay.

She threw herself back onto her bed and pulled out her phone. The spy software she had installed on Josh's phone was still going strong. It included a GPS tracking system, and she watched his little dot lingering near her old apartment. He was waiting for something, the police maybe. He must have seen her ghost account's profile. She couldn't resist giving him some clues. He was missing out on all the fun unfolding on the news about Mignon right now. Such a shame. The world would finally know her name.

She smiled wickedly as she imagined the look of horror on his face as he opened the door to the empty studio. It was time. She was only just getting started.

To Josh, she sent a question:

Do you believe in ghosts?

CHAPTER THIRTY-NINE

JOSH

Amelia. Amelia, alive this whole time. Playing with him. Framing him.

Josh fled her apartment, back down the stairs and out into the street. With shaking fingers, he dialed the unknown number despite the roar of rage in his ears.

The phone rang once, then twice, and his insides churned, until the other end picked up and Amelia sighed, light and airy, and he could envision the beautiful smile on her face even now. "Hello, Josh."

All he could do was breathe, failing to keep it under control. The muscles in his back shook with rage, he couldn't even speak.

"I see you've found my clues," she said. "Did you see the ones I left for you on my Instagram?"

"You're alive." He barely moved his lips.

"Am I? Or am I a ghost?"

Josh ground his teeth, fighting back every urge to shout and scream. "Whatever you're doing, this has to stop."

"We're well beyond that, *joshreuter.*"

His eyes went to the windows of the buildings bordering the lane. He dodged traffic, cutting across the street, hurrying home. He wondered if she was here, watching him.

"How do you know about Eureka?" he asked.

Amelia clicked her tongue. "Honestly, you need another clue? I thought you would have figured it out by now. My sister really was way smarter than you, *Bennet*."

He hadn't heard that name in years. He'd done everything in his power to push his past down into an untouchable place, an inky black pool he wouldn't dare touch at the risk of staining everything.

His thoughts went to his suitcase, her blood. She'd planted it. He doubted she'd gone as far as to make the airline lose his luggage, but she was manipulative and cunning.

To think, all this time, Mignon's sister had tracked him down, set him up, made him a fool. It turned his thoughts into static.

"Did you forget about me?" Amelia asked, her voice sickly sweet. "Did you really forget what you did to us two years ago? What you did to her?"

He let out a growl of frustration. He should have seen it coming. He'd been so confident in everything he'd done to start over with a new life in San Diego, leaving behind Eureka like shedding a second skin. "So everything was a lie?"

"It was fun for a bit though, wasn't it? But the game is almost over now. We can both stop pretending."

"Are you watching me? Are you following me?"

"I have eyes everywhere, Josh. Like I said, I'm a ghost. I'm here to haunt you."

"You can't hide forever." His laugh took on an edge of menace. "I'll find you."

"You can try. But who will help you? No one will believe you."

He had a sudden understanding that she had him exactly where she wanted him. He could go to the police, but he had nothing. An empty apartment was literally nothing. That's why the police were so confused about Amelia's life. She had erased herself from existence. Even if he showed Detective Hindmarsh the Instagram comments, the texts, this phone call, it wouldn't matter. Amelia was playing a long game.

Who would take him seriously anyway? The story would sound like the ravings of a madman driven to the brink.

"What will you do now, *joshreuter*? Will you be able to talk yourself out of this one like last time? Will your parents help you again? Or is this one missing, presumed dead girl too many?"

"You won't get away with this."

"Neither will you."

He paused for a moment, his breath a shudder. "Maybe we can work something out, strike up a deal."

"Oh, Josh. That's so cute. You really think I can stop now? You're going to be disappointed. And unless you can bring my sister back, you're out of luck."

He laughed again. His mask was slipping, cracking at the edges. "How long have you been tracking me?"

"Long enough to know you have been such a shut-in these past few weeks. Staying home, locking yourself up so as to avoid suspicion. How boring of you."

"You can't prove anything."

"Yes, I can," she said. He could hear her grit her teeth. He was getting under her skin. "You're a murderer."

"You'll never be able to prove it. Call it off before it gets out of hand."

Amelia was quiet for a moment, then, slowly, she said, "You made me this way, Josh. Don't underestimate me. I've been waiting for this for a very long time."

Josh couldn't help the chill that raked down his spine.

"I'm watching you, Josh," she said. "So are the police. You can't hide anymore. You're going to have to keep looking over your shoulder, wherever you go now, because they will come for you soon, and when they do, I will be there to watch."

Then she hung up and the line went dead.

Josh stared at the home screen, stunned. Pure, unfiltered rage roared in his ears.

She must have bugged his phone, tracked it somehow. How else would she have known he was in her apartment just now? She was a genius with computers, so it made sense. She must have done something to his phone when he wasn't paying attention. Then he remembered that day after their date at the zoo, how she was on his phone while he was in the shower. He thought she'd been looking for evidence of cheating. But it was so much worse.

She'd been watching him for months and he hadn't even noticed.

Rapidly, Josh shut off the phone, choked it out with the power button, and then—for good measure—shoved it deep into a trash can at the corner of the street and rushed home.

Whatever Amelia was planning, he had to get ahead of it.

CHAPTER FORTY

AMELIA

Amelia threw the phone onto her bed, hanging up on Josh, and a sob escaped her.

Mignon stood in her corner of the room, watching Amelia panting, gasping for air that felt like cotton. She hadn't expected to feel such a rush speaking to him, like he was somehow still the one in control. He was Josh Reuter, the charming boyfriend who could get anything he wanted with a placating smile and a dash of humility. She needed to end him. Now.

"That will be the last you hear from him," Mignon said. "He'll be extra careful now."

Amelia collapsed on the mattress and held her head in her hands. He must have found the spyware on his phone, or at least figured out that she was watching him that way. Hearing his voice after so long felt like she'd reopened a wound. She flopped back, cuddling the pillow close to her chest.

Mignon appeared in the bed next to Amelia, curled up on her side. "You're the only one who can make all this stop. The only one."

A tear slid down Amelia's face, landing in her ear. She blinked and another one followed the first's trail. Mignon reached out to wipe it away, but her hand never touched Amelia's face. It never could. Never would again.

She wasn't real, and Amelia was alone.

She just wanted her sister back, and it was the one thing in the world she couldn't have. The tears flowed hot and thick, and she choked on her spit and wailed. Mignon only watched, a deep sadness in her eyes, and couldn't do anything to stop it. Amelia didn't want to be stopped anyway. It felt good to cry.

"I can't stop, Mignon," she said. Her voice, thick with phlegm, was weak but her eyes were hard. "I'm in too deep."

"Breathe. You are still alive."

"I'm still alive."

"You won't give up."

"I won't give up.

"You'll find me."

"I'll find you."

She grabbed her phone again and posted a single picture. No caption, no tags. This one was for Josh.

It was a photo of her necklace.

CHAPTER FORTY-ONE

JOSH

Josh rushed home to find Derek standing in the living room, watching the television.

He didn't turn around, even as Josh burst in, breathless and bruised from climbing back in through his bedroom window, then peeled off his cap and jacket and tossed them on the floor. Munch scurried for cover, dodging the falling clothes.

"Hey man," Josh said. "I've got a huge problem." He didn't even know where to begin. Everything was unraveling so quickly, but he had to try. But then he noticed what Derek was watching on TV and his blood ran cold. It was the nightly news.

"—Mignon Lee, a high school student, had been last seen near Shasta Lake. Bennet Joshua Reuter was never formally charged with Mignon Lee's disappearance."

Josh could hardly believe what he was seeing. Mignon's face, her beaming smile, her silky black hair flying out behind her, as she laughed on a swing. He thought he'd never see that face again. He should have known—Amelia had her smile. They looked so similar, it raised the hairs on his arms.

"With new eyes on the case," the reporter went on, "we sent our team to the scene to get a statement from the Lee family."

The feed cut to a blond-haired woman standing on her front porch, wrapped in a cardigan and looking shocked as a camera crew rushed forward.

"Mrs. Lee!" A reporter shoved a microphone in her face. "Do you have anything to say?"

"I don't really know what's going on. What's happening?"

Derek slowly turned to him, his face pale. "What is this?" he asked, his voice shaking.

"Derek, listen, I can explain." Josh started talking before he even knew what he was going to say. All the while, Derek backed up, putting space between them.

"Who is Mignon Lee?"

"I'm being set up—"

"The news says you went by another name? Bennet? Who even are you? What is going on? What is happening?" Derek had picked up Munch, cradling him to his chest.

Josh pushed his hands out in front of him, pleadingly. "I'm being framed. This is all Amelia's fault. She's alive, she's pulling the strings." Now he regretted throwing his phone in the garbage. Without it, how was he supposed to convince Derek of anything?

Derek shook his head, backing away slowly. Even Munch sensed something was different. "I'm not sure I even know you anymore," Derek said. "I thought we were friends, but . . ."

"We are friends! You have to trust me!" Josh said. He had to use every tool in his arsenal to convince him, but it wasn't working. It was like a spell had been lifted. His charm had faded. Now he was naked and unmasked. Derek was looking at him like he saw who he really was.

A murderer.

No. No. It was an accident! He didn't mean to—it just happened!

Derek's phone rang in his pocket and he answered it, not taking his eyes off Josh. His voice cracked when he spoke. "Hey, Tori."

Hang up, Derek. Don't talk to her. Don't let her turn you against me too, Josh thought.

"Yeah, uh," Derek went on, still looking at Josh. "No problem. Uh. Sure. I can . . . meet you."

Josh clenched his teeth. He was losing his best friend to Amelia's game. He tried to keep calm, but the foundation beneath him was crumbling.

Derek hung up, his eyes shifting. "Tori wants to hang out so . . ."

"Derek, please. Don't go."

"Sorry, man," Derek said, still holding Munch close to his chest. "I'm not sure when I'll be back but . . ."

Josh called his name again but Derek had already grabbed his keys and left.

Derek was yet another thing Amelia had stolen from Josh. He watched through the front window as Derek hurried down the sidewalk, heading for Tori's, glancing back only briefly. The unmarked police car was still out front, and Josh backed away from the window.

He was running out of options.

He didn't have time to grab anything, there was nothing to take anyway. The police still had all the clothes he'd packed from his trip. All he had was his hat, jacket, and shoes, his wallet, and pure panic.

The TV was still going and his attention snagged on it as the reporter said, pulling her hand down from her ear, "Breaking news: It appears that Amelia Ashley's Instagram account was recently updated as of one minute ago. It's a picture of a compass necklace." There it was, displayed as an inset graphic. "We want to emphasize that the account may have been hacked and to leave this to the police—"

Josh stared, his heart hammering.

That necklace.

He'd seen that necklace so many times. He'd played with it around Mignon's neck. It was hers. Unique, like her. He'd never forget it.

This was a message for him.

He needed to go, now. He needed to check, to see for himself. Had Amelia found it? He couldn't leave without knowing. Without waiting a second longer, he rushed to his bedroom and climbed out the window once more, running into the night.

Maybe he did believe in ghosts.

CHAPTER FORTY-TWO

AMELIA

A hurricane raged outside the plane window. She pulled out her phone from her pocket just as the captain's voice carried through the cabin.

"Good evening, folks. This is your captain speaking. We're a little delayed with the weather, but we're going to sit here on the runway until we get the go-ahead from control. We'll be on the sunny West Coast and out of this downpour in no time."

Amelia wished she could make the flight go already. She was running out of time.

It was Josh's turn to make a move.

"What makes you think this will work?" Mignon asked, from her usual seat beside Amelia.

"He doesn't know it's mine. He'll think it's yours. You always wore it, never went anywhere without it. Most likely, you had it when you disappeared. No matter what, he's going to want to know. For sure."

The plane started to taxi down the runway. She felt the engine rumbling beneath her shoes and looked out the window at the raging storm outside. The rain splattered against the window, and the plane shook with the force of the wind.

"Ladies and gentlemen, sit back and relax. We are on our way," the captain's smooth voice said. And the plane started accelerating. Amelia's back pressed deeper into the seat. She gripped the armrests tightly and closed her eyes. If they crashed because of the storm, what would happen then? Amelia would just be another anonymous passenger, using a fake name that no one would ever look into. She willed the plane to fly.

The plane roared, engines driving them forward, and there was a lurch and Amelia's stomach swooped horribly as the wheels lifted off and they were airborne. The whole cabin shook, buffeted in the wind, and Amelia clamped her eyes shut, imagining the look on Josh's face—inevitably panicking as his life crumbled to ash between his fingers—to distract her from visions of falling out of the sky and crashing into a fireball.

The storm seemed endless, and Amelia started to wonder if they would ever make it out, but as if someone had flipped a switch, the air evened out and the plane broke through the cloud cover. Bright sunlight poured into the cabin. Rain streaked against the window, disappearing with the plane's ascent above the gray blanket churning beneath them. It was like they had emerged into another world, peaceful and bright, exactly what everyone said heaven looked like.

The knot in Amelia's stomach loosened and she allowed herself to breathe. They had made it this far; she was going home. She was going to find Mignon. Her body thrummed the same as the engine beneath her feet. In just a couple hours, she would have him.

"Josh always thinks he's smarter than everyone else in the room," Mignon said.

"Exactly. Which is why he thought he could get away with this," Amelia replied.

"He already found the tracking app on his phone, he's cocky. He thinks he caught you."

"He did. But he's missing the real tracking device."

Mignon smiled. "He was always so lazy."

Amelia remembered holding Josh's Nikes out to him, like a doting housewife. "If I pack up for the flight, would you check us out at the front desk?" She'd batted her eyes at him.

"I could get used to this," he said, smiling as he slipped on his shoes. "See you in a bit."

She gazed out the window at the dazzling sunlight. He'd never see her coming.

PART 8

TRUTH

CHAPTER FORTY-THREE

HARPER

Harper sat at her computer, staring at her work unfolding on Twitter. Thanks to her, the media had jumped on Josh's name change like sharks feeding on chum. The twist was too good to ignore.

Now both Amelia and Mignon's names filled up her whole feed. She hoped that the news outlets would honor her request to stay anonymous. She was almost positive if anyone found out how she got her information, she would be charged with something serious. But it got people talking, and that's what mattered. The more people who knew that Josh Reuter was involved in two missing persons cases, the better.

The fact that Amelia and Mignon were sisters was still a secret she intended to keep. If Amelia was planning revenge, Harper needed to be patient. It was Amelia's play now, Harper was just waiting on the sidelines.

Everyone wondered if there could be more missing girls, if Josh was a serial predator, if he was hiding more secrets. Harper had lit the match for an explosion of speculation.

"Was this your doing?" Lucy appeared at Harper's doorway, holding her phone aloft. Her feed was filled with news about the necklace too. She was in her running gear, either coming from or going on a jog. Harper had lost track of time. She glanced at the clock on her computer. It was the afternoon, so Lucy was probably heading out. "Everyone was talking about it at school," she said, coming over to Harper.

"I had nothing to do with that. I wouldn't hack into her account. Besides, she's too good. This has Amelia written all over it."

"So she's sending one final message?"

Harper nodded and Lucy braced her hand on the desk, looking at Harper's screen. She raised an eyebrow. "Planning a vacation?"

"I'm keeping an eye on flights coming in and out of San Diego." She showed Lucy the entire list of passenger manifests from every single flight heading into San Diego, with names and credit card info included. To say this was illegal was an understatement.

"What for?" asked Lucy.

"That photo she uploaded makes me think she's baiting Josh. She wants to make him sweat. We all want to go home, we can't stay gone forever. She is coming back here to finish the job."

"What job? How do you know?"

"I don't think getting Josh arrested is her ultimate game plan. I think it's part of it, but not all of it. She has unfinished business." A name caught her eye on the screen and she froze. "Holy shit," Harper said, staring.

"What?"

Harper pointed to a name on the itinerary. Seat 23A. "That's her."

"How do you know?'

"Wendy Tesoro. Wendy Darling—*darling* in Italian. She talked about *Peter Pan* being her favorite book all the time in her vlogs."

"Seriously?"

Lucy was looking at Harper, incredulously, and Harper said, "What! She's used other aliases like it before. Wendy Querida, Liebling, Cherie—all are different languages for *Darling*. Is this really beyond anything that's happened already?"

"Can you prove it?"

"No," she said. "Even I'm not that good."

"Then it could just be nobody. How do you know for sure?"

"Gut instinct."

Lucy scoffed. "Why come back? If that really is her on the flight, why risk being found out?"

Harper thought about it for a moment. It was a valid question. Harper knew that Amelia was smart. She was clever, had a whole game-play laid out for what she needed to do. If the girl was anything like Harper, she would have an itemized list and a step-by-step process for carrying out her revenge. So if she really did risk someone recognizing her, it had to be for something important.

"They never found Mignon's body, never could prove that she was dead, but . . . what if Amelia is doing this so she can get the drop on him? Maybe she's doing this so she can learn the truth. Maybe she's going to find Mignon."

"Harper, this is starting to sound beyond your pay grade. You're out of your depth. Don't you think this should be for the police to handle?"

"They've already failed her once. What's to say that she's not trying to take justice into her own hands? Do you really think they'd believe me anyway?"

"Where did they say Mignon was last seen?"

"Shasta Lake . . . California." She pulled up a Google Maps view and typed in the city name. "I can find Josh's family's cabin address. It'd be a good place to start."

"Harper. You've lost your damn mind. There's millions of acres of woods around it. How do you know you'd find anything? That's like threading a needle from space, right?" She pointed to the vast swaths of green taking up almost the entire Google Maps page. It was all national forests with rough terrain, most not seen by human eyes in a long time, if ever.

Harper jutted out her jaw, thinking. Lucy had a point. How would Amelia do it? How would she follow him? Before, Harper had been thinking like a dead girl. Now she needed to start thinking like a vengeful one. "Amelia would have a way . . . How though?" She was mostly thinking out loud.

She didn't feel like she was smarter than the average person; it was just that not everyone had the time or interest to do what she did. She understood computers, and oftentimes she didn't understand people. But for some reason, she understood Amelia. Even if she didn't think she could ever do anything that Amelia had done, she still felt a kinship that resonated within her like a harmony. Different notes, same song.

Harper wondered if there wasn't another way, a more basic way, to track Josh. She had bet that Josh might leave his phone either turned off or in airplane mode, knowing it would be tracked as it pinged the nearest cell station. So how could Amelia keep an eye on him from afar?

"The guy is smart on his own, right?" Harper asked, watching Lucy getting ready for her run. "He's avoided police for so long, so he must know what to look out for, if people are on his tail."

Lucy adjusted the armband that held her phone against her bicep; she would use it to listen to music while she ran. "I guess. So then the real question is, how do you follow someone who knows they're being followed?"

Harper didn't have a good answer.

Lucy retightened her ponytail and headed for the door. "Whatever it is, I hope she can find some closure," she said.

A thought occurred to Harper. "Lucy. What do you use when you track your running routes?"

"My phone mostly, some of my friends put stuff in their shoes to monitor their pace and gate. Why?"

Harper had been keeping tabs on Amelia's purchases before she'd disappeared. One of them was for a marathon running chip from an athletics store. What were the odds?

Lucy sensed that Harper's thoughts were miles away and she started to head out once again, but Harper stopped her.

"Hey," she said. Lucy paused at the door and looked back, waiting for Harper to say whatever was on her mind, but Harper wasn't sure she could form the words well enough. She settled instead on saying, "Be safe, okay?"

A look crossed Lucy's face, and she might have known what Harper was trying to say. All she did was nod once, her lips pressed together to make a solid line. "Sure. You too."

When Lucy left, Harper got to work. With a few clicks, she pulled up Josh's phone records. He got one phone call from an unknown number before it went dark. The only thing that could spook him enough was Amelia.

It had to be her.

With another few clicks, Harper traced the anonymous number, where it pinged off cell towers. She was here. The phone had clocked in at the San Diego Airport.

If Harper couldn't follow Josh, she could follow Amelia. She looked at the clock again. Wendy Tesoro's flight had just landed. There was no time to lose.

× × ×

Harper started up the car and the engine hummed to life. She tapped on the screen of her phone and saw the little blue dot that was Amelia at the airport.

Her heart hammered and she gripped the steering wheel of her mom's car, making her knuckles turn white and her breath shaky.

Harper didn't think of herself as a hero, so what was she doing? She knew Amelia was about to do something rash. But if Amelia was following Josh, this was a chance for Harper to do something more than find a missing girl. It felt bigger, the word itself too big to sit inside the car with her. Justice? Vengeance? Redemption?

She glanced at her phone, sitting on the empty passenger seat. Maybe Lucy was right, maybe this was above her pay grade. The cops were better equipped to handle this, even Harper had to admit. But if Amelia was planning to do something drastic, maybe going so far as to kill Josh out of revenge . . .

She grabbed her phone and started to dial. Trusting the police was starting to seem like the better play, but something held her back from hitting the green button to call just yet. She had every reason to hate Josh, but she didn't want Amelia to throw everything away because of him. There was still time.

All Amelia had been working toward was getting closure, solving this mystery. If Harper called the police now, it would all be over. And Harper could still help her.

She put the phone down on the passenger seat, backed out of the driveway, and took off toward the highway. She would call the police at the very last minute, hoping she wouldn't be too late.

CHAPTER FORTY-FOUR

AMELIA

The moment Amelia set foot in California, she felt off-kilter. The world seemed to have shifted beneath her feet. It was as if she had forgotten on the way from the terminal to the outside world that she had a body, or a name. She was remembering what it felt like to be home again, though it was more like she was at the place where home should be, like the aftermath of a fire, the foundation nothing but ash and cinder. Ruins that once held so many memories, now nothing more than a smudge of dirt on the ground.

Every step she took through the crowds of travelers, she thought she saw Mignon, standing still as the world passed, watching her with eyes full of sadness and fear.

"Go back, Amelia," she said.

"No," Amelia whispered.

Mignon watched as Amelia exited the airport, took a shuttle to the parking lot at the north side of the airport. She swayed with the shuttle as it turned a corner on the tarmac.

"Go home, Amelia," Mignon said.

"I can't," Amelia whispered.

She got off the shuttle and walked, her backpack the only possession she had left, filled with nothing but a change of clothes, her laptop, Mignon's book, and a half-eaten bag of peanuts. She kept her head low, her eyes swiveling from side to side, as she picked the right kind of car to take her to her final destination. In the long-term parking lot at the airport, she found one. No one would miss it for a while.

Mignon was leaning on it, a blue Honda Civic, her arms folded over her chest. "Leave it," she said.

"No," Amelia whispered.

She ducked low, keeping an eye on the security camera positioned at the four-spoke streetlights above. If she wasn't careful, the alarm would go off. She'd never stolen a car before, but she had learned how. What was one more crime?

Push down, latch the end, pull up until resistance, tug up firmly.

She got in the car and searched for the keys. She didn't want to have to figure out how to hot-wire an engine. The security guards might appear at any second, the parking lot would be monitored, and she had little time left. She searched the glove compartment, the cup holder, the sun visor—the keys fell into her lap.

"I'm not going with you," Mignon said.

Amelia's eyes lifted to the rearview mirror. Mignon was sitting in the back, her face turned out the window, looking at the world as if it had not yet started passing her by.

"I can do this on my own," said Amelia.

"I know."

Amelia put the car in reverse and backed out of the space. The car had a full tank of gas. Good. She followed Josh's little blue dot on the map. He was heading to Shasta Lake, wearing his idiotic Nikes with the marathon runner's chip hidden inside. He was leading her somewhere she could not escape from, a black hole of destiny.

Amelia's gaze went back to the rearview mirror, looking at Mignon.

The image of her sister didn't move, didn't blink. A life, frozen in time, frozen in Amelia's memory. Amelia wondered if she remembered her right, if she recalled the correct angle of her nose, or the brightness in her eyes, whether her lips actually turned down all the time or if they really turned up. And then Amelia realized that it was her in the mirror, staring back at herself.

Mignon was dead.

Dead and gone.

Amelia was alone. With no one. With nothing.

She was insane. She had gone nuclear. She was a ticking time bomb. Tick, tick, tick, time's almost up.

"I'll find you," Amelia said, searching in the mirror for her sister, waiting for her to reappear.

"This can only end one way." The disembodied voice floated from the back seat.

"I'll find you."

"One way."

CHAPTER FORTY-FIVE

AMELIA

Amelia drove for hours all the way up Route 5, taking breaks only when she needed to, never long enough to breathe in the crisp Northern California air as she got deeper and deeper into the green hills, leaving behind the city smog and asphalt for fresh earth and evergreens.

She'd never been to the Shasta–Trinity National Forest before, and even now she couldn't enjoy it. There was something about a towering pine that made a person feel small, insignificant, a blip in the great expanse of time it took for the tree to grow from a sapling into the giants looming over her. Amelia took the winding roads, hardly ever seeing another car pass her, coming or going. It stretched on, curving and sloping, Amelia blindly following, chasing the little blue dot of Josh's tracking device, as she gained on him.

Her breathing was the only sound in the car. She didn't play music, or talk to herself, or hum to pass the time. All she had was the road, and the trees on either side, and the dotted yellow line guiding her forward.

He was leading her somewhere, whether he knew it or not. He was leading her, and she was following.

The day shifted. From afternoon to night, casting the sky from a husky orange to a murky, bruised purple, bleeding into a black veil the farther she got from the city lights. The air changed too, from chewable to alive, as if the air had come from a different planet.

She had to turn on the headlights to see, and even then, it was only a bit at a time, the light illuminating a part of the road, obscuring the rest. The darkness seemed alive, pressing on her from all sides. The road curved, and turned away from her, and she had to keep up. Like Mignon, it danced out of reach.

She drove through the night, punching herself in the thigh to stay awake, biting her lip and pinching the thin skin behind her ear hard enough to draw blood in her fingernails. All the while, she watched her phone, checked that Josh's little blue dot was still moving north on the same road. Driving.

Movement ahead, a flash of something to her right, bounding toward her.

Amelia slammed on the brakes, grinding the car to a screeching halt.

A deer stood in the middle of the road, stock-still, staring at her car. Its tail was up, at the ready, and its nose twitched in her direction. Even in the headlights, it blended in with the forest around it, the tawny brown fur on its back like tree bark. A doe.

If she hadn't braked in time, she would have hit it head-on. She gasped, breathing heavily as she watched, daring the deer to move. She imagined what it would have felt like if she really had hit it, the deer thumping horribly on the hood of the car, the sound like a body going down a slide as blood smeared across the windshield, the squeal as it died. Deer died all the time—this one would have been one of many to suffer at the hands of bad luck. And yet, Amelia had stopped. She didn't want to hurt it, she never thought she could.

She wanted to get out, scream at it, yell at it to get out of the way, but she didn't. She sat firmly in the seat. Her lower back ached from the drive, and her bottom felt as if she'd been sitting on hard concrete all day after the long flight. She wanted to shout at the deer to run, that it was too dangerous, but the deer stared her down as if it knew exactly what it was doing.

Again, movement from the side of the road. Another deer darted out, leaping over the ditch on the shoulder. It joined the first one, pausing long enough that both stood looking at her car, before they bounded into the woods together on the other side of the road, vanishing in the solid darkness that surrounded them.

All that remained was Amelia's ragged breathing and the hum of the car's engine in idle.

Josh's little blue dot had stopped just outside of Shasta Lake. It stayed there for a long time, almost like he was waiting for her.

Morning was coming. She couldn't stop it. The sun would rise and she would meet him there.

She pushed the car onward.

× × ×

Shasta Lake was a small tourist destination in a quiet corner of suburbia. Even though she'd never been there before, the road, and strip malls, and sprawling blacktop parking lots had a hint of familiarity. She could have sworn she'd walked down these roads before, stopped at that pharmacy, shopped at that grocery store, played in that park, but it was a trick of the mind. Suburbia was safety in familiarity. There were no strangers in suburbia, only people who swore they'd been there before, and maybe they had. How would they ever really know?

Amelia took CA-151 all the way to the end of the road, toward Josh's little blue dot on the other side of Shasta Dam. The road took her through winding foothills, and she ascended higher and higher as the day grew stronger and stronger. She was nearing the end. Her heart thumped in her chest with every turn, expecting to see Josh waiting for her around every bend, until finally, she could drive no more.

The road had ended at an overlook, a small unpaved shoulder where cars could park to look out across the lake created by the dam. A car was already parked there. The cliffside below was covered in trees and underbrush, tall sugar pine and needly conifers, all green and glowing. The sun rose high enough over the surrounding mountains and made the lake sparkle like freshly cut diamonds on a blue velvet blanket. She got out of her car and admired the view.

They were only a mile away from Josh's family's cabin. An easy walk along the shore.

Josh's blue dot was here. She only had to walk a little farther.

She glanced at her phone, then took a photo.

Remember this place. Remember her.

A dirt path cut through the underbrush, and Amelia followed the trail, followed the little blue dot all the way to the bottom.

She heard him before she saw him.

Josh Reuter, digging, hauling up dirt. His back was to her, his shirt drenched in sweat. He hadn't heard her coming.

She watched him for a moment, cradling a pressing feeling to her chest. Was it victory? Or anguish? Or vicious rage? She didn't know. All she knew was the feeling of her chest about to collapse on itself. The flush of her skin despite the cool morning air, the cacophony raging in her head of a thousand things she wanted to say to him, the venom that she wanted to spit.

Josh stopped digging his hole for a moment and rested against his shovel. He must have heard something, perhaps the beating of her feverish heart, because he turned and looked at her. His hair was damp with sweat, the long ends hanging in his eyes; his chin was smeared with dirt, his chest heaved with the exertion.

Standing before him now, she couldn't move.

Terrible, handsome, grotesque, charming. His expression didn't change as he took in the sight of her. The girl standing before him now was not the same girl he thought he'd known. She'd put him through hell, but, then again, he'd done the same to her. It was only fair.

"You," he said.

His voice made something inside her crack. She'd always been a little broken, but now she was missing a chunk, like a porcelain doll dropped on her head. She blinked rapidly, tears stinging her eyes.

"Where is she?" she asked, barely above a whisper.

She couldn't take her eyes off the shovel. Was he burying something? Or digging something up?

"How did you find me?" he asked.

A hard lump formed in the back of her throat, choking her out. The edges of her vision were starting to darken, just like the night on the road. Breathe in, breathe out.

Josh barely moved. "Were you tracking me? I turned my phone off . . ." A shadow settled on his eyes. He straightened his shoulders. "It doesn't matter now, I suppose."

"Where's my sister?" she asked.

"Whatever you're doing won't bring Mignon back."

Hearing her name come out of his mouth made her feel like she'd gone insane, as if she would start foaming at the mouth. "Don't. Say. Her. Name."

"Let's talk about this," he said. "We can sort this out—"

"Where is she?" Amelia asked again, stronger now.

Josh's hand flexed instinctually. His jeans were covered in dirt, his arms filthy up to his elbows. The look in his eyes was dark, uncanny, a far cry from the charming façade he used around everyone else. This was the real Josh. "You were bluffing this whole time?"

At one time, she might have imagined herself being the unhinged, laughing, maniacal mastermind, revealing her ultimate plan while Josh cowered in fear. But now, all she could manage was staying upright. She wasn't as strong as she thought she was. She wasn't as strong as she wanted to be.

"Is this where . . . Just tell me. Be honest with me for once in your whole life . . ." Her words trembled as she said them. "Is she here?"

He worked his jaw, inspecting her. What did he have to gain from this? What did he have to lose? His gaze pierced through her and still she stood her ground. She knew the answer. He knew she did. So he stepped aside, like a gentleman, and gestured to the earth at his feet.

Amelia barely registered that she was stepping forward. It was as if her body had become detached from her mind. The hole was shallow, the dirt recently overturned, the smell lingering in the air the closer she got to it.

As she kneeled down in the soft earth, the world melted away. All that ever existed, all that ever mattered was the small copse of trees hidden away in a desolate forest, where secrets had been buried. She scraped her fingers through the dirt, clawing at it slowly, methodically, painfully. Her fingers snagged on something hard and smooth, and then on something thin, a chain. She pulled and brought it into the light.

A silver necklace, a compass.

Mignon.

She was right here.

Amelia didn't feel like she herself was alive anymore, like she was real, or ever existed. She was a ghost, come back to haunt the world, and no matter what she did, it wouldn't change that. She breathed, but no air came in. She gasped, but she was suffocating. She cried, but no tears fell. There weren't any left.

A minute could have passed, maybe an hour, but she kneeled in the shallow grave, staring at the soft brown dirt below her. She couldn't dig any farther. She knew Mignon was here, she could feel her, the life of her had seeped out into the ground beneath her splayed palms.

Had she tried to fight him? Did she know what was going to happen to her? Had she seen the lake, sparkling like diamonds on a blue velvet blanket, and known where she was going?

Did she know how much Amelia loved her?

Amelia stood, slowly, operating on mechanical hinges and faced Josh.

He kept his distance, standing a few paces away from her, and watched her with a neutral expression. No regret, no remorse, no grief. Absolutely nothing.

There was a flash of silver in his hand and Josh showed her the knife. He'd come prepared. He must have known it would end like this.

"Now that you know . . . ," he said.

Slowly, she raised her empty hands. Amelia had known it would end like this too, and still she hadn't brought anything to protect herself. She knew this was how it was supposed to go, where she would always end up. It was the way things always were.

CHAPTER FORTY-SIX

AMELIA

"Why?" she asked. She was surprised that she was calm enough to speak.

That was the ultimate question. Why, why, why. She didn't care how. She didn't care when. She wanted to know *why*. Make it make sense.

Josh stared at her. "Are the police coming? Are they here to take me away?"

"No," she said. "No one's coming. It's just you and me."

"Really? All of this, everything you've done, and you don't even bother to see it all through?"

"Believe me or not. It doesn't matter. All I want to know is why."

Josh paused, barely breathing. She thought maybe he was listening for the distant sound of sirens headed their way, but instead all that could be heard was the chipper morning songs of birds overhead. No one was coming. She didn't believe in the police anymore. She didn't believe they could have helped her at all. Not in ways that meant anything.

She'd left everything behind for this one moment, and she wasn't going to waste it.

Josh scrubbed his chin with the back of his wrist, smearing more dirt onto his skin. "I loved her. And she didn't love me back. She wanted to break up with me. She tried to run. I couldn't let her leave. I grabbed her, and held her down, and she screamed, and she wouldn't stop screaming, and I had to make her quiet so she would listen. I loved her so much, and she wouldn't listen."

Saying it out loud, his chin quivered. Amelia got the distinct impression this was the first and the last time he would ever say those words to another person.

Amelia didn't have anything to say. Hearing him admit it made everything snap into focus, clear as the lake water. He could be lying, he could be telling the truth. Either way, it didn't change the fact that Mignon was dead. And it was his fault.

Once Josh had started, it seemed like he couldn't stop. He waved the knife as he spoke. "It was an accident. It was done. She was so quiet. I didn't even realize what happened until . . . I couldn't throw away my entire future because of one mistake. I had a life, and I couldn't spend it in jail."

"So did she," Amelia said, barely able to maintain control of her voice. "She had a life, a future too."

Josh actually smiled. She saw a flash of the Josh he put on for the world, the Josh who disarmed and charmed.

"I got a chance to start over. Don't we all deserve that? Don't we all deserve to be the person we want to be? One mistake, and that's it?

"I'm sorry about what I did. I truly am," he said. *Liar! Liar liar liar liar.* "But it couldn't ruin my life. I couldn't let it happen. Is there a chance you'll forgive me?"

Amelia met his eyes. "No," she said. "I won't forgive you."

Josh's expression remained unchanged. He operated on a different playing field than the rest of the world. "Well then, that's a problem. Because I can't let this get out, so I can't let you go." The knife glinted in the morning light.

The Mignon of her imagination had pleaded with her not to go through with this, and she hadn't listened. She wanted this. Maybe Amelia too had died the second Mignon disappeared and Amelia was only a ghost operating her own meat suit. Dying now wasn't the worst thing that could happen to her. The worst had already happened.

Before she could react, Josh lunged forward and Amelia put her hands out. They both screamed and slammed into each other, immovable objects, frozen in a vicious embrace.

They stood, facing one another, staring each other down, almost as if they were about to kiss. A bright, white-hot pain bloomed in Amelia's stomach as she looked deep into Josh's eyes, somehow more agonizing than the wound in her gut. It felt like she was staring down a bottomless, eternal pit, to the end of the world itself. She felt the closest she'd ever been to Mignon since she'd vanished. The world was not a fair place. It was not made for girls like Amelia before her sister had disappeared. She had needed to become something else, and it only ended here, at this inevitable point.

Josh's cheek twitched, and his hand shook as he held the knife in her body. How beautiful and horrible it was to look at him. She drowned in the smell of him, of earth and decay, sweat and hot breath.

Blood drenched the front of her shirt, seeping from her gut where the blade had gone in.

He'd stabbed her someplace deep, the acid of her own body eating her from the inside out. Her knees gave out and she fell forward into him. He held her for a moment, just as he had so many times before. Then he let go of the knife and stepped back as she dropped to the ground.

She'd imagined dying to be a lot like being born, thrust into a new world screaming and crying and confused, but she was still and silent and calm. The hilt of the knife protruding from her belly looked alien, a sight she couldn't process. Josh stood back, looking at her, his skin taut against his cheekbones like a skull, his hand coated in her blood.

She'd never felt anything like it before. Dying was a one-way experience. Sweat drenched her face and she looked at him, kneeling in Mignon's grave, and still she smiled.

"Look what you made me do," he said.

Blood filled her hands as she cupped her stomach, dripped through her fingers. It was so warm, and sticky, and full of life that left her.

Josh took another step back, then turned and ran. Amelia only heard the sound of him crashing through the underbrush, fleeing the scene. She put her hand on the soft earth of Mignon's grave. It was getting harder to breathe. Darkness had started to creep along the edges of her vision, Death's black robe skirting the outskirts of her mind.

With all the energy she had left, she clawed her fingers through the dirt and grasped onto Mignon's necklace once more and pulled it free. She crawled toward the base of a great sugar pine, near Mignon's final resting place, and pressed her back against the trunk. A gentle breeze whispered through the treetops, making them sway and sigh, tickling the bright blue sky of a new day.

It was quiet now, save for her hollow, ragged breathing.

With sticky red fingers, she tugged her own necklace off her neck, breaking the chain. At last, the necklaces were reunited, and she clenched the pair in her fist, soaking them in blood. Together at last.

Then Amelia laughed, wheezing and coughing. She tasted the blood on the back of her tongue.

To die was not the end for her.

Before she'd confronted Josh, she'd made one last move.

She had scheduled a post for her Instagram account. It was the picture of Shasta Lake, glistening in the morning light, geo-tagged with her exact coordinates, knowing it would be the eventual place of her own death. Millions of followers would see exactly where she was, where she'd been, where she was going.

The caption read:

Here we are, at the end of all things.

Where have we gone? Find us here.

Everyone will know. Millions will learn the truth. Josh cannot stop it. He can try to run, he can try to hide, but eventually he will be found. He will be caught. He will be known for exactly what he is: a monster at the lake in the woods.

Amelia smiled, though it had turned into a grimace. It hurt to die. She rested against the tree, the knife still inside her, staring at Mignon's shallow grave. Being here finally felt like being home.

She laughed, but the hole in her gut made her stop. She didn't want to pull out the knife. Everything hurt too much. Instead, she started to talk.

"I found you, Min. It's been a long time. I didn't know I'd even make it this far."

Every word felt like it would be her last, but Amelia kept talking. It was like Mignon was right there with her.

A bird flew overhead, coasting on the breeze. Amelia blinked against the sunlight, finding tears gathering at the corner of her eyes.

"Remember how we used to play hide-and-seek? You were way better at it than I was. I think you cheated though. I remember getting so mad at you, because I'd look and look and look and couldn't find you anywhere, and then you'd pop out and scare me from a place I thought I'd already checked before. Like our tree house. I think I just was too scared to really find you, knowing you'd be waiting to pop out anyway. That tree house out back, our headquarters, our secret base. I never changed a thing, even when you went missing. Remember when we'd count falling stars to make a wish? Well, I wish I could have you back . . . Guess I had to come find you, just like old times."

A tear slid down her face, but she didn't bother wiping it away. Her body felt heavy, like she could sink into the earth and sprout flowers, become covered in moss, grow roots. Time had slowed to a trickle, same as her blood.

"People will know what happened to you. About time, really. I'm sorry, Min," she said. Her voice cracked. "I'm sorry I didn't find you sooner. I tried. I really did. But you can rest now. It's over. You can go someplace better."

Amelia thought about her mom, and her dad. Crying for them felt like it would take too much out of her. The earth was soft under her legs, the tree sturdy at her back, the air full of pine and wildflowers. This wasn't a bad place to die at all.

Mignon appeared in the distance, getting closer. But she didn't look like Mignon anymore. Mignon was something else now. She was free.

The dark closed in. Amelia couldn't keep her eyes open. She thought she heard someone calling her name. It sounded like Mignon, but the voice was closer, something else beside her imagination. She almost thought it was real.

Amelia! Amelia Lee! The voice was getting louder, but the dark was getting darker.

Someone was coming through the woods, someone who'd been trying to find her all this time.

And then there was another voice. Many voices. Radio static. Policemen with shields and the sound of Josh yelling, screaming. Screaming that he'd been set up, that he didn't do it, that it was an accident.

Then someone was there, with a hand on her stomach, stopping the bleeding.

"Mignon?" Amelia whispered.

"No, I'm Harper," said a girl Amelia had never seen before. Dark-haired, dark-eyed, like her sister. "You're okay. We've got you."

Amelia smiled. It was over.

She looked up and saw a streak of light cross the sky. Amelia squeezed the hand holding hers. The stars were so bright. And she wanted to count every last one.

ACKNOWLEDGMENTS

So many thanks to my amazing editor, Laura Schreiber, and my dear friend and publisher, Emily Meehan, who believed in this book from the beginning. Thank you to Richard Abate for always cooking up the most fun books together. Thank you to Hannah Carrande at 3Arts for keeping my lights on. Thank you to Ellen Goldsmith-Vein and everyone at Gotham. Thank you to my friends and family, most esss-pecially my two, Mike and Mattie.